# Fearless LOVE

## KG Fletcher

VINCI
BOOKS

## By KG Fletcher

### The Bennetts of Langston Falls

*Faultless Love*

*Shameless Love*

*Breathless Love*

*Reckless Love*

*Fearless Love*

### The Stardust Duet

*Love's Refrain*

*Love's Reverie*

*For my dad who has always believed in me.*

Vinci Books

vinci-books.com

Published by Vinci Books Ltd in 2026

1

A CIP catalogue record for this book is available from the British Library.
Paperback ISBN: 9781036708207
The EU GPSR authorised representative is Logos Europe, 9 rue Nicolas Poussion, 17000 La Rochelle, France contact@logoseurope.eu

# Chapter One

JAMES BENNETT

Sometimes, the universe makes it crystal clear when it's time to make a move. Like the kind you make in a good game of chess. But before you get started, you should consider all aspects of a move since the consequences cannot be undone. James Bennett believed the advantages of his decision outweighed the disadvantages, and his next move was not a mistake but an essential milestone in his and Samantha's relationship.

And he was ready for a checkmate.

Entering the five-star Speckled Trout Restaurant on the outskirts of Langston Falls, his heart blipped with hope. The interior was intentionally dim; the candlelight glows from each table giving off a quixotic vibe for those weekend couples looking for a little more romance. Although he didn't get the specific table he requested, he thought the romantic atmosphere might work in his favor. It couldn't hurt, right?

He stared longingly at the view beyond the large

windows across the expansive terrace, wishing for a spot where he and Samantha could dine al-fresco among the big porch heaters and crackling fire in the outdoor fireplace. Hues of pink and orange highlighted the stunning backdrop of the long-range mountain view, the winter sunset clocking out at half past six.

But the outdoor space was already filled; reservations for a prime table required weeks in advance before the Valentine's Day weekend surge. Still, the interior was nice, the vibe everything James wanted it to be for this important milestone in his life. Now, if he could only calm his nerves.

James waited for Samantha for almost forty-five minutes. She was usually irritatingly punctual, a pet peeve of hers in her law enforcement career monitoring her assigned parolees fresh out of jail. But since the holidays, his brother Walt's New Year's Eve wedding in Atlanta, and his father's cardiac arrest and hospital stay, it felt like they hadn't seen each other in weeks, hence the romantic dinner reservation and the decision to take things to the next level.

He was anxious to talk to her about moving in together once and for all. Having a few drawers in his dresser and closet space for some hanging clothes wasn't cutting it anymore. At least she'd texted, letting him know she was running late and would be there as soon as possible.

He wondered what delayed her. Was she at a halfway house getting someone signed in? Or maybe she had to collect another urine sample from one of her parolees for a drug test? Perhaps she was helping a colleague take a violator back to rehab or the county jail?

James had never been fond of Samantha's job, which often put her in dangerous situations. And don't get him started on how it seemed like she was on call twenty-four hours a day, including weekends. He'd never understood her willingness to help out the low-life thugs in her occupation. But hadn't she helped his oldest brother, Teddy, when he was released and out on parole? And he was *nothing* like most of the degenerates Sam worked with daily.

He remembered the moment they met, like it was yesterday. Samantha "Sam" McNeil was Ted's assigned parole officer and she visited Bennett Farms to check in on him. When his big dog, Jaxson, jumped up on her, she lost her footing and fell flat on her ass. From the moment he touched her hand to help her up from the ground, he knew she was someone special. Their connection was instant. It was magic.

Too bad they had to wait until her time as Teddy's parole officer was completed before they could officially date; relationships between officers and members of a parolee's family frowned upon. Still, they managed to keep things on the down low, meeting for coffee or lunch and biding their time with lengthy phone conversations when she was off the clock.

Samantha was instrumental in helping his family through the legal mumbo jumbo when Ted unintentionally violated his parole after an unfortunate incident at the Harvest Hoedown a year and a half ago. It was the same night family neighbor and nemesis, Glen Kirby, punched Sam in the face during a barnyard fight, resulting in a sinister black eye.

But all those painful memories were behind them now —or were they?

It seemed everyone in the Bennett family had moved on and found love. Teddy was free and married to his high school sweetheart, Robyn. Walt was also a newlywed, his recent New Year's Eve wedding in Atlanta to television producer Elyse Farrell, a huge family celebration. His youngest brother Hank was engaged to famous country music songwriter Ella Mae Miller, and his sister, Becky, was in a relationship with their former feuding farming neighbor, Glen Kirby. How the heck did that happen?

"Hey." Samantha whooshed in and sat across from him, the candles flickering and highlighting her flushed cheeks.

James was taken aback and arose from his seat to assist with her winter coat. "Here, let me help."

Samantha waved him off and scowled. "I've got it." She demonstrated her independence, never allowing him to fuss over her.

He reluctantly sat down and watched her fumble with the heavy fabric. Her dark hair was pulled back into a tight bun, and she was still dressed in her work clothes and sensible shoes. Picking up a thick menu, she peered at the specials from behind black-rimmed glasses—her *work* glasses.

"Have you ordered anything yet? I'm starving."

James frowned and eyed the empty table setting in front of him. He'd been sipping on nothing but water while he patiently waited for her.

"No, I haven't."

Samantha glanced over the top of the menu at him with wide eyes. "Then what have you been doing here for the last forty-five minutes? Staring into space?" She laughed at his expense.

James cleared his throat and tried hard not to come across as a grumpy boyfriend. "I've been waiting for you. I thought maybe you'd gone home to change, but I can tell you're still in work mode. What happened this time?"

Samantha sighed, took her glasses off, and set them on the white tablecloth. Before she could respond, a waitress appeared and took their drink order. Sam was cordial, smiling as she ordered a champagne cocktail and an expedited crab cake for starters. James decided on a recommended local craft beer.

"You don't want an appetizer?" she asked as the waitress flitted away.

James reached for her hand across from him and squeezed. "I want to know what's been happening between us, Sam."

She averted his gaze and pulled her hand from his grip, grabbing her linen napkin to clean her glasses. "I'm fine, James. I'm just… late."

"Are you going to tell me why?"

"Maybe."

"Maybe?" James chuckled. He decided to change the subject. "I miss you, darlin'. I feel like we haven't spent any quality time together since Walt's wedding and Daddy's hospitalization."

"By the way, how's your dad doing? How's Roy?" Her brow furrowed as if she was genuinely concerned.

But Sam hadn't made it to the hospital since his dad was admitted over two weeks ago. She'd told him she was too slammed, and by the time she got off work, visiting hours at the hospital were over. Still, he was glad she asked about him.

James offered a small smile. "He's okay. He's chomping at the bit, ready to come home tomorrow."

"That's tomorrow?"

"Yes." James frowned. "I told you to put it on your calendar. The whole family is welcoming him home. Please, Sam. I need you there with all of us."

The waitress reappeared with their drinks and Sam's crab cake. Her attention was immediately diverted to the food, and she dug in with her fork, moaning after the first bite. James watched, perplexed by her behavior. She was more interested in eating than hearing about his father's homecoming.

"It's so good. You want a bite?" She took a quick sip from her champagne flute and licked her lips.

"No, thank you."

"Suit yourself." She chewed another mouthful, the silence between them deafening.

James held up his hand when the waitress came by to take their order. "Could you please give us a few more minutes?"

"No problem."

Samantha watched the waitress walk away before she shot James a look of confusion. "Aren't you hungry? Don't you want to order?"

James sat upright in his chair, his jaw clenched with determination. "I want to know what's going on between us. You've been... distant."

Samantha exhaled steadily through her nose and laid her fork next to her half-eaten appetizer. "I guess now's as good a time as ever to tell you."

"Tell me what?" James steeled himself in his chair, ready to hear about her latest work frustrations.

"I'm leaving Langston Falls."

Her comment wasn't what he expected, and he stared back at her, puzzled. "Say again?"

"I said, I'm leaving Langston Falls."

James blinked. "When? Where are you going? Do you have another court case in Atlanta? Are you vacationing with your family again?"

Sam bided some time before she answered and drained the pink bubbly in her glass. Wiping her lips with the napkin, she finally stared right at him, her expression giving nothing away. No remorse. No emotion. No love.

"I'm leaving Langston Falls tomorrow for Quantico, Virginia, to begin training at the FBI Academy."

All the color drained from James's face. Sam had mentioned her interest in working with the FBI when they first started dating, but that was well over a year ago. For her to make such a drastic decision without him felt like a sucker punch in the gut.

"You passed the preliminary tests?" His throat felt dry, and he reached for his beer to take a sip.

"Of course."

James swallowed hard and carefully set his glass on the table. "Why didn't you tell me?"

Samantha tilted her head and shrugged. "Because I knew you wouldn't like it. You've never been a fan of my work."

Her comment struck a nerve. "Now, hold on, Samantha. That's not fair. I'm not a fan when you get *hurt*, okay? When you get punched in the face or slapped and ridiculed by a bunch of convicts. You said it yourself: it's a tough career, especially for a woman."

"I know what I said. And that's part of the reason I'm turning the page. James…," She paused, pressing her lips together for a beat.

"James, I can't be tied down to Langston Falls anymore. I need a fresh start. I've always thought about a career in the FBI, and the timing feels right. The intensive training is for twenty weeks while I live on campus."

"I'll come visit you."

Sam shook her head. "I need to concentrate on my training. It'll be taxing on so many levels—academically, physically, and mentally—and success is far from guaranteed. I... I don't need any distractions."

"Then I'll wait for you to finish—"

"You're not listening to me," she interrupted curtly. "I'm ready to level up in my career. I'm looking forward to the intense training regimen necessary to prepare me as a new agent to carry out the FBI's complex mission to... to..."

"To what?" He could tell she was flustered, but so was he.

Sam stared at him with unmistakable determination in her eyes, her knowledge of the FBI impressive. "To carry out complex missions protecting the nation from criminal threats from terrorists, spies, hackers, gangs, and more—while upholding civil rights and the Constitution of the United States. This is serious business, James."

She leaned back in her chair and sighed. "I'm not ready to commit to a relationship with you and settle in a small town like Langston Falls. There's no future for me here."

He was stunned, his voice croaking with emotion. "You mean no future with *me*. Ouch, that hurts."

"James, please see this from a career perspective. Don't take it personally."

He was flabbergasted she felt so little for him. Looking back, it all made sense now. He had always been the instigator in their relationship. She was just biding her time.

"So that's it, then? We're through?"

She nodded, undeterred. "I'm sorry. Please believe me when I say this: I didn't want what we had to end this way. Everything happened so fast."

"Well, you should go. If that's what you want, you should go and do it. I won't try to stop you." He pulled several twenties from his wallet and threw them on the table. "I'm not hungry anymore. I'll follow you home and help you pack the rest of your things."

Sam pursed her lips together and shook her head. Right then, he saw goodbye in her eyes.

"No need. I already got everything."

James pinned her with his stare as the finality of her words closed the door on their relationship.

"That's why I was late."

# Chapter Two

## SARA LARSON

"Are we there yet?" Noah asked.

A cheeky grin was plastered across her son's face, his eyes lighting up from behind his glasses. Sara shook her head and offered him an exaggerated eyeroll in the rearview mirror.

"You've asked me that for the one-hundredth time, Mr. Snuggle-bunny. We have about another thirty miles to go."

"Thirty miles?" he whined.

"Yes, sir. But it'll go by in a flash if you read one more book from your bag. You don't want to be behind when you start school next week, do you?"

Her empty threat seemed to do the trick. Her smart little boy was a regular book nerd, and devoured books on all their road trips, including this one.

Sara was a travel nurse by trade, and her next assignment was in the small town of Langston Falls. She'd never traveled this far north, the mountainous area of Georgia bordering the North Carolina state line a refreshing change of scenery.

She was to care for a man by the name of Roy Bennett, who'd suffered cardiac arrest a few weeks prior. His prognosis was good, but only with ongoing at-home care and physical therapy. She was commissioned for the job, happy for another clean slate and adventure with Noah.

The winter scenery in Georgia's northeast corner whizzed by in hues of forest evergreen and gray clouds. But the dreary weather wasn't about to tamper her excitement, the anticipation for what lay ahead filling her with hope.

Noah had always been a trooper the times they'd packed up and moved before. How many was it now? She'd lost count. At least a dozen. But this particular move had left him agitated and grumpy. He wasn't his usual fun-loving self, often mopey and depressed. She knew it was because he was getting older and had become opinionated and vocal about things.

He'd grown up on her in the blink of an eye. He was on the cusp of his eighth birthday and had finally made friends in his second-grade class at the local school, classmates he didn't want to leave behind. Sara assured him he'd make new friends at their destination, promising him a festive birthday party where he could invite his entire class to celebrate.

Still, he wasn't convinced, begging her to reconsider and wait to move at least until his birthday was over. She knew he was ready to settle down and plant roots. Her, not so much. But she couldn't wait; the ink on her next contract already dried, and her new patient was about to be discharged from the hospital. She'd have to make it up to Noah with an over-the-top birthday bash to cheer him up during the transition.

The two-lane highway circled the mountain, her car climbing to a higher elevation, the dramatic overlooks from the Blue Ridge Parkway breathtaking. Her last assignment had been in suburban Atlanta, the congested traffic and never-ending road construction something she wouldn't miss. Some might consider Sara a vagabond, never staying in one place for more than a year. Her nomadic lifestyle suited her.

Peaks and valleys punctuated the landscape, the stretch of small towns so charming, they seemed like they came straight out of the pages of one of Noah's storybooks. She was tempted to wander the picturesque downtown districts and explore the rolling countryside. From her investigation into the new area she and Noah were to call home, she imagined romanticized weekends picking apples, riding the scenic railway, or strolling through the changing seasons.

She'd lived her fair share in plenty of Georgia towns, the Southern hospitality warm and friendly. But to live in this particular stretch of the Peach State mountain region where most folks trekked for a weekend getaway seemed like the perfect fit. Quiet with room to grow and a lower cost of living. No more bumper-to-bumper traffic or news of gun violence and car-jackings. Fresh, clean air and unobstructed views. She looked forward to the beckoning mountains and foliage, festivals, and the lively community of Langston Falls, the small population of less than five hundred, a nice change of pace.

Sara wanted to get them checked in at the little roadside motel she'd found online before the sun went down. But the slower speed limits up the mountain messed with her timing, especially with a small trailer hitched to the back of her car.

She took each turn slowly, the daylight slipping behind the thick foliage and elevation. Finally, her headlights illuminated a small sign in the distance that read, "Langston Falls, five miles."

Glancing in the rearview mirror at her son again, she smiled. He held a small flashlight and aimed it at the pages of his book, his little brow furrowed with concentration.

"We're almost there, sweetie. Once we check in, I'll order us a pizza for dinner."

"Hooray!"

The exterior of the two-story Langston Falls Economy Motel held a classic roadside motel vibe, the building modest and situated along the main highway. A bright neon orange "vacancy" sign was lit up above the entrance, the communal space outside featuring a fire pit with several Adirondack chairs perfectly spaced around the perimeter.

Sara was intentional with her choice, opting for a more affordable alternative to a traditional hotel in town. And she needed to find a storage facility for everything in their packed trailer while she scoped out the perfect short-term lease. She'd learned the hard way about signing a contract for a place to live sight unseen and wasn't about to do that again. A walk-through and a thorough inspection were top priorities, and she wanted to find someplace cozy to hang her scrubs, at least through the end of the school year.

"Cool!" Noah exclaimed. The orange neon made his glasses glow over his eyes.

Sara parked near a big rig, her car and trailer dwarfed by the giant machine. Breathing in the crisp mountain air, she stretched her back and sighed, ready to call it a night after their long travel day.

"Come on. Let's go check this place out. I'll bet they have a stocked soda and snack machine."

"Can I get a soda to go with my pizza?" His warm little

hand slipped into hers as they approached the large lobby doors.

"I don't see why not. We can make a toast to our new town."

They laughed and entered the building, a doorbell chime announcing their arrival. A tiny dog with a blinged-out collar yipped and stood guard, the front desk vacant.

"Hey, little doggie," Noah said in a high-pitched tone. He'd wanted a dog since he could speak and immediately kneeled, gently holding out his hand. "Come here. I won't hurt you."

"Careful, son. I don't want it to bite you."

"Tinkerbelle won't bite."

Sara and Noah flicked their heads in unison to see a middle-aged blonde coming toward them. Her hair was in a bouffant style, and her breasts were pushed up to expose her extraordinary cleavage from under her tight pink tee. Skin-tight jeans and sky-high heels finished off the woman's outfit.

But Sara wasn't looking at her clothes or boobs. Nope. She was fascinated by her pretty face adorned with false eyelashes and shiny ruby-red lips.

The woman scooped up her little dog and held out her hand, her bright fuchsia nails looking like they could fillet a fish caught from the local pond.

"Hey there. I'm Crystal Cavanaugh, the proprietor of this lovely establishment. But everybody around here calls me CC. And you've already met Tink. Say hello to our new guests, princess." The little dog yipped as if she understood every word Crystal said.

Sara shook her hand and smiled. She was usually a good judge of character and knew right away she and Crystal would get along just fine.

"Happy to meet you, CC. This here is my son, Noah." She palmed his shoulders and presented him with pride.

Crystal beveled her stance in her impressive heels and rested one hand on her hip while holding her dog in the other. "Well, hi there, handsome. How old are you?"

Noah didn't miss a beat, his voice confident with self-assurance. "I'm seven, but my birthday's coming up, and I'll be eight."

"Eight years old. Oh my. What a great age."

Sara and Noah followed her to the front desk, where she deposited Tinkerbelle on a small bed right on top. They were definitely not in Atlanta anymore.

"Go ahead and pet her. She won't bite, though she might fall asleep on ya. It's been Grand Central Station here all evening with some regulars coming in for the weekend."

Noah stood on his tiptoes and happily patted Tinker-belle on the head. Crystal's long nails tapped away on a keyboard as she continued talking.

"You're Sara Larson, correct?"

"Yes, ma'am."

Crystal waved her off. "Please. No one around here calls me 'ma'am.' Makes me feel like I need to be knittin' baby booties or rockin' in a chair." She laughed, her Southern accent oddly comforting. "I've got you upstairs, away from the ice machine, per your request. Room number twelve."

"Twelve's my favorite number," Noah admitted. He continued petting Tink on the head, the little dog nodding off.

"Mine too!" Crystal grinned. She handed Sara a keycard and a piece of paper. "I need you to fill out this form, and I'll need a credit card on file for incidentals."

Sara frowned, looking at the printed form with blank

spaces for her information. "I, uh, thought I filled this out online already?"

"Oh, honey, everyone who comes here says the same thing. But the internet in these parts is spotty, and I'm lucky to get those completed forms in my inbox. Unfortunately, yours didn't make it. But I did get your reservation, so there's that."

"Oh."

"Here you go." Crystal plucked a pen from a mason jar that looked like it held a bouquet of flowers. But upon further inspection, Sara realized they were all pens with bright plastic flowers taped to the ends.

"Y'all are welcome to sit here in the lobby and watch television anytime you want to. I've got satellite TV with over one hundred channels, including Disney." She leaned forward with glee assessing Noah's reaction, her boobs dangerously close to spilling out of her top.

"Did you hear that, Mom? She's got the Disney Channel!"

"Super." Sara concentrated on filling out the form. She wrote in the space for her current address, "undetermined." Clearing her throat, she asked, "Do y'all get the local paper? We're currently between houses, and I'll be looking for local leasing options before I start my new job this week."

Crystal didn't press her for details, her sweet nature underneath all her hair and makeup endearing. "Honey, I'm friends with everybody in this town, including a few realtors. We'll get you hooked up in no time."

"Thank you." She signed the form before handing off her credit card. "And one more thing. Are there any pizza places that deliver around here?"

Crystal ran her card through a machine and handed it

back to her. "This is a tourist town. Of course, we have pizza."

She leaned forward again with intention, motioning for Sara to come closer. "And I've got a stash of hard seltzers in the back if you ever need a cold one after a hard day's work. You just holler, and I'm your gal. Happy time is my favorite time of the day if you know what I mean." She winked.

Sara knew right then she'd made her first official friend in Langston Falls.

# Chapter Three

## JAMES

The pickup truck headlights highlighted the wraparound front porch of the main house at Bennett Farms as James accelerated up the hill, eager to call it a night. Knowing the home was vacant while his father recovered in the hospital, he was determined to go straight to bed.

With the engine turned off, he gripped the steering wheel and thought about his final moments with Samantha.

There was no romantic dinner. In fact, there'd been no dinner at all. No hug goodbye. No kiss. She shook his hand before getting into her car and driving off. He'd stood in the parking lot of the fancy restaurant and watched until her taillights disappeared into the dark woods of the surrounding mountains.

She was gone.

Jaxson barked a greeting from inside as James fumbled with the key into the front door lock. Being alone on the property felt odd, his siblings off living or playing house with their better halves. James was by himself for the first time in his life, the feeling peculiar and foreign to him.

Thank goodness for his black and yellow labs, Jaxson and Delia.

"Hey, boy," he greeted, stroking Jaxson's sable fur. The excited animal's entire body moved to the rhythm of his wagging tail as Delia stood nearby. She was a few years older than Jaxson and waited patiently for her turn.

"Come here, D," he requested. He knelt and allowed the yellow Labrador to lick his face, making him smile.

That's the thing about having dogs. Jaxson and Delia were pleased with nothing more than a treat, a scratch behind their ears, or a pat on the head. James wasn't sure where his love of dogs came from, but he found himself calmer around his companions, and his stress and anxiety alleviated, at least for a little while.

The more he loved on his canines, the more they paid him back in ways nobody else could. He felt it deep down, the term "man's best friend" hitting him in the feels. He knew he was melancholy from his break-up with Samantha and could swear his dogs knew instinctively something was up. Still wearing his coat, he sat silently on the floor and spent time with the animals, showering them with love.

Delia laid her head in his lap, enjoying the belly rubs, while Jaxson got the zoomies and repeatedly fetched a tattered toy James tossed across the expansive great room. He knew he was a more disciplined person because of his adorable and loyal dogs. They made him fully appreciate unconditional love, commitment, and life itself. Like clock-work, they let him know when they needed to go outside or be fed.

And they were his trusty sidekicks when it came to working on the farm; his favorite times spent hiking through the pinewood forest with them following obediently from behind at the end of a long workday. Their excitement and boundless energy reminded him how important freedom was, even to them.

And wasn't that what he was now? Free? He wasn't all that surprised. It seemed like he and Samantha had been going that direction for a while. Still, the sting of rejection filled him with melancholy

James hoisted his tired body up from the floor. "Come on. Time to get home."

On his way to the back door through the kitchen, he noticed a note left behind on the island. It was from his sister, Becky.

*I'll have a big breakfast for everyone in the morning before we get Daddy from the hospital. Eight sharp. Love you!*

James smiled, knowing his sister was excited about bringing their father home after all this time. The big house and farm weren't the same without his presence. But he knew his dad had a long road of recovery ahead. They'd already made plans to bring in a nurse to help him through the transition and to make sure he kept up with his meds and physical therapy.

Roy Bennett's cardiac arrest rocked everyone to their core, especially James. His dad was the patriarch and their only parent since their mother died years ago. He was James's confidant and best friend. Just the thought of losing him left him shaking in his cowboy boots.

But they hadn't lost him. The man had been given a second chance, and he was grateful.

James locked up the main house and trudged across the chilly path with his big dogs by his side toward the carriage house where he resided full-time on the property. He once shared the space with his brother, Walt, until he and his new wife, Elyse, made their own home a few miles down the road on the same land as Teddy and Robyn.

But James hadn't been alone for long. Samantha changed all that. She'd stayed with him at Bennett Farms for much of their relationship while working in and around the Langston Falls area. Her career often took her to other cities, including Atlanta. And the more he thought about it, he realized she hadn't spent much time with him on the farm since before the holidays. That should've been the first warning.

The interior of his home was cold, like his heart. The dogs stopped by their food bowls and cocked their heads in confusion as James ignored them and continued toward his bedroom. Not bothering to take off his coat, he flicked on the lights to see the evidence of his relationship's demise for himself.

The dresser drawers Sam once occupied were wide open as if she'd been in a rush to clean them out. A few wire hangers hung empty in the closet space they shared, and the vanity in the adjoining bathroom was bare, the faint scent of her shampoo lingering in the air.

James swallowed a lump the size of a wine barrel in his throat, determined to keep his emotions in check. The realization she'd packed up and exited his life for good left him heartbroken. Closing his eyes, he breathed in the last traces of Sam's femininity and resolved he'd have to man up and work harder and smarter from here on out, determined to get over her.

"Screw relationships," he muttered to himself.

Digging his hand into his coat, he retrieved the red velvet ring box burning a hole in his pocket all evening. Flicking it open, blood roared in his ears as he stared at the small, solitary Princess-cut diamond set in a gold band.

His dad helped him pick it out a few months ago, and he'd planned on giving it to Samantha at dinner, preferably during a decadent dessert served with a bottle of expensive champagne. He was ready to take their relationship to the next level. Little did he know, she'd already decided to pack up and move on, leaving him standing there with his heart in his hands.

Shrugging off his coat, James gave himself an inner pep talk. He didn't need a woman to make his life complete. He had everything a guy could ever ask for. A thriving family winery and Christmas tree farm working alongside his siblings. His father's miraculous recovery and homecoming to look forward to. Two big, loyal dogs who loved him unconditionally.

Speaking of dogs...

James whipped his head around at the sound of canine nails clicking against the hardwood floors. Jaxson and Delia obediently sat in the doorway as if trying to figure him out. Squeezing the back of his neck, he realized he hadn't fed them before he rushed off to the restaurant to meet Sam.

He settled the ring box into one of the empty dresser drawers, shoved it closed, and snapped his fingers, realizing he hadn't eaten either.

"Come on, Jax. Come on, D. I'm starved. Let's eat."

———————————

The following day, James leaned against a porch post outside the main house and pressed his chin into the warm fabric of his winter coat. He lifted a steaming mug of coffee to his lips and stared out across the expanse of family land spread out before him in the cold, golden morning, the winery trellises barren, and the green carpet of Christmas pines rolling up the hills as far as the eye could see. Jaxson and Delia cantered through the vineyard, their hot breath noticeable in clouds of vapor coming from their muzzles.

"James?" Becky hollered.

He turned at the sound of his name and plastered a smile on his face.

"Yeah?"

"It's freezing out there. Why don't you come back inside? I just took the monkey bread out of the oven."

James nodded. "I'll come in a sec."

The back door closed with a thump, giving James a few more seconds to sulk. He wasn't ready to face his family, especially after a fitful night's sleep. He'd tossed and turned all night, rechecking his phone for a text message or call from Samantha—anything to let him know she might've changed her mind and wanted him to wait for her.

But there was nothing but radio silence.

Flinging the last dregs of his coffee into the yard, he headed inside with his dogs, thankful for the warm interior. Setting his mug on the counter, he shrugged off his coat, smiled, and nodded at everyone before hanging it up in the mudroom.

"Do we know how long Dad needs a nurse?" Walt asked.

His brothers Walt and Teddy, their wives, and his sister Becky were gathered around the island, filling their plates with an assortment of breakfast choices. Hank and Ella Mae were in Nashville but planned on welcoming their dad home later over FaceTime.

Even Glen Kirby was in attendance, the former nemesis of the family helping Becky with the spread. And why wouldn't he be here? The man was in a full-blown relationship with his little sister now, and she'd practically moved in with him down the road at his apple farm.

And James would *never* forget how Glen was the reason their father was still alive. He'd resuscitated his dad after he collapsed near the barn two weeks ago. He would forever be indebted to Glen and his heroic behavior, just like the rest of the family.

"It will depend on how well he does with his physical therapy," Teddy replied. He tossed a blueberry into his mouth and chewed.

James plopped a large spoonful of scrambled eggs and a few sausage links onto his plate while he listened to the conversation.

"I heard it can take several months before he's given the all-clear," Robyn added.

"Knowing Roy, he'll totally beat the odds and be up and at it in a few weeks, flirting with his nurse and cracking dad jokes," Elyse said. This induced a few hopeful chuckles and giggles throughout the kitchen.

James kept quiet and grabbed a gooey bite of Becky's famous monkey bread. Shoving it into his mouth, he almost choked when Walt asked him a question point blank.

"Where's Sam?"

All eyes were on him as he chewed slowly and finally swallowed. "She's, uh, not here."

"No shit, Sherlock," Walt laughed. "Is she on her way?"

James set his full plate of food on the island, suddenly not hungry anymore. "I guess you could say that."

"Well? When will she be here? We need to leave in the next thirty minutes," Becky said, glancing at her wristwatch.

He ran a hand across his stubbly jaw, knowing he looked like crap this morning. His usually combed hair was mussed, and he hadn't felt like shaving. Even his shirt was untucked, which was very unlike him.

"You okay, brother?" Teddy asked. He came up beside James and palmed his shoulder.

Clearing his throat, he tried to sound nonchalant and said the words fast. "We broke up last night. She already packed up and moved out. Hey, Becks, you got any more coffee?"

His family appeared stunned, his sister going into fix-it mode. "Um, sure, Jimmy. Coming right up."

"Bro? What happened?" Walt asked.

James scanned the faces in the room and shook his head. "She's on her way to Quantico, Virginia, to begin training at the FBI Academy. She's starting a whole new life —without me."

Becky handed off a mug of fresh coffee and squeezed his bicep. "I'm sorry, Jimmy. It's her loss." She looked around the room. "Right, y'all?"

The room interrupted in unison.

"Of course."

"She's a fool."

"Big mistake, James. She didn't know what she had."

"I'm so sorry. You'll find someone else."

He waved them all off. "I'm fine. Really. It's no big deal. Please don't make a fuss. And please don't tell Dad on his first day home. I'll get around to telling him at some point. Let's make sure today is a *good* day." He brought the mug to his lips and took a big gulp, the hot coffee scalding his mouth.

"Damn!" he sputtered.

"Sorry, Jimmy," Becky lamented. "Here, eat this."

She quickly offered him another gooey piece of monkey bread. The cinnamon sugar, butter, and dough melted in his mouth, easing the pain.

If only he could find something delicious to ease the ache in his heart.

# Chapter Four

JAMES

"Here we go, Mr. Bennett. Let's take it nice and easy."

A sweet hospital nurse named Susan instructed James and Walt as they flanked either side of their father and helped him out of a wheelchair, guiding him into James's truck. Teddy kept a firm grip on the chair and moved it out of the way once Roy was on solid ground. The girls and Glen were all smiles, coaching Roy with every step he took.

James kept a steady grip on his father's wrist and elbow, a childhood memory suddenly flashing through his mind. His dad once helped him into a truck after he'd sprained his ankle falling out of a tree. He was thirteen and had shimmied up a tall Georgia pine on a dare from his brothers.

He remembered losing his grasp on a limb and falling from the sky, his young life flashing before his eyes. The hard and unforgiving ground knocked the breath right out of him, and he flailed in pain as his brothers took off in search of help. Roy Bennett came to the rescue, driving through the fields like a madman in a pickup truck with the Bennett Farms logo on the sides. Lifting James to his feet, his dad held the same grip on his wrist and elbow. Same soft words of encouragement...

"You're doing great, Dad. A few more steps, and you'll be in the truck."

Every move his father made was achingly slow, his frail body hunched over while he concentrated on each intentional step. When he was finally settled in his seat, James clicked his seatbelt across his lap and breathed a deep sigh of relief.

Nurse Susan handed off a plastic bag of meds to Becky before she offered Roy his signature black cowboy hat. He immediately pressed it on top of his head, looking a little more like himself, not like someone who almost died mere weeks ago. White, thick scruff peppered his aging face, evidence he hadn't shaved since the incident, and his strength was non-existent, his hands shaking with concerted effort with every lift and grasp.

"Thank you, darlin'. I don't know what I'm gonna do without you," he said to Susan. His words came out slow with a hint of a slur to them.

"Oh, you'll be just fine. Your new nurse will be over tomorrow, and she'll keep you on track with your physical therapy. And you've got your entire beautiful family to help you too." Her Southern voice pinged with a happy tone. "You're a blessed man, Mr. Bennett. You've done a mighty fine job."

Roy nodded, his eyes misting with emotion. He'd become way more emotional since his cardiac arrest too. "Can I have one more hug?"

Nurse Susan's laugh was full of joy as she leaned in and embraced Roy one last time. With the family gathered around the truck, he looked at each of his children and their partners with a broad smile before his eyes landed on James, who sat in the driver's seat.

"Home, James."

They rode through town in a caravan of trucks going from asphalt to country roads, the gray winter sky somber in the late afternoon. James glanced over at his dad and then at the road several times. He wanted this version of his happy father in his memory always. Dormant meadows flashing by the windows, cowboy hat perched on his head. Fisted hands resting in his lap and tired eyes hooded but glimmering with a second chance at life.

He didn't know if it was the flashback of his childhood, the barbed wire on fence posts, Becky's colorful homemade welcome sign strung across the porch railing, or his dad's extended time away from Bennett Farms while in the hospital. But James felt his wayward emotions finally settling down.

He knew this was a slight respite, and he had a long way to go, especially knowing they almost lost their dad. And his sudden breakup with Samantha was still a fresh wound. But he was willing to return to some semblance of normalcy. To settle into the precious moments of his life when they happened and being okay when things didn't turn out how he planned.

James slowed the truck, and the entrance of the family homestead greeted them with gratifying contentment.

"Home is a sight for sore eyes," Roy crooned.

"Welcome back, Dad." His heart swelled with pride as they drove under the curve of the custom, heavy-gauge steel letters spelling "Bennett Farms." And as he pulled right up to the front porch, Becky's homemade sign left his father in tears.

"Dad?" James turned the truck off and shifted his body,

concerned his father's emotions might send him into another medical situation.

"I'm fine. I get weepy, is all. I've been told it's part of the healing process. I'm just glad to be home, son."

"I know. I know." He patted his dad's arm and watched his siblings park and hurry toward them. "Let's get you inside, okay?"

Roy nodded and swiped at the tears rolling down his weatherworn face. "Now, don't you be tellin' everyone about my leaky eyes, ya here?"

James chuckled. "I won't tell a soul, Daddy."

The guys managed to get Roy up the porch stairs and inside the house. Once inside, Becky showed him the comfortable lounge chair she positioned in front of the television with a small side table nearby for his medication, snacks, and water. But he was more interested in retiring to his bedroom on the main level, ready for a nap.

"If you boys could help him to his room, us girls can get him situated," Becky instructed. She was still the lady of the house, even if she didn't live there full-time anymore.

James and Walt held on to their father's arms and took their sweet time helping him shuffle down the hallway toward his bedroom. Nurse Susan had mentioned their dad would need a walker while he recovered—something to aid him because of his decreased strength and coordination. A walker would also help him be safer and more independent in his daily activities at home as he grew stronger over the next few months. But that was something the new nurse would be bringing the next day. For now, it would have to be the brute strength of Roy Bennett's strapping young sons helping him get from point A to point B.

"Careful," Walt warned as they lowered him to the edge of the bed.

"Thank you, son. Whew. I'm exhausted."

James ensured his father was safely seated before letting go of his arm. "You did good, Dad. Are you hungry? You want the TV on?"

"No. I think I'd like to take a long nap in my own bed if that's okay. But you can help me pull off my boots if you don't mind."

"No problem."

With his boots off, Roy handed his cowboy hat to James and lay back among a bevy of fluffy pillows. A genuine smile was on his face as he interlocked his fingers across his belly and closed his eyes.

"This feels good, boys. Real good."

Walt's hands were on his hips, his mouth jacked up in a smirk. "If you need anything, just holler."

"Will do."

The boys passed Becky on their way out of the bedroom. "Is he okay?" she asked.

"I think he's asleep," James replied.

"Good." She peered into the room, leaving the door open a crack. "This was a lot for him on his first day home. I guess we'll have to play it by ear at dinner."

"You may have to serve it to him in his room like Mom did when we were sick," Teddy offered.

James agreed. "Let's not push him until his new nurse can assess him. We can all take turns keeping him company like in the hospital."

Becky chewed on her lower lip, indicating she was thinking things through. "Good idea."

They started down the hallway toward the great room and kitchen, James asking a legitimate question. "Becks? Are you staying at the main house while Dad recovers, so he's not alone? Or are we taking turns being with him? One night you stay, the next night I stay, or something like that. I can always sleep in Hank's old room."

He paused. "And, of course, Glen is welcome to stay here too."

Becky stopped in her tracks and looked up at him, her lips turned up into a grin. "You're sweet, James. I've already thought about it. Of course, I'll be here for Daddy while he recovers. Glen might stay over occasionally, but he won't be moving in or anything. There's no need for you to sleep in Hank's room."

"Cool."

"And just so you know, you won't be alone either." She pressed her dainty hand against his flannel-covered forearm, the meaning behind her words touching him deeply.

"Thanks, Becks. Come here." He opened his arms wide, and she shuffled into his embrace.

A part of him was relieved the worst was over for their father. But there was also a part of him that carried the weight of the world on his shoulders, his future without Samantha leaving him feeling a little bit lost.

"You need to shave," Becky admonished, running her fingernails across his hairy face.

James stepped back from her and chuckled, stroking his jaw. "No, I don't. Didn't you know? I'm going for the Glen Kirby look."

"Stop," she laughed. "Only Teddy and Glen can pull off a full beard. Besides, his hairy face is soft. You might have left scratch marks on my skin during that hug."

Later, with his brothers and their wives gone home for the evening, James bid Glen and Becky goodnight before ambling down the hallway to check on his dad one last time.

Roy had slept most of the afternoon, exhausted from the effort it took on his frail body to get from the hospital to the farm. Becky brought his dinner to him on a tray, served on his wedding china with a linen napkin and a tiny votive filled with purple pansies.

It took their father a long time to eat, the shaky lift of his fork or spoon excruciatingly slow as he brought each bite to his mouth and chewed. James knew his recovery would take time, but to watch his father incapacitated in such a way was heartbreaking. But if anyone knew his dad like he did, he knew he wasn't a quitter and would bounce back when he was strong enough.

The bedroom door creaked, and James was surprised to see him sitting up in the bed. Earlier, the girls had helped him change into his pajamas. They washed his face and coached him while he attempted to brush his teeth, ending the evening with several tender kisses goodnight.

"Hey there. Has everyone gone home for the night?"

"Hey yourself, Dad. Everyone is gone except me, Becks, and Glen. What are you doing up?"

Roy chuckled and swiped his reading glasses from his face, setting them on a closed book on the side table. "I was looking through an old book." He patted the empty space next to him on the bed. "Come and sit for a spell."

James sheepishly sat down, his body making a divot in the soft mattress. "You missed Hank and Ella Mae's call. They said they're gonna try again tomorrow."

He nodded. "That'll be great. Now tell me, how'd it go?"

"With what, Dad?" He was confused, thinking his father was asking about Hank.

"You know with what. With Samantha and a certain ring? How did your proposal go at the Speckled Trout?"

James swallowed hard, not able to answer. He was amazed his father still remembered, especially after his cardiac arrest. He couldn't look him in the eye; his gaze focused on his father's hand covering his and squeezing. His dad seemed to know the answer without him having to say it out loud.

"I'm sorry, son." His sigh was deep.

"Me too."

They sat in silence for several seconds, the heaviness surrounding James's heart returning.

"I'm glad you're here. Like me, you'll need time to heal and process your emotions." His words came out slow and with intention.

"You might be sad or angry for a little while. But don't fight those feelings or avoid them. They're normal, and it's better to accept them and talk about them with someone who loves you."

James lifted his head and eyed his father. "Like you, Dad?"

His face beamed with fatherly love, his white whiskers a stark contrast from his salt-and-pepper hair. "Yep. Like me. I'm gonna have a lot of time on my hands." He squeezed James's fingers again.

"We can heal… together."

# Chapter Five

## JAMES

James lay in his bed and flicked open the red velvet box, the diamond ring inside glimmering in the morning light of a new day. His father was right. He needed to take some time to heal and start processing the loss of Samantha, the woman he thought he was ready to spend the rest of his life with.

Taking the ring out of the box, he slipped the diamond onto his pinky finger, his eyes capturing the simple yet stunning jewel. He clenched his jaw, triggered by the unwanted memories of the life they once shared and the future he pined for.

He knew it would hinder his progress in starting over if he hung onto the ring. Maybe he should sell it? With the funds he'd gain back, he could enjoy a much-needed mental break, like a vacation where he could take some time alone with his emotions, away from his family.

But he didn't want to dwell on things that didn't go how he wanted. And holding onto the beautiful ring would only remind him of his past with Sam, the painful memories haunting him. With his mind made up, he stuffed the ring into the box and shut the lid. He was definitely selling the engagement ring. He needed a clean break so he could move on.

Settling the box in the empty drawer of his dresser, he eyed himself in the attached mirror. Dark circles were prominent under his brown eyes, his lack of sleep evident. His usually coifed hair was a mess, and the shadow of an incoming beard peppered the lower part of his jaw, the scruffy look very unlike him.

Scrubbing a hand down the coarse hair, his bare chest lifted in a deep sigh. He didn't have the energy to shave, nor did he really want to. Maybe he and his father could start a beard-growing contest while they recovered? Now, there was a fun idea.

Delia greeted him with a wagging tail in the kitchen of the small carriage house, the sturdy doggie door near the refrigerator swinging open with Jaxson coming in after an early romp outside.

"Good morning," James hummed, stroking the beasts.

He was quick with their breakfast while waiting for a cup of coffee from his single-serve machine. The good coffee would be hot and ready in the main house, Becky getting the morning breakfast spread prepared for him and his brothers and the long-tenured farmhands.

Life on Bennett Farms never stopped, not even for a recovering cardiac arrest victim or a heartbroken winemaker.

Thankful for his routine, James dressed warmly and clomped across the pebbled path with his canine friends by his side. He breathed in the crisp morning air and marveled at the fog lifting from the mountains beyond the vineyard. His life was here, on the farm, and he was proud of what they'd accomplished with their thriving family business.

In a few short months, the first glimpses of spring would appear, the season one of the most beautiful and refreshing in the Langston Falls area. The transition from cold winter weather to warm and pleasant temperatures was something James looked forward to most. Springtime was also a time of reflection and rebirth, not only at the Bennett Farms winery but also in his daily life. He was ready to jump head-first into outdoor activities and get his hands dirty in the vineyards.

Even though spring was a quieter time of year for winery tastings, and the vines had yet to grow grapes for the next harvest, some folks assumed this was the time to sit back and relax, which couldn't be further from the truth. If anything, springtime was a crucial period in the vineyard's annual cycle and could decide the success of the vine's fruit growth.

Managing it all took James and his brothers countless hours of hard work and dedication. There was lots of soil tilling and pruning to be done, setting the stage for the upcoming growing season. They also worked on cleaning up the vineyard and the entire property from the fall and winter rains.

They'd mow weeds, trim trees, and tend to the land-scape, making the whole estate a tidy and manicured place for their guests. And he looked forward to bottling their new apple-infused wine named after his sister, Rebecca Rose, which rested comfortably in one of the warehouses on site with an expected debut around their April wine club shipment.

James loved to educate and share with the tourists about what went on in the vineyards. There was nothing quite like seeing the springtime growth firsthand, the expansive vineyard views eventually exploding with different stages of bud break, flowering, fruit set, and the ripening of the grapes. Weekend outdoor wine tastings would start again soon, their tasting room in the big red barn welcoming with Becky's treats and the family wine. Folks were also encouraged to bring their furry friends, the farm dog-friendly, much to Jaxson and Delia's delight.

As James trotted up the last few stairs to the back porch area outside of the kitchen, he was taken aback by the sight of a young boy. He couldn't have been more than seven or eight, his dark eyes behind thick glasses going wide when he noticed the big dogs.

James immediately grabbed Jaxson and Delia by the collars so they wouldn't knock the poor lad over and scare him. Much to his surprise, the little boy grinned from ear to ear. He wasn't afraid at all, came right up to the canine duo, and patted their heads. When Jaxson licked the boy's face, his ensuing giggling was contagious.

James kneeled and smiled at the boy. "You like dogs?"

"Yes, sir. What's their names?"

He ruffled the fur on Jaxson's neck first. "The black one is Jaxson, and this here yellow one is Delia."

"Jaxson and Delia," the boy repeated.

"Yup." He watched him lavish his dogs with eager pats and hugs around their necks, mesmerized by his joy.

Standing, he cleared his throat. "My name is James. I'm Jaxson and Delia's doggie-daddy."

The boy looked up at him with warmth and ease. "My name is Noah."

"It's nice to meet you, Noah. What are you doing out here all by yourself?"

"My mom told me I could come out here and look at the big red barn. Do you have any tractors?"

James squatted again, unsure why a young boy's mama would be at the farm this early in the morning. The winery wasn't even open this time of the year.

"We've got several tractors at Bennett Farms. We've also got a few ATVs and pickup trucks." He eyed the boy with resolution, eager to understand why he was there.

"Noah, what are you and your mama doing here this morning?"

"My mom's a nurse. She's helping the man inside."

It all made sense now. Noah's mother was the new nurse looking after his father. That she brought her young son to the farm while she was on the clock perplexed him.

"What do you say we go inside so you can introduce me to her?"

"Can't," Noah simply said.

"Why not?"

"She's helping him in the bathroom."

"Oh." James stood again and ran his hand down his scruffy chin. Knowing Noah's mother and his father probably didn't want to be disturbed, he got an idea.

"You want to see the inside of the barn while you wait? I've got some doggie treats in there you can give Jaxson and D too. They'll love you forever if you give them a treat."

Noah's eyes lit up as he pushed his glasses up his nose. "I want to give them a treat."

"Okay, but hold up for a minute so I can let your mama know."

James left the boy loving on his dogs and slipped inside the kitchen. Becky was busy putting the finishing touches on the morning breakfast buffet spread across the kitchen island.

"Hey," he greeted. "I just met Noah. He's outside with the dogs."

She grinned and set a large plate of breakfast burritos wrapped in foil on the island. "I knew he'd spot you and the dogs. He's a sweetie, isn't he?"

James grabbed two burritos and tucked them inside his coat pocket for later. "Nice kid. But why is he even here? I mean, he told me his mama is the nurse helping Dad. Why would she bring her kid to work with her?"

Becky explained while filling a travel mug with hot coffee. "Sara just moved into town."

"Sara?"

"Yes, Noah's mother is Sara Larson. It's winter break, so Noah won't start school at Langston Falls Elementary until next week. Until then, she asked if it'd be alright if he came with her for the first few days while she took care of Daddy. I told her it was fine with me. Do you have a problem with it, James?"

He shook his head. "No problem at all. Where are they from?"

"I'm not sure." She twisted a lid on the mug and handed it off to him.

"Thanks. Do you mind telling Sara that her son wanted to see the inside of the barn, and I'm taking him? We won't be long."

Becky offered a sunny smile and nodded. "Great idea. But keep an eye on him. Little boys are known for getting into mischief if you know what I mean." She playfully punched him in the arm, alluding to James and their three brothers' antics over the years.

"I will," he chuckled.

Outside, James scanned the back porch and scowled when he realized Noah and the dogs had disappeared. Trotting down the steps, he breathed a sigh of relief when a flash of sable and golden fur caught his eye on the edge of the pine forest. Much to his chagrin, Noah happily threw sticks for his dogs to retrieve.

Bringing two fingers up to his mouth, he whistled, startling the boy. "Come on!" he hollered, pointing toward the barn.

Noah immediately grinned and ran toward him. A few trucks were parked in the lot next to the barn, indicating some farm workers had arrived for the workday. Out of breath, the little boy looked up at James with awe etched across his flushed features.

"Can we go inside?"

"Sure."

James hoisted the heavy door open, running the ancient wood along a refurbished track system. The interior of the barn was frigid, the smell of earth and sweet wine permeating through the rafters. Flicking on a switch, the Edison-style string lights illuminated the space in a soft glow.

"Cool," Noah said, craning his little neck to take it all in.

James came around the end of a long bar and set his coffee mug on the counter. He reached under and pulled a plastic bucket from a lower shelf. "Do you want to give Jax and D a treat?"

"Yes!" The little boy was full of energy and curiosity and came up beside him, watching his every move.

"We get lots of dog visitors here at the winery. We keep a stash of treats just for them."

He took the lid off and peered inside the recently replenished bucket. Jaxson and Delia eagerly sat on their haunches, tails wagging wildly against the hard dirt floor.

Taking two bone-shaped treats from the bin, he handed them off to Noah.

"Here you go."

Noah giggled and held them out to the dogs. Jaxson swiped the treat from his hands and gulped his in an instant. Delia was more gentle and slower in her actions, crunching her biscuit with ease as if enjoying every bite.

"Can I give them another one?" How he eagerly looked up at James with permission left him flushed with warmth, the child's innocence and naivety beguiling.

"No, sir. It's a treat, not a meal. Too many treats aren't good for them. How about you? Are you hungry? I swiped a couple of breakfast burritos from the kitchen." He pulled one of the foil-wrapped burritos from his coat pocket and handed it off.

"Thanks."

"What do you say we sit on a tractor and have our own breakfast treat this morning?"

"A real tractor?" Noah asked, his youthful voice cracking with excitement.

"Yup. A real farm tractor. Come on." Palming the boy's shoulder, he guided him through the barn, thankful for the unexpectedness of the new day.

Truth be told, it was turning out to be a good one.

# Chapter Six

## JAMES

James never did meet Noah's mother that day. He was sidetracked by a bottle delivery and a malfunctioning label machine at the winery. At least the little boy seemed pleased he got to sit on a tractor, his breakfast burrito cast to the side, tiny hands gripping the worn steering wheel in imaginative play.

Not long after, Becky texted James, telling him to return Noah to the house per his mother's request. He'd forgotten about the boy until after supper when he paid his dad a visit before retiring for the night.

Roy was propped up against a thick pillow. The bedside lamp was on, but his eyes were closed, his chest rising and falling in steady breaths. His face was freshly shaven, and his hair was neatly combed and parted to the side. As James bent over to turn the lamp off, his dad blinked open his eyes and smiled groggily at him.

"Hey," he exhaled.

"Hey, Dad. Sorry if I woke you."

"You didn't wake me. I was just dozing on and off like I do most days."

James sat on the edge of the bed and grinned. "You look good, Dad. Fresh."

Roy chuckled. "Miss Sara helped me out today. Feels good to show my face again." He ran his crooked fingers down his smooth jaw. "Did you get to meet her?"

"Sara? No. But I met her son, Noah. We hung out for a little bit this morning."

Roy nodded. "He's a good boy. He sat right over there and told me all about you letting him sit on the old tractor behind the barn. That was a good thing you did for him."

James frowned. "Why?"

"Because he's the new kid in town and hasn't made any friends yet. He went on and on about how you let him give the dogs a treat, showed him all the gadgets on the tractor, and explained how they worked."

"Well, truth be told, Noah didn't need to be here while his mother was helping you. I'm not sure I'm too keen on her bringing her kid to work if you know what I mean."

Roy sank lower into the bed and sighed. "Hush. It's only for a few days. He'll be in school soon enough. Give the boy a break and have a little fun with him when you see him around, okay? Once upon a time, you were a little half-pint following me around the farm too."

James laughed. "As long as he doesn't get into trouble, I guess I'm fine with it." He patted his father on the arm. "Get some rest. Goodnight, Dad."

"Goodnight."

He flicked off the light and was about to close the door when his father's voice stopped him.

"James?"

"Yes?"

"Don't forget, when one door shuts, another opens."

James sighed. "I know."

"Just don't stare at that closed door for too long, or you might miss out on the one next to it opening up for you."

He furrowed his brow, unsure what his father was getting at but thankful for his little pep-talk. It meant he was feeling more like himself, which was a blessing.

"Whatever you say, Dad."

---

In the early morning hour, James awoke to a wretched smell curling around his nostrils, waking him from a deep sleep. Sitting upright in the bed, he rubbed his eyes and sniffed the air, grimacing with dread.

"Dog shit," he mumbled. Swinging his legs over the sides of the mattress, he tucked his bare feet into well-worn slippers.

The sunrise was still an hour away, and he was in no mood for cleaning up poop in the middle of the night. There was a doggy door for his dogs to go outside and take care of business. That they couldn't hold it in meant two things: snow, or they were sick.

Shrugging on a sweatshirt, he padded through the hall-way, the unmistakable stench growing stronger and stronger with each step. Turning on the kitchen light, he stopped in his tracks, his face morphing with horror at the scene before him.

There was dog crap *everywhere*, a trail of poo running out the doggy door as if Jaxson or Delia tried to make it outside before the shitstorm invaded. But alas, one or both dogs didn't make it.

James slapped a hand over his nose and mouth, his gag

reflex engaging as his body attempted to eliminate the stench from his system.

Two panting muzzles lifted the heavy plastic of the doggy door open, Jaxson and Delia peering inside the kitchen. The dogs didn't dare return inside as if knowing they'd done something wrong.

"Stay back!" He hollered through splayed fingers across his face, his other hand fixed in a rigid stop motion.

Jaxson whined as James carefully crossed the floor, avoiding the crap mines along the way. The entire scene looked like something out of a grotesque horror film.

"Oh. My. God," he mumbled, unsure of what to do first. With the doggy door secure, he knew he needed to act quickly as it was cold outside, and he didn't want the animals out in the elements for too long, especially if they were sick.

Grabbing a kitchen towel, he wrapped it around his face to help with the stench and filled the sink with hot, sudsy water. Upon further inspection, he was thankful the shit-storm hadn't spread through the rest of the house. The worst of it was in the kitchen area nearest the doggie door.

Using an entire roll of paper towels, James got most of it off the linoleum floor and disposed of it in a tightly knotted garbage bag. He scrubbed and mopped the area and followed up with a potent bleach concoction that burned his eyes. But the residual stench lingered in his nostrils, making him grumpy.

His hand shook as he finally opened the door, his big dogs shivering on the welcome mat. A paternal instinct took over as he coaxed the animals through the hallway and into the tub, where he scrubbed them in a warm bath. They seemed exhausted and rested on the bathmat as James took his shower, relieved the worst was over.

His phone rang in the bedroom, and he wrapped a towel around his middle, leaving the dogs sequestered in the bathroom so he could answer it.

"Bro, where are you at?" Walt asked. "Becky said you didn't show up for breakfast. You okay?"

James clenched his jaw, his arm and neck muscles tired from scrubbing and cleaning for the past few hours. "The dogs shit all over the kitchen. I've been cleaning up crap for hours."

"Fuck, that's horrible," Walt laughed.

"It's not funny. I'm not sure what instigated it. I didn't feed them anything out of the ordinary yesterday."

"Well... You didn't, by chance, forget to put the lid on the dog treat bin in the barn, did you?"

He tensed. "No. Why?"

Walt chuckled. "When I came in this morning, I noticed the bin was tipped over and empty. Unless your dogs know how to open it, someone else might've given them the entire bucket yesterday."

James gasped, shocked by the news. "Walter, that was an entire ten-pound bag! Are you telling me they're all gone?"

"Yup."

He closed his eyes and groaned. "Noah..."

"Go easy on him, Jimmy. He's just a kid."

"A kid that made my dogs sick. I gotta go." He tossed the phone onto his bed and hurriedly dressed.

When he left the carriage house with his dogs following from behind, he noticed Nurse Sara's white sedan parked near the main house, which meant Noah was probably somewhere nearby. He still couldn't understand why a professional nurse would bring her kid to work.

Spotting the boy on the back porch, James waved his hand to gain his attention.

"Hey! Noah! Come over here."

The little boy's face lit up at the sight of the dogs, and he eagerly descended the steps in his faded red sneakers. He was all smiles until James spoke in a low, menacing voice.

"Did you feed my dogs the entire bucket of treats yesterday?"

Noah's eyes went wide from behind his glasses as he looked up at him, the boyish grin from his chapped lips fading.

"Answer me."

"I… I thought they were hungry."

The two dogs seemed to look at the exchange between boy and man, Jaxson whining with unease.

"Noah, what you did was *very* bad, do you understand?" He pointed at him like a stern teacher. "My dogs were sick all night long because of you. They shit all over my kitchen, and I've been cleaning it up for hours! Do you know how awful it is to clean up dog shit? Huh? I should've found you and had *you* clean it up—"

Noah's lower lip trembled before he turned and dashed up the steps toward the house, fleeing James's rant.

"*You owe Jaxson and Delia an apology!*" he yelled after him. "And you owe me one too," he mumbled, kicking at a stone with the pointy tip of his cowboy boot.

He harrumphed, rolled his eyes, and moseyed into the barn, evidence of Noah's generous handout lying empty on the dirt floor. Picking up the plastic bin, James eyed his dogs.

"No more treats for a while, understand?"

Jaxson barked in protest as Delia sat on her haunches and wagged her tail.

"Give the boy a break, my ass," he muttered.

His nose itched with the faint smell of dog crap lingering in his sinuses. What a shitty start to his day.

# Chapter Seven

## SARA

Sara set the one-pound hand weights on the floor and stretched her back while waiting for Mr. Bennett to finish his business in the bathroom. She'd started him on a few simple exercises to regain strength since his hospital stay, and he quickly caught on.

Roy was undoubtedly charming, and he was definitely sweet, like a good Southern tea. The man was constantly making small talk about life and his big family. She'd met two of the Bennett brothers, Teddy and Walt. And on both mornings, she was pleasantly greeted by their sister, Becky, who offered her hot coffee and an assortment of breakfast items, including homemade pastries, much to Noah's pleasure.

She had yet to meet Hank, who she learned resided in Nashville, and of course, "Mr. James," as Noah called him, the man with the big dogs.

As she tucked her son in bed the previous night, he couldn't stop talking about his farm adventure. Sara was grateful James had taken Noah under his wing and paid attention to him. That's all her son ever wanted—a friend to call his own. And it didn't even bother her that James was a grown man and not an eight-year-old boy.

Splaying her hand against her hip, she winced from the lower back pain brought on from a fitful night's sleep on the less-than-comfortable bed in the economy motel where they were staying. It was slim pickings in the real estate market. Between her job at Bennett Farms in the mornings, and her other part-time job at the local clinic she was about to start once Noah was in school, she didn't have much time to house hunt.

Still, she hoped she might score something over the weekend after Noah's birthday party when she finally had some scheduled time off. But she was already disappointed by the meager choices she'd found through the newspaper and online when she perused the internet when the motel Wi-Fi worked. The small town's housing inventory was definitely depleted.

Sara reminded herself the first week in a new town was always the hardest, finding a residence and enrolling Noah into the local school. Once he was settled around some kids his age, enjoyed his party, and she found them their own space, she knew things would calm down.

Being a travel nurse had its perks. The money was fantastic, and the travel took her and her son to places she might not have ever explored if she was a permanent employee at a doctor's office or a hospital. They usually ended up staying in a location for nine to twelve months, most of her patients elderly and in need of home care, physical therapy, and assistance in their daily routines. Half her day was spent in a patient's home, the other half working part-time at the local clinic. She'd always had an innate desire to help people, her empathy and patience a plus in her field.

But there was also a downside to being a travel nurse: Noah.

The poor boy had lived in at least ten towns since birth. Every time they moved on to her next assignment, the second grader seemed up for an adventure. But she could tell not having a permanent home to call their own was starting to take a toll on him, especially with his birthday coming up.

"What do you want this year, snuggle bunny?" she'd asked him.

"I want a big party with lots of friends. You know, the kind of party with balloons and games and a great big cake with a giant number eight!"

Sara bit her lip, unsure how to make her child's birthday wish come true. "What about presents? Is there anything you've been thinking about? Anything you've got your eye on?"

Noah shook his head. "I don't want any presents this year. I just want a party with friends…"

The door to Mr. Bennett's bathroom opened, and Sara was back in work mode, quickly sliding the new walker toward him.

"Do you remember how I showed you?" she asked.

"I think so." With a firm grip, he placed his hands on both sides of the walker.

"Good job. Now, move slowly a short distance, keeping your weight on the palms of your hands."

Mr. Bennett did as she instructed, moving forward with ease.

"Piece of cake," he joked, grinning at her.

"I'm impressed."

Before she could coach him any further, the bedroom door burst open, startling Mr. Bennett and causing him to teeter on his feet. Sara was fast and gently grabbed him by the arm in a sturdy grip so he wouldn't fall.

"I've got you."

"*Mom!*" Noah hollered. "Mr. James screamed at me and used a bad word!"

Sara was mortified by her son's loud voice in the presence of her client and apologized, her face exploding with heat. "I'm so sorry, Mr. Bennett. Let's get you situated so I can get my son under control."

Obviously agitated, Noah yanked at the edges of her pink scrubs, not letting up. "Mr. James said the bad word twice and didn't even apologize. It's not my fault his dogs got sick. He told me I could give them treats. He even showed me where they were in the big red barn."

Sara barely understood what her son was saying, his speech fast and high pitched. With Mr. Bennett sitting safely in a chair, she turned and squinted at Noah, her voice low and firm.

"You need to wait for me outside this bedroom, do you understand? I'm with my patient—"

"He's fine, Sara. He can come in here anytime he wants to, especially if he needs his mama," Roy interrupted.

"Thank you, sir. But Noah understands the rules while I'm working. I can assure you this won't happen again. Now, if you'll excuse me, I'll find out what's going on and then bring you back a mid-morning snack. How does that sound?" She offered him an uneasy smile.

Mr. Bennett's cheeks turned ruddy, his chuckle deep and infectious. "You go right ahead. I'm not going anywhere. And for the record, I find it highly unusual for my son, James, to use bad language. He's usually a

complete gentleman. Fill me in when you get the full story."
He winked.

Sara herded her son out of the bedroom like a mother
hen and shut the door. "Noah Michael Larson, what in the
world were you thinking barging into the bedroom like that?
You scared the daylights out of Mr. Bennett, and he almost
fell down." Her hands were planted on her hips as she
scolded her son; her voice turned down a notch in case
other family members were nearby.

"But mom, Mr. James is really mad at me. He *cursed* at
me! He said the 'S' word."

Sara wasn't sure what word he meant, knowing he'd
never been around folks who used profanity. And Roy
assured her James wasn't like that.

"What word? Stupid? Smelly?"

"*Shit,*" his little eyes lit up, saying the word out loud as if
knowing it was taboo.

"What?" She was stunned. "Why... who... grrrrr.
Come with me."

She grabbed him by the hand and pulled him through
the house and out the back door, thankful she didn't run
into any other Bennetts along the way. The bright sun was
blinding, and the weather was frigid without a coat.

Scanning the area in front of the barn, she spotted two
big dogs, and a man she assumed was Mr. James chatting
with Walt. Squatting to Noah's level, she held his forearms
and looked right at him.

"You stay right here while I go have a chat with Mr.
James, okay?"

"Okay."

Standing tall, she clenched her jaw and marched down
the stairs with fisted hands. No man was going to yell
obscenities at her son.

"*Excuse me!*" she hollered.

The two men turned their heads in unison, their cowboy hats shadowing their features.

Huffing, she came right up to them. "You must be James Bennett, am I right?"

The man smiled and took off his hat, thrusting his hand out in a greeting. "Yes, ma'am. I'm James. You must be Sara."

"Yes. I'm Sara Larson, mother of Noah Larson." She raised her eyebrows and crossed her arms in front of her bosom. There was no way she was going to shake his hand.

Walt snickered and sheepishly shoved his hands into his front jean's pockets. "I told you to go easy on the kid," he mumbled toward James.

"Shut up, Walt."

"Did you just yell at my boy?" She watched him slowly anchor his hat back on his head and step away from her.

"No, I did not yell at him. But I admit I did use a stern tone in my voice to get my point across. I apologize."

"Did you use profanity in front of him—*twice*?"

"Aw, Jimmy. You didn't," Walt teased.

"Walter, shut up," James said again through gritted teeth.

Sara watched the long column of his throat move in a swallow. He was a handsome cowboy, no doubt. That she took in his good looks during a confrontation made her even more miffed. Huffing a stray auburn hair escaping her claw clip, she steeled herself against the man's charming disposition.

"Answer the question, please. Either you did, or you did not use profanity in front of my child."

James tilted his hat back and squinted in the sunlight.

55

"Well, that depends on your definition of profanity. What word did your son say I used?"

Sara looked over her shoulder and up the hill at Noah. He sat on the top step with his elbows propped on his knees, chin in his hands. He looked so young and innocent, although she did notice a gleeful smile taking up half his face.

Turning back toward James, she let the word exit her mouth in an exhale of hot breath.

"*Shit*. And he said you used it *twice*."

James nodded. "Yes. I did use that particular word, but it was used in context with the situation."

"Excuse me?"

He pointed toward Noah. "Yesterday, I showed your son where I keep the dog treats in the barn and let him give one to Jaxson and Delia. I explained to him that a treat was *not* a meal. Later in the day, when he was obviously out of your supervision…"

Sara winced at the back-handed comment, reminding her how unprofessional she was bringing Noah to her job. But she had no choice until school started back after winter break.

"… Noah took it upon himself to wander into the barn without my permission and feed my dogs an entire ten-pound bag of treats."

She gasped, bringing her cold fingers up to cover her mouth. "The entire bag?"

"Yes, ma'am. As you can imagine, this did a number on my dogs' digestive systems, and they ended up…," he cleared his throat, "… *shitting* all over my kitchen floor last night."

He stepped toward her and tipped his hat back to where she could make out his dark eyes and angular jawline covered in scruff. "Have you ever had to clean up an entire ten-pound bag's worth of dog shit?"

Sara shook her head, mortified by this information.

"I can assure you, it's not a pleasant experience. So, yes, I used the word 'shit' when I explained to Noah about his actions having consequences. He's lucky they're okay and not at the vet. And furthermore, he offered no apology or remorse whatsoever."

Heat flared across her cheeks. "I'm… I'm so sorry, James. I had no idea."

His features softened, and he took his hat off again, the move chivalrous. "I'm sorry too. But I want you to understand, I used the word in the correct context. It was not used as a form of profanity directed toward your son. I would never, ever do such a thing, I promise."

"I understand."

Walt intervened, interrupting the apologetic gaze Sara and James shared. "You should get back inside without a coat on, Miss Sara. It can get pretty darn cold in the mountains during the winter."

She hadn't noticed the cold, her body blushing from top to bottom with noticeable heat. "Yes. I need to get back inside. I've got physical therapy exercises to do with your father." She looked right at James. "And don't worry about Noah. I promise he won't be a problem again."

He offered her a generous smile. "He's not a problem child. He's just a little boy. All's forgiven." He winked at her.

Stunned, her mouth fell open as she stood there. "Thanks."

Walt looked back and forth between the two and cleared his throat. "You should get inside before you catch a chill, Miss Sara."

She sucked in a breath and nodded. "Yes. You're right. Brrr," she giggled, wrapping her arms across her chest. "I'll, uh… see y'all around."

Turning her back on the pair, she hurried up the stairs in her clunky nursing clogs, knowing the brothers were watching. Pushing her hair back from her face, she pressed her lips together to thwart a slight grin.

She hadn't had a handsome fella wink at her in ages.

# Chapter Eight

## JAMES

"Can you please pass the potatoes?" Teddy asked. He sat beside his wife, Robyn, at the dining room table.

James sat across from his brother and sister-in-law and passed off a chafing dish. Every Thursday night, without fail, the entire family gathered for a meal, and this week was extra special, having their father back home to join them. The only couple missing was Hank and Ella Mae.

"Thanks. Say, I heard you got into a little scuffle with Miss Sara this week." Ted grinned, plopping a massive mound of mashed potatoes onto his plate.

"There was no scuffle, Teddy."

Walt snickered next to his wife, Elyse. "Oh, come on. I was there. Y'all were like two peacocks sizing each other up."

"We were not." James forked a big bite of meatloaf and shoved it into his mouth. Talking with his mouth full, he said, "I explained the situation, apologized for my profanity, and she was fine with it."

Roy sat at the head of the table, his smile indicating he felt better and was undoubtedly enjoying the usual Bennett sibling banter. "What did you say, Jimmy? Miss Sara wouldn't tell me. I've been dying to know."

"Don't say 'dying,' Daddy," Becky admonished. Her pretty brow furrowed with worry.

"Sorry, darlin'." He patted her hand next to his.

"I'm not going to say the word or the context in which I used it at the dinner table because we're eating, and it's inappropriate. Let's just forget about it and enjoy this fine meal Becky made with all your favorites, Dad," James insisted.

Glen cleared his throat, all eyes turning toward him. "I remember the first time I ever cussed in front of my ma. She wasn't having it one bit. Sat me in the corner and told me to open my mouth wide. Next thing I know, I'm sitting there with a bar of soap between my lips."

"She didn't!" Elyse gasped.

"Oh, yes, she did. I'll never forget it. It was that green Irish bar soap too. Tasted nasty."

The family erupted in a bout of hearty laughter. The focus shifted from James, and he was glad.

Looking around the table at his siblings and their partners, a pang of sympathy dinged his heart when his eyes landed on his father at the head of the table. He looked smaller—almost fragile among them. He was a widower going through a health crisis without their beloved mother by his side.

At least he had all of them and, of course, Miss Sara. On the bright side, there was a familiar gleam in his eyes since he'd come home, and he seemed happy as a lark taking in the energetic conversation around the dinner table about curse words and the taste of soap.

James sat back and swirled his glass of Bennett Farms wine, his thoughts shifting to Samantha. He wondered what she was doing at that moment. Was she over-stimulated being in a new environment in Virginia? Was she overdoing it like always, trying to prove herself? Had she made any friends?

Was there a single second she ever thought about—him?

"Besides your little scuffle with Sara, what did you think of her, Jimmy? Do you like her?" Becky asked. Leave it to his little sister to play matchmaker.

"I like her," Roy chimed in.

"I know you do, Daddy," Becky laughed. "And I'm glad."

"She's a good girl. And her son, Noah, reminds me a lot of all you boys when y'all were his age."

"How so, Roy?" Robyn asked.

"Curious. *Loud*," he chuckled. The entire table laughed with him. James was happy he'd dodged another bullet.

"I sure do miss those days when your mama kissed your boo-boos and tucked y'all in at night after bath-time with a story. When you'd ask a million questions about any 'ole thing, and she'd patiently come up with an answer until you were satisfied." His eyes misted, and he sniffled, bringing his napkin to his face. "I sure do miss her."

"We all do," James comforted.

The group turned quiet, and he noticed Robyn lean her head against Ted's shoulder and the way Walt wrapped an arm around Elyse. Glancing at Glen, he was surprised to see the big lug of a man swiping a wayward tear from his bearded face and the way Becks offered him a sympathetic smile, while tenderly holding his hand.

Teddy changed the subject to something more mundane as James kept his emotions in check and sipped from his glass, his thoughts shifting from Samantha to Sara Larson and her son. What was her story? Was there a Mr. Larson? If there was, why did she bring Noah to work with her and not leave him with his father?

Sara was a pretty woman, and knowing his dad trusted her was a bonus. Even though their encounter was brief, he'd noticed the barren ring finger of her left hand. And her rosy cheeks below those heartbreaker blue eyes. And the way her auburn hair glinted in the sunlight with hints of gold interspersed in the reddish-brown tresses. Even her mama-bear attitude made him respect her from the get-go.

Draining his glass, he decided to scope her out in the morning and get some of his questions answered. Either that, or he'd have to do a deep dive and investigate the woman online.

---

James was already on his second tumbler of coffee, his nerves on high alert as he kept an eye out for Sara's arrival. A cold front had come through in the night, the vineyard and Christmas tree fields covered in light frost glinting like diamonds in the morning sun. Thankful for the warmth of the main house kitchen and hot coffee running through his veins, he leaned his forearms against the island and took his time scanning his iPad.

Unlike his sister, Becky, Sara Larson didn't have a social media presence. No Facebook, no Insta, no tweets. She wasn't even listed on LinkedIn. When he typed her name in the search engine, he scrolled through dozens of women with similar names. Images of coaches, writers, fashion designers, students, and mothers stared back at him, none of whom held the likeness of the woman caring for his father.

He was about to give up when he came across an article from the South Georgia Medical Center in Valdosta, Georgia, a "staff spotlight" highlighting a Georgia College State University nursing graduate named Sara Larson. The article recognized her compassionate care, presenting her with The Daisy Award for Extraordinary Nurses. He learned the award highlighted nurses who provided skillful care to patients and families, reinforcing the importance of compassion in health care. His Sara was definitely compassionate.

James inhaled sharply when the screen landed on a picture of her wearing bright blue scrubs. A stethoscope hung around her neck, and she was smiling. James smiled right back.

"Boom," he muttered under his breath. He'd found his Sara.

She was gorgeous, her auburn hair resting on her shoulders in perfect waves and her blue eyes vibrant with pride. She stood tall, her hands clutched around a plaque with her name on it. Even though he didn't personally know Sara, he was delighted she'd been recognized.

He continued reading the short article, thrilled he'd found something about her online. She was even quoted in the article saying, *"I work in a department where not all of my patients have the ability to remember the care I provide them, so this award holds a special place in my heart."*

She was pretty *and* well-spoken.

"Is that Sara?"

James was startled and stood tall, almost knocking over his coffee. Becky was right next to him, staring at the screen.

Unable to hide the evidence, he cleared his throat and said simply, "Yup. That's her."

Becky eyed him inquisitively. "Why are you looking her up online?"

Flicking off the screen, he shrugged. "I don't know. Curious, I guess. Gotta make sure whoever's in our home is on the up and up. You can't be too careful these days."

Becky harrumphed. "You know the hospital has strict policies about who they send for home care, right? She's been vetted and approved by a reputable agency."

"I know."

"You want to know what I think? I think you like Sara, and you're checking her out." There was a teasing tone in his sister's voice.

James rolled his eyes. "Yeah, right. I thought I'd scope her out so she could be my rebound babe."

"Jimmy!"

"What?" He laughed. "Even if I was attracted to her, I'm not asking her out. No way. Not after my recent breakup with Sam. And besides, she's got a kid, and I am *not* in the market for an instant family. No thanks."

Becky puckered her lips to the side, and he could almost see the wheels turning in her head. "Still, you admit she's attractive, right?"

He shook his head, tucked his iPad under his arm, grabbed his coffee, and hoofed it toward the mudroom to get his coat. "This conversation is over, Becks."

Coming around the corner to the space packed with work boots, coats, hats, and gloves, he almost collided with Sara.

"Oh!"

"Shit! My bad." With his free hand, he gripped her arm to steady her.

"He said it again, Mom! See?" Noah was right beside her and pointed a mittened hand at him.

"I am so sorry. What is wrong with me?" His chuckle was forced, and he was embarrassed he'd used profanity again, called out by the little boy.

"Good morning, Sara. Hey there, Noah," Becky sing-songed from behind James's shoulder. "I have a glazed doughnut with your name on it."

She summoned the kid with a crooked finger. James had never been so happy for a diversion in his entire life.

"Goodie!" Noah squealed.

"Mittens in your coat pockets," Sara yelled after him.

"Okay, mom!"

James finally let go and stepped back when it was just the two of them in the mud room. A subtle smile was etched across Sara's face as she blinked at him, her blue eyes wide with wonder.

"Good morning, Mr. Shit," she giggled. At least she wasn't mad at him this time around.

"Good morning. And I deserve that." He watched her unroll a scarf from around her neck and hang it on an empty peg. When she shrugged off her coat, he was quick with his manners.

"Here. Allow me."

"Thanks." She handed off her coat, and he hung it up for her. There was an awkward silence for a beat before she spoke again.

"Well, I should check in with your dad and see how he did last night."

"Yes. You probably should."

She smiled again and started to walk past him. James caught her by the wrist, and she jerked to a stop, a gentle whiff of her perfume snaking its way under his nose in the cramped quarters. It was sweet with a subtle hint of citrus.

"I have questions," he said.

Her lips were dewy in the morning light, her azure gaze doing funny things to his stomach—or maybe it was the exorbitant amount of coffee he'd already consumed?

"What kind of questions?" She pinned him with her stare, the space between her pretty brows indenting. Even dressed in navy scrubs and funny-looking shoes, she was a pretty woman.

"What kind of pizza does Noah like?"

Her lips twerked into another amazing smile. "Why?"

"It's my way of apologizing. And it's Friday, and we won't see y'all again until Monday. With your permission, I'd like to take him out on one of the ATVs and show him the farm. Maybe have a little pizza party for lunch?"

Sara nodded as if pleased. "Pepperoni."

"Then pepperoni it is." He grinned.

"And you won't see him on Monday because he'll be starting school. But this will be a great treat for him, because his eighth birthday is tomorrow."

"Get out! His birthday is tomorrow?"

"It sure is."

"I'll bet he's excited, huh?"

"Excited for his birthday and nervous about school." She glanced at her watch. "Anything else? You said you had questions, which is plural."

"Hmmm. I did, didn't I?" He leaned his shoulder against the wall. "Just one more."

He paused for a beat, hoping against hope she'd give him an honest answer.

"Are you married?"

"Nope."

Her one-word response was all he needed. "Good to know."

"And you?"

"Nope."

She nodded slowly. "Duly noted, Mr. Shit." She stifled another laugh and disappeared, leaving James pressed against the wall.

Things were getting interesting.

# Chapter Nine

## SARA

Sara stood in the doorway of the small meeting space of the economy motel and surveyed the room. Brightly colored streamers were strung from the corners into the center light fixture, and helium balloons in all shapes and sizes bobbed up and down against the walls. A rectangular table was set up with snacks ranging from popcorn and pretzels to pepperoni pizza bites, cookies, and juice boxes.

She had bingo cards made, hung a piñata in the shape of a tractor, and set up a small speaker in the corner to play musical chairs. There was even a table with little goodie bags for each party guest to take home filled with stickers, mini chocolate bars, and bubble blowers.

But the party's focal point was a mammoth sheet cake she'd ordered from the local bakery decorated with a giant number eight in bright yellow frosting. It was precisely what Noah wanted, and she couldn't wait to see his reaction. The only thing missing was the "friends."

Noah was officially enrolled in Miss Dodge's second-grade class at Langston Falls Elementary School, set to start his first day on Monday, after the shorter week of winter break and teacher workdays. Sara had gone out of her way to deliver a stack of birthday invitations to Miss Dodge's teacher's mailbox, inviting every child from his new class to the party. She figured meeting his classmates before his first day at the new school was a win-win. And what kid wouldn't want to come to a fun birthday party?

The school receptionist assured her the invitations would be delivered on time. And she congratulated Sara for being such a thoughtful parent, especially with her son being a new student in the middle of the school year.

"Hey! Lookin' good, mama!" Crystal Cavanaugh peered over Sara's shoulder into the room.

"You think? Am I missing anything?" The two ambled inside.

"No, honey. The place looks great." Her accent was thick, and her makeup thicker. "Has Noah seen it yet?"

Sara shook her head. "No. I gave him extra screen time on my computer. He's in the room playing video games while I set up."

"Smart."

The two had become fast "happy time" friends in the last week when Sara hung out in the lobby with Noah, watching the Disney channel on the big screen TV. She didn't like keeping him cooped up in the tiny motel room and thought a change of scenery would do her son some good.

Crystal was thrilled and offered Sara a hard seltzer— and the empty meeting room off the check-in desk for Noah's party. She said it was all hers whenever she wanted. She also offered a discount when she learned Sara had struck out again, finding any affordable lease in town.

"You stay here as long as you want. I'll look after y'all," she'd said.

Sara was thankful for a new friend of her own; the two of them total opposites. She'd learned in the short time they'd been hanging out that Crystal was a widow, her husband Waylon, the love of her life, killed in a tragic hunting accident. They'd never had any children, but Crystal's motherly instincts were intact with how she cared for her little dog and how she doted on Noah as if he were her own.

The vibrant woman never pried or asked questions, allowing Sara to share things from her life on her own terms. They laughed a lot and kept each other company in the evenings while hanging out in the lobby near the big screen TV Noah was obsessed with.

Sara was always in scrubs, while Crystal wore tight pants, high heels, and revealing tops that accentuated her double-d's. She was a regular Dolly Parton with big blonde hair and vibrant, painted nails.

But Sara learned real quick not to judge a book by its cover. CC was a savvy businesswoman and didn't take any crap from anyone, especially the truckers and loggers who often stayed at her establishment for extended periods. She knew them by first name and even asked about their wives and children.

It was common knowledge Crystal knew everyone in town, and she was always befriending those who were just passing through. She knew Sara was a travel nurse—a "noble profession," as she'd called it. But she didn't know Sara cared for Roy Bennett, who she probably knew. That part was patient confidentiality, and she planned to keep it that way.

Because it was a Saturday, Sara wore regular clothes,

her well-worn blue jeans comfortable and her button-down denim shirt over her turtleneck sweater open and loose. Glancing at her wristwatch, she nodded and smiled.

"It's about that time. I'll go get the birthday boy." A sudden rush of emotions swept through her, and her voice cracked. "I can't believe he's eight years old today."

Crystal tilted her head and offered an empathetic smile, her red lips popping against her pale complexion. Tinker-belle looked on from the crook of her arm.

"You go on and get him. I'll keep watch for the early little princes and princesses."

"Thank you."

Sara unlocked the door to her room and noticed Noah sprawled on his tummy, wearing headphones. He was oblivious to her entrance, spellbound by the colorful images on the computer screen reflecting in his glasses. She sat down, making a divot in the mattress, and rubbed his back, her touch bringing him back to reality. He sat upright and flung the headphones off with excitement.

"Is everybody here? Is it time for my party?"

She smoothed his unruly hair back from his face and nodded. "Almost. Go wash up and get your shoes on."

"Yippee!"

By the time they got downstairs, Sara was perplexed when she made eye contact with Crystal, who shook her head. Glancing at her watch again, she frowned. The party guests were late.

"Wow!" Noah exclaimed.

He rushed inside the meeting room and went from table to table, checking everything out, the perpetual smile on his youthful face making Sara's heart clench.

"Do you like your cake? I had it made exactly the way you wanted."

Noah approached the cake in awe, his little tongue darting out of his mouth and licking his lips. The distinct aroma of sugar and chocolate was prevalent in the small space, the anticipation of a sugar high sure to keep him up way past his bedtime. But it was his eighth birthday, after all. There were those special times when rules were made to be broken.

"It's perfect," he whispered.

Sara glanced at Crystal, who leaned in the doorway cradling her Chihuahua close as she took in his joy.

"I bought pointy hats, but if you don't like them, you don't have to wear them."

"I want a hat!"

She laughed and watched Noah pick up the cone-shaped cardboard.

"Careful with the chin strap. Don't let it snap your skin."

He nodded and carefully placed the hat on his head while pulling on the thin elastic strip. He continued to roam, thanking her profusely. Then he dragged a chair right in front of the cake table and sat down, intent on inhaling the sweet smell of chocolate and marveling at the giant yellow eight repeatedly.

Sara pulled her phone out of her back pocket and snapped a picture. It was then she noticed the actual time. Furrowing her brow, she approached Crystal with wide eyes and pressed her teeth into her lower lip. The start time of the party was twenty minutes ago.

"They'll be here," she reassured, stroking Tink's fur.

"You sure about that?" she whispered.

"Mom?"

Sara jerked her head to look at her son. "Yes?"

"Where is everybody? You dropped off the invitations at the school, right?"

Her heart hammered in her chest. "Yes, baby. I did. Folks must be running late, is all."

The front door to the lobby dinged, making Tinkerbelle yip. Noah rushed to the doorway with a wide grin on his face. But it was short-lived when he realized it was a strange man and woman probably checking in.

"I'll be back in a jiff," Crystal said, going into hotel manager mode.

Noah leaned against Sara's legs, and she pressed her hands into his shoulders, her mind reeling with what was happening. Surely, the entire second-grade class wouldn't forego his party. What kind of small-town families would do such a thing?

Another twenty minutes later, Noah's pointy hat was askew as he shuffled his feet, sat back down in front of his cake, and sulked. With his elbow on the table, he rested his chin in his hand, looking so forlorn and sad, Sara thought her heart might break into a million pieces.

Anger replaced her sadness in a flash, and she pulled her phone out again and captured the woeful moment. She had a right mind to show his new teacher what she and the rest of the class had done to him.

Tears welled in her eyes, and she had to dig deep to muster the energy to salvage the day. Standing tall, she forced herself forward and stood in front of the cake with her hands on her hips.

"What do you say we dig into this giant monstrosity, huh?" Her grin was forced, and she noticed Crystal in the doorway again, her lips pressed together with disappointment.

"I'm not hungry."

"Okay. Maybe later?"

"Sure." He looked up at her with big puppy-dog eyes from behind his glasses, his lower lip quivering. "Can I go back to the room and play video games."

Sara swallowed hard and nodded. "Miss Crystal? Do you mind taking Noah back to our room while I get this giant cake back in the box so we can have it for later?"

"Don't mind at all." Her heels clicked on the linoleum floor as she crossed the space. "Can you please hold Tinker-belle for me?"

"Sure."

Crystal passed off her pet to Noah, and he cradled her in his arms, pressing his cheek against the top of her head. Tink licked a lone tear making a path down his face, the action so sweet and profound, Sara thought she might lose it.

"Come on, handsome. I'll take you back." Crystal palmed his shoulder and maneuvered him toward the exit.

Noah stopped as the two crossed the threshold and looked over his shoulder.

"You did good, Mom. Thank you. It's not your fault no one came. They just don't know me yet. Maybe next year?"

Sara blinked back tears, her lips trembling in a forced smile. "Sure, snuggle bunny. Next year."

When he turned and disappeared, she clamped her hand over her mouth to muffle the sob she'd been hold-ing in.

# Chapter Ten

## JAMES

There was a definite pep in James's step, knowing Sara was due at the farm any minute. He was anxious to hear all about Noah's birthday party—and to lay eyes on the pretty auburn-haired nurse whose blue gaze did funny things to his insides.

"Good morning," Becky sing-songed while standing at the giant stove. She was flipping pancakes, the scent of maple syrup warming on the back burner, filling the kitchen with homemade goodness.

"Mornin' Becks. Sure smells good in here."

"I've got sausage links too. Everything will be ready in about five minutes."

"Cool." He strolled to the coffee pot and poured a cup. Leaning against the kitchen counter, he asked, "Do you need any help?"

"No thanks."

James didn't bother removing his coat and took his mug outside on the front porch with his big dogs trailing from behind. Plucking a worn tennis ball out of a basket, he jerked his arm back and flung it into the air. Jaxson took off in a flash of sable fur as he noticed Sara's white car crest the hill. His smile was immediate.

"Good boy," he said to Jax, vigorously rubbing the fur on his neck. He held onto his collar and gave Delia a turn, tossing the ball across the vast stretch of dormant lawn. As soon as she fetched the ball, he stood tall and leaned against a post from where he could watch Sara exit her vehicle.

"Mornin'," he hollered with enthusiasm.

Looking up at him, her expression appeared downtrodden. "Hey, James."

"Hey." She continued down the pebbled path and up the steps, walking right past him.

"Hold up, Sara. How was the drop-off at the school this morning? I'll bet Noah was super excited. And how was his birthday party?"

Her shoulders lifted in a heavy sigh before she turned around, her azure eyes shimmering with unshed tears.

James frowned and set his coffee on a side table beside several outdoor chairs. "Uh-oh. What happened?"

Sara shook her head and looked everywhere but at him.

"Come here." He reached for her hand and led her to one of the chairs, motioning for her to sit down. "Tell me what happened."

Wringing her hands in her lap, she spoke softly. "I messed up, James. I messed up bad."

"What do you mean?"

He watched her fish her phone out of her purse, fire it up, and pass it off to him. A photo of Noah sitting before a giant birthday cake was on the tiny screen. He held his chin in his hand, his pointy birthday hat crooked on his head, and his sad expression a sign things had not gone as planned.

"I dropped off the invitations at the school last week during a teacher work day, and I watched the receptionist put them in Miss Dodge's teacher mailbox. She assured me she'd get them and pass them out to the class before the weekend."

His eyebrows raised. "Miss Dodge is still teaching second grade? Wow. I had her back when I was at Langston Falls Elementary School."

Sara shot him a surprised look. "Well, maybe she shouldn't be teaching anymore after all these years. Apparently, she called out for a substitute teacher when the students came back after winter break ended because her arthritis was acting up again—"

"Oh no," James interrupted.

"Oh yes."

She pinned him with her stare, and he watched a lone tear escape the corner of her eye. He wanted to lean in and swipe the tear with the pad of his thumb, the thought of touching her skin leaving him reeling in his boots.

"Of course, the substitute teacher didn't know to check the mailbox, which meant the invitations never got delivered to the students. Nobody showed up."

"Nobody?"

She shook her head again. "Not a one."

James returned the phone to her, his excitement replaced with pure disappointment for the little boy. "How did Noah take it?"

Sara sniffled and ran her hand under her nose. "Like a champ. He never cried. In fact, he tried to console me. He said it wasn't my fault."

"Because it wasn't."

"Yes, it was." She stood and looked out over the lawn with her hands on her hips.

"What am I doing, James?" Her voice cracked with emotion.

He didn't know how to answer. Instead, he came up beside her and squeezed her shoulder. They stood there in silence for a good thirty seconds. And then she surprised him by turning in a rush of emotion and gripped the lapels of his coat, burying her face into the fabric. Her sobs were soft and pitiful.

James was tender in his actions and wrapped his arms around her, allowing her to cry against him. Her soft hair smelled like flowers, and he pressed his nose into her tresses where it was strongest. He held her tighter, feeling sorry for the pretty single mom and her son. Feeling an undeniable need to want to help.

When she finally pulled back a bit, her muddled baby blues held his. And what he saw there was something like confusion or embarrassment. Licking his bottom lip, his eyes mapped the curve of her cheek and the tangle of auburn hair hanging over her shoulders.

"I'm sorry," she muttered.

"Don't be." He held her by the forearms. "Seriously, what can I do to help make things better?"

"Nothing. It's over. I just hope his first day as the new kid in school goes well."

"It will."

"And thanks again for buying him pizza on Friday and taking him on an ATV ride. He hasn't stopped talking about it since. At least you gave him a birthday to remember."

James offered her a crooked smile. "Don't you remember? I'm the shit."

His comment induced a laugh from Sara's pouty lips. "You sure are."

He was bold and leaned low, swiping an escaped tear from her cheek with his thumb, eyes never leaving hers. "Come inside and warm up. Becks made pancakes and sausage. A little comfort food will perk you right up."

"The only thing that will perk me up is a Saturday do-over."

James held the front door open, allowing her to walk through first. The dogs followed, and he paused.

A do-over was just the type of thing he was good at.

———————

"James?"

"Yeah?"

"What's wrong with Sara today? She seemed off at breakfast." Becky wiped down the kitchen island, her face pinched with worry.

James sat at the table, scribbling notes on a pad of paper. "None of the kids from Langston Elementary showed up for Noah's birthday party on Saturday."

"*What?*" Becky was shocked and marched over to the table. "You've got to be kidding me. Is Noah okay? Oh, my gosh. He must've been devastated."

"He was. But I've got a plan. Have a seat." He motioned with his head toward the empty chair across from him.

"What have you got in mind?"

James shifted the pad of paper to where Becky could see it.

"*Surprise party for Noah,*" she read from the top line. "Really?" Her excited gaze flicked to his, the enthusiasm in her voice noticeable.

"Absolutely. We can do it this Saturday. I'll rally our

brothers and farming friends. I also want to contact the local fire station and see if they can do a drive-by with one of their big rigs. Let's go all out and make it a surprise-slash-welcome party he and his mama will never forget."

"Do you think you should talk to Sara about this first?"

"Nope. I kind of want it to be a surprise for her as well. Maybe we disguise it as a fake Bennett family supper, and they show up to a regular country fair welcoming them moving to town and Noah turning eight."

Becky's eyes danced with joy. "You really like him, don't you? Even after the stunt he pulled, feeding your dogs all those treats? Or do you have an ulterior motive and you're trying to impress his mama?"

James laughed. "Of course, I like him." He left it at that, not about to confess to his little sister he was also infatuated with Sara. Damn, she was pretty.

"Whatdoyousay? Can I count on you to be on board with this? It'd be good for Dad too. You know how he loves a good party."

"Count me in."

"Cool."

He showed her his notes and how he planned on turning the big red barn into a carnival-like atmosphere with games and prizes. There'd be tractor rides, hayrides through the fields, and tons of pizza and kid snacks. He even thought about having adult nibbles and wine samples for the parents. And Becky suggested asking Glen to bring over his classic 1960s powder-blue refurbished pickup truck for the kids to gawk over.

"Great idea, Becks. We could gather and stack all the birthday presents in the truck's backend. Sara told me Noah likes anything with wheels on it."

"Just like Glen and all my big brothers growing up on the farm," she giggled.

James passed his phone across the table and showed Becky the picture of Noah in front of his birthday cake. He'd asked Sara to forward the photo for the cake example. It was also an excellent way to get her number.

"Do you think you'd have time to make a cake that looks like this?"

Becky scanned the picture, her smile immediately fading.

"Poor Noah. Of course, I can make a chocolate cake with a giant yellow eight for him. Anything to bring back a smile to that little face." She handed him his phone.

"You're going to be blessed by this, Jimmy. Noah and Sara are going to be blown away."

"I sure hope so."

"I know so." She grinned.

# Chapter Eleven

## SARA

Sara rolled a thin layer of gloss across her lips and eyed herself in the giant mirror of the motel bathroom. She'd been counting down the days and hours until Saturday, the dinner invitation to Bennett Farms a pleasant diversion from the recent birthday party catastrophe.

James had invited them, saying it was the least he could do after what happened to Noah. He even told her how his thoughtful sister, Becky, was recreating the birthday cake Noah requested, complete with the giant yellow number eight. This left her speechless. No wonder he'd insisted she forward the picture she took of Noah in front of his cake on that fateful day, even though a part of her secretly hoped he'd asked for the photo as a sneaky way to get her phone number.

Eyeing her toiletries on the cramped sink vanity, she sighed. Too bad she hadn't found a permanent residence yet. Her address was still at Crystal's motel off the main highway into Langston Falls. CC assured her something would open up when the timing was right. In the meantime, most of her belongings sat boxed up in a storage unit across town.

At least Noah's first week of school went well, her son adjusting to his new routine like a champ. He'd even made a new friend, a red-headed boy named Billy.

Fluffing her hair one last time, she focused on the positive and was excited about having something to look forward to. The entire Bennett family had welcomed her and Noah into their fold, and for the first time in years, she felt… wanted.

Suffice it to say, she enjoyed her client's family more than any other she'd served over the last decade in nursing. It was as if they were her family. And James Bennett was an added bonus; he was always a total flirt making her giggle with his "shitty" side comments and boyish grin. And his biceps and handsome good looks weren't too shabby either.

"Mom? You coming?"

Sara inhaled sharply, her cheeks flaring with heat, knowing she'd been daydreaming about James again. It was kind of hard not to.

"Yes!"

Ten minutes later, she drove under the Bennett Farms sign and sped up the hill toward the main house. Several cars and trucks lined the drive, making her frown. Had she misunderstood James and his dinner invitation? Perhaps her thoughts had been diverted to his full lips and charming smile when he'd first invited her. Had she completely gotten the wrong impression?

This looked like a party.

"What's going on here tonight?' Noah asked. He craned his neck to look out the back window at the numerous pickups and SUVs.

"I'm not sure. James said it was a family dinner."

"Well, Mr. James sure has a big family."

His comment made her smile as she pulled into an empty space. "You got that right."

The two of them marched hand in hand up to the front door, the faint sounds of music pinging the air. And was that popcorn she smelled?

"Hey!" James greeted with a mega-watt smile. "Come on in."

He immediately took off his black cowboy hat and welcomed them inside. He was dressed in dark jeans with a thick coat covering his plaid button-down, and his face was chiseled and smooth from a recent shave. She'd never seen his whole face before, his normally thick scruff obscuring his undeniably handsome features. Her tummy pooled with warmth as she scanned his features and ushered Noah ahead of her.

James held out a splayed hand in an attempt at a high-five. "How are you doing, birthday boy?"

Noah stopped and didn't reciprocate, shoving his little hands into his pockets with force. "My birthday is over."

"Are you sure about that?" The grin on his face was infectious.

"Mom? What's he talking about?"

"I'm not sure." She looked James right in the eye. "What's going on here? It looks like you're having a party."

He chuckled and leaned in, giving her a peck on the cheek, the smooth skin of his cheek making contact with hers. "Oh, it's a party alright. Come on and I'll show you." He ushered them through the main house to the rear entrance off the kitchen, not even stopping to ask for their coats.

When he opened the door wide, Sara was startled by the

spectacle that appeared beyond the stairs leading to the area in front of the big red barn.

"My family and I would like to officially welcome y'all to Langston Falls with a special party. Of course, we had to make it birthday-themed," he said simply.

Noah audibly gasped at seeing the carnival-like celebration prepared just for him.

Sara's eyes immediately welled with tears as she squeezed her son's shoulders. "Well, go on then. Mr. James went to a lot of trouble for you."

"It's no trouble at all. The entire family was in on it."

She was dumbfounded and stared at him as if he had two heads.

Noah broke free from her and bear-hugged his thigh. "Thank you, Mr. James. Thank you so much!"

"You're welcome, son."

They watched him rush out the door and stand at the top of the stairs, waving his arms frantically while shouting, "I'm here, everybody! I'm here!"

All eyes looked up, and a pronounced cheer swelled as folks waved and clapped for the guest of honor. He trotted down the stairs more confidently than a prize fighter after a knockout in the final round. Sara had never seen her boy happier.

"How did you… *why* did you…"

"Surprise," he grinned.

The crinkled skin in the corners of his eyes when he smiled made her heart drop to her stomach. The only thing she knew to do at the moment was to give him a bear hug.

"Whoa!" he exclaimed in a happy tone, losing his footing for a second from the force of her embrace. "I take it you're happy too?"

"You have no idea," she mumbled against the thick fabric covering his shoulder.

He smelled of pine and earth, and she had to hold back the sudden urge to run her fingertips across the smooth skin of his face and full lips. Breaking their connection, she stared back at him with wide eyes and wondered if he could see the outline of her heart hammering from beneath her coat.

"Just so you know, this isn't all about Noah. This is for you too."

"Me?"

"Yes. We've got adult beverages, food, and tables set up for big kids like us. I thought you deserved a little something special too." The pride in his gorgeous expression said it all.

There was much to see; the party spread across the property and already underway with kids and parents, Bennett family members, and dogs enjoying the festive atmosphere.

Twinkle lights were strung across the area in front of the barn, with a few outdoor heaters and firepits glowing in the late day. Several kids gathered around the small flames holding enormous marshmallows on sticks for S'mores, Becky Bennett supervising the gooey chaos. The local fire department was present, the gleaming red rig carrying ladders and curled hoses a beacon for little boys and girls trying on flame-resistant jackets and oversized fire helmets.

Sara couldn't take it all in fast enough. The air was heavy with the scent of popcorn and burning wood mixed with evergreen and upbeat music, thick with joy and cele-bration. Between the happy sounds of children and the backdrop of the magnificent mountains, she was over-whelmed with gratitude.

She spotted Roy Bennett holding court with a few of the adults. He wore his signature cowboy hat and sat comfortably on a bar stool at a wine-tasting table. Exhaling a deep sigh, Sara palmed her heart, grateful he felt good enough to join the party.

The sound of an ATV cut through the air with Walt behind the wheel. Three children were strapped in and waved at their parents as he took the vehicle in a fast turn through the Christmas tree fields and disappeared into the pine forest. Colorful balloons outlined the entrance to the barn, and a vintage 1960s pickup truck was parked nearby, the back stacked with wrapped presents. The entire scene looked like something out of a movie.

"I... I don't know what to say," Sara whispered, her voice hoarse with emotion. "Thank you."

Palming his hat onto his head, James reached for her hand and linked his fingers through hers, squeezing gently. "You're welcome. Now, why don't you leave your purse in the kitchen, and I'll show you around."

"Okay." She followed him back inside and set her purse by the refrigerator, holding his hand tight, not ready to let go.

He faced her, his coat stretched across his broad shoulders, smooth cheeks notched with a cockeyed grin. "Would you like to watch the kids go wild and wear themselves out while we relax by one of the firepits with a glass of Bennett Farms Merlot? I hear it's delicious."

"Sounds amazing."

The kitchen lingered with the aroma of sweet sugar, the island crowded with remnants of baking utensils and frosting tools smeared in yellow. She knew in her gut there was a birthday cake somewhere in the vicinity made by Becky Bennett herself.

But right now, she was more interested in the way James looked at her with those warm brown eyes and how his handsome grin left her feeling lightheaded as if she'd already consumed a glass or two of celebratory wine. And the steady squeeze of his hot fingers linked through hers wasn't foreign to her. He was... familiar. Comfortable. For a man to go to so much trouble bringing joy to her son was everything she dreamed of.

Gratitude flooded her system, and she squeezed back, unsure if she could ever let go.

# Chapter Twelve

## JAMES

The satisfied grin on James's face couldn't be helped. He knew he'd hit a grand slam with this birthday party celebration, overjoyed he'd made Sara and her son happy. The way her face lit up like the fireworks on the fourth of July was enchanting, the pretty nurse experiencing happiness after a long, deflated week.

He'd do it all over again just to see her smile like that.

Leading her down the stairs, they greeted several parents and kids, including Noah's new friend, Billy. He was a cute little boy with fiery red hair and a smattering of freckles across his nose and chubby cheeks. Seeing Noah completely animated and excited reminded James of when he was a boy at one of his birthday parties, the youthful buzz in the air contagious.

They bellied up to the bar inside the red barn, and he caught the attention of one of the hired servers. "Two merlots, please."

Sara stood right next to him, and the way she leaned

against his shoulder was very telling. "If I forget to tell you later, I had the best time tonight."

James shoulder-bumped her gently. "The night has just begun."

He knew today wasn't about scoring with the auburn-haired mother. Today was about kindness and showing her how much he believed in family and birthday party celebrations, friendship, and small-town neighbors. He wanted her to experience an authentic community and how everyone came together to show their support for one of their own. And wasn't she one of them now?

They had a connection. Sparks. A rolling thunder building beneath the surface. It didn't matter he knew relatively little about her. Heck, he didn't even know where she and Noah lived. But he planned to find out, and tonight was only the beginning.

Handing her a glass, James held his in the air. "To you, Sara. Welcome to the neighborhood. And to Noah's eighth trip around the sun."

Her flawless cheeks flushed with gratitude, and she demurely angled her head. "And I'd like to add, cheers to you, James, for making Noah's birthday dream come true."

As if on cue, Walt drove by the entrance to the barn in an ATV and honked, Noah waving from the passenger seat with glee.

"Hi, Mom!"

"Hi, baby! Hold on."

"I will."

Pride bubbled up in James's chest as they laughed, dinged glasses, and sipped, the bold flavors of his family's wine filtering through his senses. Her deep blue, appreciative gaze held his, and she hummed with pleasure.

"Mmmm. This *is* delicious."

"Told ya."

They meandered outside, the laughter of children prevalent against the backdrop of the sun setting beyond the mountains.

"Wow," Sara uttered.

She stared at the sky for several seconds, the swaths of orange and violet creating a breathtaking view. "I always leave the farm after lunch to work at the clinic in the afternoons. I had no idea the sunsets were this beautiful here."

His eyes traced the sky, knowing how blessed he was all these years growing up with the tapestry of beauty right outside his front door. He often took the simple act of noticing and rejoicing in the ethereal splendor of the sunset for granted. For him to stop, relax, and take time out of his often busy farming day to appreciate the colors was a gift. And he was undoubtedly savoring the added beauty of Sara Larson standing right next to him.

Before he could delve into a clumsy speech about the symbolic meaning of what a sunset meant to him, Sara pressed her hand against his bicep.

"I'm going to say hello to Roy and make sure he's doing okay. I'll be right back."

"Okay," he chuckled.

He watched her leave, her auburn hair glowing in the golden hour. Inhaling a deep breath through his nose, he took a hefty swig from his wine glass, thankful he hadn't said anything stupid.

"Hey, Jimmy. Nice job on the party." Teddy had his arm around Robyn, the two looking cozy and very much in love.

"You really outdid yourself with the theme," she added. "I've never seen so many happy kids bouncing around the farm, except when you and your brothers were little."

"They're probably all on a sugar high. I went a little overboard with the kid treats for tonight," James admitted.

"Definitely," Teddy laughed. "You know I'm a sucker for S'mores. I've probably had at least four in the last hour."

Robyn giggled and swiped her hand down Ted's beard. "You still have bits of marshmallow and graham cracker crumbs stuck in your whiskers."

"Snacks for later, babe."

The threesome chuckled as James palmed the back of his neck with chagrin. "Well, when I found out nobody showed up for Noah's party last week, I felt awful for the little fella. I had to do something."

"I know what you mean." Teddy nodded. "I just spoke to Miss Dodge, and she feels real bad Noah had to go through that. She blames herself for being absent and not informing the substitute teacher to check her mailbox."

"Miss Dodge made it tonight?" James was surprised. He hadn't seen his second-grade teacher in decades.

Robyn pointed toward Glen Kirby's vintage pickup truck parked near the barn. "She's standing right over there talking to Becky and Glen. She's very sweet..."

"—and very old," Teddy interrupted.

James laughed. "This I gotta see." He moseyed over to the truck, surprised to find Miss Dodge chatting with a few of her former students, including Glen and Becky.

"James Bennett, as I live and breathe." Her Southern accent lilted with pleasure at the sight of him.

"Hello, Miss Dodge. It's been a long time." James moved in for a polite hug.

"It sure has. My, oh my, look at you all grown up. I was just telling your sister it seems like yesterday I was teaching all of you Bennett boys in my classroom."

"And now you get to teach a new generation, which includes Noah Larson."

The smile on her wrinkled face faded, and she looked away. "My apologies for ruining Noah's first birthday party in Langston Falls. I feel terrible about it."

James waved her off. "It's not your fault."

Becky chimed in, palming the elderly woman on the shoulder. "No one blames you, Miss Dodge. I mean, look at him right now."

She pointed toward the vineyard where Walt drove the ATV around a trellis of dormant vines. Noah had both hands in the air as if on a roller coaster about to go down the first stomach-dropping hill, his boyish giggles infectious.

"Does that look like a sad little boy to you?"

Miss Dodge suppressed a small smile. "He looks like he's having a good time."

"He's having the time of his life," Glen added.

Several slim cocktail tables and stools had been spread out in front of the barn for parents and farming neighbors to enjoy the crisp evening. James caught a glimpse of Sara helping his father up from his seat.

"Well, it was good to see you, Miss Dodge. Please excuse me."

"Nice to see you too, James."

He trotted over to his dad and Sara just in time to grab him by the elbow as he teetered on his feet.

"He didn't bring his walker outside," Sara scolded.

"I had help," Roy explained. "Teddy and Walt drove me down here before the party started. It's all good."

James and Sara were slow in their movements, guiding his father toward a familiar pickup truck with the red peeling letters of the Bennett Farms logo painted on the side.

"The fresh air is good for him, but he's pretty tired. I'd like to get him settled inside for the night," she mumbled toward his ear.

James frowned. "My brothers and I can handle this. You need to stay here and enjoy your party."

His dad grunted, gripping the truck's sides to angle his body inside. "Sara, please listen to James. He can drive me back up the hill and get me inside. I don't want to take any more of your time today. You're off the clock, darlin'."

She bent over and lifted his booted feet one by one and settled them on the floorboard. "You are my responsibility, Roy, even if I'm not on the clock. Please don't argue with me."

James looked at his father with eyebrows raised. Roy chuckled and held his cowboy hat in his lap as Sara snapped his seatbelt in place. "Yes, ma'am."

She approached the driver's side and was about to get in. "Hold on. Let me let Noah know where I'm at, okay?"

He was playing a game near the barn with Billy. Waving her hand to gain his attention, she hollered, "Noah!"

He spotted her and immediately grinned. She pointed at the truck. "I'm taking Mr. Bennett back to the house. You good?"

"I'm great!"

She gave him a thumbs up and scooted across the leather, sitting in the middle of the bench seat so James could drive.

"I'm sorry I'm taking you away from your party…"

"—stop, Mr. Bennett," she interrupted. "I'm your nurse, and it's my duty and pleasure to care for you. I'll return to the party as soon as I get you situated. I promise." She patted his thigh.

Getting his father out of the truck and up the front

porch steps of the main house took extra effort. Sara grabbed his walker from inside, and James helplessly watched as he shuffled across the pinewood floors like a tortoise—slow and painful. Sara assured him she didn't need help getting him settled for the night, leaving him biding some time.

He waited for her in the kitchen, helping himself to another glass of wine. When she finally came out, her smile was immediate.

"He's good. Resting in bed with a book in his hands." She seemed to notice the wine. "May I?"

She held her hand out, and he passed his glass off to her, chuckling as she took a hefty swig.

"Mmmm," she moaned. "You know this is my new favorite wine now, don't you?"

James wasn't sure if it was her azure gaze directed at him, the wine compliment, or the way her lips glistened with the sweet taste of merlot. But he found himself moving stealthily toward her and cupping her cheeks in his hands.

He'd been so close to kissing her when she told him about last week's failed birthday party. On the porch, with her beguiling blue eyes muddled with tears before she cried in his arms. Tonight, with her hand curled around his as they looked up into the sky, sunset colors highlighting her pretty face. And now, in the kitchen, with his hips mere inches away from hers, wine staining her lower lip. He wanted to do more than kiss her.

"What are you waiting for?" she whispered.

Beneath her wide and watchful stare, he glimpsed a spark of something that sent heat surging through his stomach. Leaning lower, his mouth brushed against hers in the faintest touch, her breath a gentle puff against his skin.

Before he could plunder her mouth with his tongue, the

back door opened, and they jumped back from each other, guilty expressions sure to give them away.

"Time for the birthday cake!" Becky announced with a wide grin.

# Chapter Thirteen

## SARA

Sara was feeling no pain, comfortably numb with a wine buzz humming through her system. She angled her head against an Adirondack chair and stared at the inky black sky smattered with a million twinkling stars.

Noah rested against her chest, tuckered out from the energetic party playing with all his new school friends. His hair smelled of wood smoke and baby shampoo, his mouth smeared with chocolate and frosting. Jaxson and Delia lay near them, small flames and embers from the firepit glowing in their black eyes as they kept watch.

"I've never seen the stars shine so bright. Is it because of the higher elevation?" she asked.

James shifted in his seat next to hers, the three of them waiting for the staff to finish cleaning up. All the parents, kids, and the rest of the Bennett family had called it a night a half hour ago, leaving them to decompress by the warm fire.

"Probably. There's less atmospheric distortion the

higher up you go. And Langston Falls is not a big city pumping out tons of air pollution."

"Hmmm," she mumbled, staring into the night sky. She stroked Noah's hair and kissed his cheek, whispering, "Did you have fun tonight?"

"Mmhm."

"Are you tired, snuggle bunny?"

His answer came in the form of a big yawn. Sara turned toward James and smiled. He was staring right at her, his voice low and husky.

"Time to go?"

She nodded. "Would it be okay if I left my car here overnight? I've had my fair share of merlot and probably shouldn't get behind the wheel, especially on these dark country roads. I'll just call us an Uber home."

James shook his head. "Not possible."

"Why not?"

"We don't have Uber in these parts."

"Really? Wow. Well… what about a taxi service? Surely you've got a few cabbies in town?"

"Nope."

"You're kidding me?"

"But I do have something I can offer—a spare bedroom in the carriage house where I live. You and Noah are welcome to spend the night."

Noah bolted upright, causing the big dogs to lift their heads in unison. "Can we, Mom? Please? This has been the best night of my life. I want to stay here on the farm. I don't want to go back to the motel."

"Motel?" James questioned.

Sara helped Noah off her lap and stood, waving off his question. "If you're sure you don't mind, we'd love to take you up on your spare bedroom. I don't want to take any chances driving tonight."

"I don't mind at all." He stood and placed a large lid over the firepit, snuffing out the lingering flames. "Come on."

Sara was more than curious to see the refurbished carriage house near the main home at Bennett Farms where James lived. A narrow staircase led them up to the second floor, where he and his brother Walt had roomed together above the oversized garage for several years. Now that Walt was married to Elyse and residing at the Morgan compound in a big farmhouse down the road, James and his dogs had the place all to themselves.

"It's not much, but it's home." He flicked on the lights revealing a spick-and-span kitchen.

"Nice." She smiled and followed him into the main living space.

A comfortable L-shaped sofa took up most of the room, and a big-screen television was attached to the wall next to a mounted deer head with Mardi-Gras beads hanging from its antlers. Two doggie beds were in the corner, and she watched Jaxson and Delia obediently hunker down for the night.

"I've got three bedrooms: mine, a room we turned into a workout space, and Walt's old room, now the guest room. It's right through here."

They entered the room, and she was surprised at how cozy and inviting the space appeared. Although the dark furniture and bedding held a masculine edge, the place was clean with a made-up queen-size bed. Pictures of old barns hung on the walls, and the shelves and dresser were empty where Walt's personal items must have been.

"This bedroom has its own bathroom like mine. And

you'll find clean towels under the sink. Please, help yourself to anything I've got. You and Noah can borrow some extra T-shirts in the top drawer to sleep in if you want."

"Thanks, James. I really appreciate it." She noticed Noah shift from one foot to another, cupping his hands at his crotch. "Sweetie? You need to go potty?"

"Yes!"

She unzipped his coat, and he bolted out of the heavy fabric straight into the bathroom like a rocket, slamming the door behind him.

"I swear he forgets to go when he's having so much fun," she giggled.

James nodded. "I know the feeling." He paused and looked at his wristwatch. "It's still early. Would you like a nightcap with me after you get him tucked in?"

Immediate heat warmed her cheeks. "I'd love one."

He grinned. "Great. I'll meet you in the family room. Take your time." He politely shut the bedroom door behind him.

Sara shucked off her shoes and hung her coat in the empty closet. Curious, she opened the dresser's top drawer, pleased to find an assortment of tees for her and Noah to borrow. Bringing the fabric up to her face, she inhaled deeply. The shirt smelled like James and made her smile.

She peeled off her sweater and bra and slipped the soft, faded material over her head. She kept her pants and socks on and knocked on the bathroom door.

"Noah? Can I come in?"

"Yes, Mom."

She opened the door to find her son fumbling with the top button of his jeans. "No, baby. You can take those off. But first, let's untie your shoes."

"Mom, I'm eight years old now. I'm not a baby anymore," he pushed back.

She stifled a smile and helped him wash his dirty hands and undress, slipping the extra T-shirt over his head. The fabric reached his knees and swallowed his tiny body, making her laugh.

"This looks like a dress," Noah complained.

"But you know it's not a dress. It's James's T-shirt, and he said you could borrow it. Look, it even has a tractor on the front."

He pressed his chin into his chest and peered over his glasses for a good look. "Cool."

Sara held a washcloth under the faucet and drenched it with warm water. She removed his glasses and ran the fabric across his skin, making him grimace.

"Almost done."

His eyes were closed when she finally tucked the comforter around him and kissed him on the forehead. Tracing her finger through his hair, she smiled and whispered, "I love you, birthday boy."

"I love you too, Mom."

"I'll be in the next room for a little bit, winding down. Get some sleep. Good night."

"Night."

She tip-toed out and gently shut the door, surprised to see James standing by a bar cart stocked with family wine and whiskey. A soft melody played from an ancient record player in a corner unit with colorful albums lined up neatly underneath. And she noticed an uncorked bottle of wine, two glasses, and a tray holding grapes, cheese, and crackers displayed on the coffee table.

"You didn't have to go to all this trouble," she grinned.

But secretly, she was thrilled. The man had poured a lot

of attention into the details of the surprise party, including an exact replica of Noah's birthday cake. For him to throw together a mini-charcuterie board wasn't by happenstance —it was well planned, she was sure of it.

Sara sat on the edge of the sofa and watched him pour the wine. With his coat and flannel button-down off, the long-sleeved shirt he wore underneath fit him like a glove, outlining the dips and valleys of his bulging arm muscles.

"Here you go." He handed her a glass.

"Thank you."

"My pleasure."

They sat and sipped, the quiet sounds of a jazz trumpet humming through the home.

"Is it true you and Noah are living in a motel?" he finally asked.

Sara licked her lips and answered him matter-of-factly. "Yes. I'm having difficulty finding a short-term rental in these parts."

"I'll bet." He cupped the wineglass with one hand. "Which one?"

"Which one, what?"

"Which motel?"

"Oh. It's the economy motel off the main highway at the Langston Falls exit."

"Crystal Cavanaugh's place, right?"

"You know her?"

James chuckled. "Of course, I know her. It's a small town, remember? My dad used to go hunting with her late husband, Waylon. He was a great guy."

"Yeah, she's told me all about him. CC has become a good friend to me. I've enjoyed getting to know her, and she's totally helped me out by giving me a great rate for as long as I need."

She took a hefty swig of wine, thankful to be talking about the elephant in the room.

"Not that I need any sort of help with money. I mean... I make great money working as a travel nurse. I've saved up a ton. Someday, I want to buy a house for Noah and me. You know, a permanent home to call our own."

"Have you been living out of a suitcase for a while?" His forehead furrowed with curiosity.

"Not really. Only now because the motel room doesn't have enough space for all of our stuff. I've rented a storage unit nearby. I usually don't have this much trouble landing a short-term lease. I always find us a place and unpack everything to make it our temporary home."

"Hmmm. Temporary, huh? How long is your assignment with my dad in Langston Falls?"

A gusty sigh escaped her mouth.

"I'm sorry. I'm just... curious, okay? I like you, Sara. I like your son, Noah too. I'd like to learn more about you and your story."

"My story?"

"Yes. What made you decide to become a travel nurse? Do you like moving around this much or is there another reason? What are you... never mind." He shook his head and lifted his glass of wine to his mouth.

Her gaze fixated on his handsome face. "Go ahead, James. What were you going to ask me?"

She sat erect on the sofa, her heart thumping madly beneath the soft tee covering her bare breasts. Of course, James would be the one to get to the root of her story. And she was ready.

He placed his glass on the table and scooted closer to her. Picking up her hand, he squeezed. His voice was low and whispered, his eyes pinning her with his stare.

"What are you running from, Sara?"

# Chapter Fourteen

## JAMES

"I'm not running," Sara replied, pulling her hand out of his grasp.

"You sure about that?" He watched her tuck a thick strand of hair over her ear, her unease noticeable. He must have hit a nerve.

"My story is… complicated. You'd never understand."

"Try me."

She whipped her head to look right at him, the blue in her eyes eclipsed by dark pupils. They were in a stare-off, neither one of them moving. When her shoulders sagged, his pulse blipped with anticipation she was about to tell him everything. Instead, she reached for the wine bottle and topped off her glass.

"I think I'd rather get to know you better before I reveal my deep, dark secrets."

James leaned back and rested his ankle on his opposite knee. "Dark secrets? Well, now I'm downright intrigued." She punched him in the arm with playfulness, and he laughed. "I'm an open book, darlin'. You can ask me anything."

"Anything?"

He nodded. "Sure. Fire away."

"Okay." She sipped and thought for a moment. "Why are you still single?"

"Wow, going straight for the jugular aren't you."

His comment made her giggle. "I'm sorry. I just don't understand how a kind and loving family man like you is still unattached. Is it because you live in a small town? Because everyone around here is spoken for?"

James shifted and leaned his forearms on his knees, cupping his wine glass with both hands. "I was in a committed relationship. She recently broke it off with me over Valentine's weekend."

"Oh, wow. That's harsh. I'm so sorry."

"It's fine. There were red flags all along."

"What kind of red flags?"

"Isn't it my turn to ask you a question now?" He sat up and rested an arm against the back of the sofa, his fingers dangerously close to Sara's hair.

"Okay. I'll let you have a turn. Fire away."

James edged his hand closer to her head and boldly caressed a lock of her hair between his fingers. She didn't pull back, her eyes wide, and her breathing turned shallow.

"Tell me about Noah's father."

She looked away and twisted her hands in her lap. "That's not a question."

"Hey." James set his glass down and leaned low to make eye contact. "It's me, Mr. Shit. Talk to me. I promise whatever you say won't leave this room."

Her mouth tweaked, and her stormy eyes held his as he

reached out and boldly traced the swell of her lower lip with his thumb.

"You sure?"

"I'm sure."

He leaned in for a hug and kissed her cheek with reassurance, tucking his nose below her ear. Her hair smelled like citrus and fire. He dragged his face lower and pressed a tender kiss against her creamy throat.

She tilted her head back, giving him full access, and hummed, "Don't stop."

The tips of her fingers forged through his hair, sending ripples of pleasure to his core. He caged her in his arms and nipped her lips before he moved full steam ahead and devoured her mouth with a searing-hot kiss.

They gave in to the rush together, sucking face on the sofa like two horny teenagers on a first date. Hot staccato breaths. Nipping and licking. His blood-gorged penis tenting his sweatpants.

Coming up for air, they studied their fingers laced together.

"You're dangerous," she whispered.

"Me?" His lips tingled from the kiss, surprised by her comment. He was a puppy dog compared to most men.

"Yes. I've never been this open with anyone, especially a man."

"Well, I hope you know by now I'm not just any man." He kissed her knuckles, his gaze never leaving hers.

She paused as if making up her mind, the floodgates suddenly opening.

"Noah's father was a doctor at the hospital I worked at in Valdosta, Georgia." She focused on his face, her voice breathy and even-tempered. No emotion. No regrets.

"You never married him?" James asked.

Sara rolled her eyes and let go of his hand. She reached for her wine and took a sip. "Nope. We were never married. Russell didn't want children. He was very vocal about it."

James frowned. "So, he left you to raise Noah on your own?"

"Hmm." She pulled her knees up to her chest and swirled the wine in her glass. "I raised Noah on my own by *choice*."

Confused, he ran a hand along his jaw. "Forgive me, Sara. I'm not exactly following you. Is Russell a part of Noah's life or not? Does he at least pay you child support? I mean, he's got the money if he's a doctor."

"Oh, he's got the money all right. But no, he doesn't pay me a dime."

"Well, why not?"

Sara looked right at him again, the words exiting her mouth, shocking him to his core.

"Because he never knew I gave birth to his child."

James became agitated and pulled back in disgust. "Why wouldn't you tell the guy you had sex with that he knocked you up?"

He couldn't fathom her reasoning. Did she do it on purpose? Was there an ulterior motive? His tone must've frightened her because her words came out quickly in a heartbreaking confession.

"Russell was a lot older than me. He was a player. All the nursing staff warned me about getting involved with him, but I didn't listen. I was infatuated he was an elite doctor on staff interested in *me*. We went on a few dates, and that was it. When I missed my period and took a pregnancy test to confirm what I already knew, I *did* do the right thing, and I told him."

"What did he say?" James asked through gritted teeth.

She held her fingers up and mocked quotation marks, her eyes muddled with unshed tears. "He told me in no uncertain terms to 'get rid of it.' I took a leave of absence and weighed my options."

"Your options?" He was crushed. "You mean you almost got rid of your beautiful baby boy because some older egocentric doctor told you to?"

"No. I mean… yes. I thought about it. But I couldn't go through with it. I'd always wanted a child, but I suffered from… female problems and was told the odds weren't in my favor. And I was already twenty-six."

He held up his hand. "Whoa, hold up. If you were twenty-six when you got pregnant…"

"I'm thirty-four now. Noah just turned eight. You do the math."

They were silent for a beat, James processing this information. It was hard to believe she was two years older than him. He had no idea.

Sara continued. "I was floored I was even able to get pregnant. It was a miracle, really. Please believe me when I tell you this. I *wanted* a committed relationship. I *wanted* a devoted father for my child. But Russell made it clear he didn't want any part of it, so… I lied."

"You lied?"

She nodded. "I told him it was a false alarm, and I wasn't pregnant."

"Why would you do that, Sara? He deserved to know. I would want to know."

"Yeah, but you're *nothing* like Russ. I was young and stupid. I thought with his money and his clout, he'd find a way to badger me and force my hand. And that's not what I felt I should do in my heart and soul."

"How did he not eventually find out with you both working in the same hospital?"

Sara sniffled. "I quit my job and stayed with my grandmother in Atlanta until Noah was born. I told no one but my grandmother."

"Not even your own parents?"

She laughed through her tears. "Ha! That's a story for another night, James. I was an only child raised by my grandmother. She died right after Noah was born. I've been alone ever since. I never had a big family like yours."

His muscles vibrated with the urge to throw something. He wanted to flip the table. Shatter the wine bottle against the wall. He rubbed his palm across his forehead, grieved by Sara's loss and tragic story. No wonder she protected her unborn child and lied to that son of a bitch. Noah was the only family she might ever have.

"I never heard from Russell again. But it's probably because I deleted my social media and changed my phone number. I also have a job that keeps me moving from town to town. Don't get me wrong, I still spy on him occasionally to make sure he's stayed put, so I'm never worried I'll run into him at the same Georgia hospital. Even so, he's never tried to find me. He probably assumed he'd dodged a bullet and was in the clear, thankful he could screw around with some other poor unsuspecting young nurse." Her voice cracked with pent-up emotion, her confession finally out in the open.

"But ultimately, it's his loss. I have the most beautiful son to share my life with. And I'd do it all over again in a heartbeat."

Sara's shoulders shook as she broke down and cried. James was instantly beside her, folding her into his arms and holding her tightly.

"We all make choices," she sobbed into his shoulder. "I've learned to live with mine. Noah and I may not be a conventional family like yours, but we make it work just fine."

"I know, darlin'. It's obvious Noah loves you to the moon and back," he reassured.

"And I love him. I'd sacrifice everything for my son. He's all I have. Please don't worry about us. I'll figure out our next steps. I always do."

James was shaken, her heartfelt confession making his head spin.

The record player stopped, and the half-empty wine bottle and charcuterie board were left untouched on the coffee table. Sara stretched out across the couch and laid her head in James's lap. He was numb, stroking her hair back from her face in a slow, deliberate motion until she fell asleep.

Once again, his mind went into fix-it mode. There had to be a way he could help Sara and Noah find housing while they were here in Langston Falls.

He just needed a little more time to figure it out.

# Chapter Fifteen

## SARA

"Why the long face?" Crystal Cavanaugh asked. She handed Sara a hard seltzer in a can, their regular motel midweek get-together right on schedule.

Sara glumly rested her chin in the palm of her hand, her elbow crinkling the newspaper she'd been sorting through laid across the big lobby table. "I've called every single one of these realtors about housing in Langston Falls multiple times. What is it about small towns and short-term leases, huh?"

"What do you mean?" Crystal parked herself opposite Sara and cocked her blonde head. Her nails were painted a bold red, several bracelets jingling as she brought the seltzer up to her over-glossed lips and took a sip.

Sara glanced at her own nails, embarrassed by the rough edges and chapped skin from one too many hand washings while on the job. "It seems the homeowners in this town have long-standing commitments with the Floridians getting ready to pack up and come north for the spring and summer months so they don't melt in their home state. There's hardly a single lease available."

Crystal laughed. "You got that right. Do you know how hot and humid it gets down south?"

"Uh, yeah, I do. I worked in Valdosta, Georgia, for several years. It's about fifteen miles from the Florida state line. I got a facial from the humidity every time I walked outside to get the mail."

"Lord, have mercy. How did you manage those awful summers living there? My hair would've never recovered." She palmed her over-sprayed up-do to ensure not a single hair was out of place.

"It wasn't so bad because I was holed up in a freezing hospital most days."

Noah approached the table and dug his hands into a tote bag Sara had brought down from their room. She kept the bag filled with his favorite snacks, a sweatshirt, and a refillable water bottle.

"Thirsty?" she asked, ruffling his hair.

"Uh-huh." He grabbed the bottle and trotted back to his seat in front of the lobby television. Sucking water through the built-in straw, his eyes were fixated on the screen as the animated cars sang about life being a highway.

Crystal smiled. "I'm so happy the Bennett family came through for Noah and surprised him with a big party. And I'm glad you're the one nursing Roy Bennett back to health."

Sara had come clean about her nursing assignment taking care of Mr. Bennett, glad she could share details with CC about the fantastic party the family had thrown for them.

Her cheeks heated, the mere mention of the Bennett

name taking her back to James's place. The way he listened when she told him her story. The way he held her when she completely lost it, strong arms comforting her with lips pressed against her forehead. The way he promised he'd help her find housing so she could settle down in Langston Falls.

"I know y'all want a place to call your own while you're in town," Crystal continued. "But let me ask you a question. Are you married to the idea of a short-term lease? Why not think outside the box?"

Sara swallowed a mouthful of passion fruit flavor, thankful for the cocktail Crystal shared. Grateful for her friendship. Intrigued, she nodded.

CC sat up a little straighter, her giant bosom magnificent against her tight sweater. The woman was a regular pin-up girl with her big hair and overly done makeup face; the regulars at her hotel often using the nicknames "Backwoods Barbie" or "Bombshell."

"Noah likes his new school, right?" she asked. "And didn't you say he has a little buddy now?"

"Yes. His name is Billy, and they're inseparable."

Crystal's blue eyes lit up from beneath her heavy false eyelashes. "What if you made a list of pros and cons and…" she paused.

"And what?"

She leaned forward and pressed her bejeweled hand on Sara's. "And considered staying in Langston Falls long term yourself? Why not *buy* a house?"

Sara took a hefty swig of her drink and eyed Noah sprawled on the big sofa. He didn't care if he was watching a show in a motel lobby as long as his favorite channel was on.

Unbeknownst to Crystal, she *had* thought about putting down roots in Langston Falls several times. The small town was just the right place to raise a young boy. Country living agreed with him. The mountains. The small classroom size with friends. The tractors and barns.

The Bennett farm.

"I'm considering it," she mumbled, locking eyes with Crystal.

She squealed. "Well, hot tamale!" She set her can on the table and grabbed a sheet of newspaper. Sara was shocked when she pulled a pair of reading glasses from her tight britches and settled them across her nose. Crystal looked like a sexy school teacher.

"You don't want anything on the south side. The trains will keep you up all night in the summertime. There's a cute little neighborhood on the north side of town, within walking distance of Main Street. You could find a place with a nice front porch and put together some flower containers. Maybe even hang up a porch swing and some ferns. You know, stay a while?"

The excitement in Crystal's voice was contagious. Sara always imagined she and Noah would permanently land somewhere quiet and friendly when the timing was right. Could her new home potentially be in Langston Falls? Was this the end of her running?

"I've never wanted to settle down until we came here," she confessed.

"I know, honey. There's something magical about our little slice of heaven up here." Crystal concentrated on the newspaper and circled a property with a big fat marker.

Sara never saw herself as the type with a white picket fence dug into the ground or flower-filled planters on a front porch. The thought made her skin prickle with nerves. Or maybe it was excitement? She'd saved enough money over the last decade to put a substantial down payment on a house but never felt the urge to settle down in any of the towns they'd lived in before.

Never till now.

Crystal stopped perusing the newspaper and tapped the end of the pen against her cheek. "Mark my word, sweetie. We're gonna find you something special. And don't be afraid to start all over again. You just might like your new story way better."

Sara pursed her lips together and offered her friend a quick nod. Was her anxiety over the lack of short-term leases? Or the guilt that Crystal was right; a home purchase might be better suited for her and Noah now that he was older?

No. She knew what this was about.

James.

She blamed her carriage house confession on the exorbitant amount of wine she'd consumed the night of the birthday party and apologized profusely to him the next day. He wasn't having it and told her in no uncertain terms he would always be there for her and Noah, no matter what.

And what kind of man would sacrifice his weekend planning a massive party for virtual strangers anyway, just to make a little boy happy? She knew what kind. A compassionate man. A man with morals and family values. A man whose kisses ignited a fire in her belly, making her crave so much more.

Glancing at her innocent son, who always went along with whatever adventurous career choices she'd made over the years, she knew he'd be happy if she decided to stay put. Living in and out of motels and rentals his entire life had taken a toll on him. Maybe CC was right? Perhaps it was time to start a new story and put down roots. But she needed to muster the willpower to open her mind to this possibility.

Langston Falls would undoubtedly be the place to do it. Her heart and mind felt safe here. Protected not only by the mountainous region in the small town off the beaten path but by the folks she'd befriended and trusted in such a short time. She'd never experienced anything like it.

If she was meant to stay in Langston Falls with her son, finding a home would be the easy part. The hard part was changing her attitude. She was the walking definition of unsettled and restless, the needle in her compass pointing anywhere but here. She'd never wanted to settle down before, always having one foot out the door. But now?

Now, she'd caught a glimpse of what she envisioned home could be: the sweet scent of pine and the sound of laughter. Dirt roads and miles of fence posts. Big dogs and colorful mountain sunsets. James's lips generous and warm.

Sara hadn't known him very long but some secret part of her unlocked thinking about him. He felt like coming home. But this feeling wasn't about a place. It was a sense of peace and joy better than any fairytale or dream. The intangible feeling wasn't lost on her. She knew she and her son were welcome in this town. And James Bennett undoubtedly made her feel wanted.

But there was still one niggling thought in the back of her mind spoiling her reverie—Dr. Russell Chambers, Noah's biological father.

"Let me take a look," she said, grasping the edge of the newspaper.

Crystal winked. "Atta girl."

The front door of the hotel chimed with a customer, causing Tinkerbelle's head to pop up from the backside of the sofa where she lounged with Noah.

"I'll be right back." CC excused herself to check them in.

Sara pushed the newspaper aside and fished her iPad from her tote bag. She hadn't done an internet search on Russ in a while. Checking up on him was a habit she'd formed early on, a defense mechanism keeping her and Noah distanced from the man who didn't want them.

She'd scour the local newspaper and his social media online like a spy, ensuring he hadn't moved or relocated to another hospital anywhere near them. Knowing he'd stayed put in Valdosta all these years gave her a sense of peace.

But she knew she was overreacting. A guy like Russell probably never gave her a second thought—out of sight, out of mind, right? Still, she kept her distance and moved at least once a year to keep the hound dog off her scent.

Her eyes traced the bright screen in front of her, and she stopped scrolling, her search landing in the obituary section of the *Valdosta Herald* newspaper. Frowning, she quickly read,

*Russell "Russ" Chambers, age 45, passed away peacefully at his home in Valdosta, Georgia, on January 23 after a brief illness...*

Her inhale was sharp, her eyes instantly muddling with tears, making the rest of the obituary regarding his history and achievements in medicine hard to read.

Russell, the father of her son, was—*dead?*

How many times had she thought things might be easier if Russell disappeared? Honestly, too many to count. But she didn't mean it. She would never, *ever* wish death on the man even though he insisted she terminate her son.

Sara looked over at Noah, his boyish figure sprawled on the hotel sofa with Tink nestled in his lap. The sight of him anchored her in her confusion, but the foreign feeling of guilt stabbed at her heart, knowing her son would never get to meet his biological father now. But hadn't that been the plan all along? She and Noah never talked about Russell. So why was she suddenly filled with shame and remorse for running away from him all these years?

"Sorry about that," Crystal said, sliding back into her seat.

Sara swiped at her cheeks, her confounded tears evidence of her shock and disbelief. What had she done?

"Honey? You okay?"

Sara offered Crystal a timid smile as she tried to hold it together. "Sure. I'm just slightly overwhelmed with this big decision, is all. Buying a house has been a lifelong dream of mine."

Crystal reached across the table and patted her forearm. "Awww, sweetie, you're not alone in this. I'll help you. My friends in the realtor business will help too."

She leaned forward and whispered, "And when you tell Noah the news, he'll be happy as a pig in mud."

Crystal was right. And even though Sara felt caught in a figurative tornado with her world seemingly disorganized and strange, she knew she needed stability and a safe place to land.

She nodded, lips pressed together with resolution. Noah's happiness had always been her motivation for the unconventional choices she'd made in her life. And for the first time in forever, she knew exactly where she was headed next...

Home.

# Chapter Sixteen

## JAMES

The old saying about March coming in like a lion and going out like a lamb rang true for the farmers of Langston Falls. In fact, it was a succinct summation of the weather changing from winter to spring in the mountainous region. Granted, James knew they'd have a few more cold snaps before spring firmly took hold. But he was excited to see signs the vines were preparing to exit their dormancy period. Bud break was a mere week or two away.

To see the vineyard magically transform from its bare and brown state to a flourishing field of green within just a few weeks was the ultimate preview of what was to come for this year's harvest. Bud break was the first stage of what he hoped would be another fantastic season in their thriving winery business.

Traipsing along the paths parallel to the trellises, he smiled as he oversaw the latest changes in the vineyard. He was anxious for spring. For new beginnings on the farm. For his father to continue to get stronger and more independent. For his relationship with Sara to blossom into the next phase if she was up for it.

He wanted to ask her out on a date.

They'd been like two ships passing in the mornings when he'd see her with his father before she left for her afternoon clinic shift. The day after Noah's birthday party, she'd woken up apologetic about her wine-induced confession and begged him not to tell anyone. Of course, he wasn't about to go back on his word.

But after two weeks went by and they still hadn't spent any time together, he was beginning to wonder if the kiss they shared was nothing more than a tipsy moment of passion she'd rather forget.

He was true to his promise and never spoke to his family about her story. The only thing he might've mentioned was how Sara was actively looking for a place in town to rent. His brothers said they'd keep their eyes and ears open, while his sister Becky was the only one poking him for more details, of course.

"I don't understand. Why is Sara looking for a place to rent?" she'd asked.

James told her the truth. "She's having a hard time finding a lease in town."

Becky seemed perplexed. "Well, where are they living right now?"

"The economy motel on the outskirts of town."

"You mean Crystal's place?"

"Yes. She's helping with the search too."

Becky smiled. "I've always liked Crystal. Daddy still talks about those hunting trips he and Waylon used to go on. It's so sad he died."

"It is," James replied.

"And how awful for Sara and Noah to live in a motel. They must be going stir-crazy."

"I know, right?"

"It's too bad they couldn't stay here. With our brothers all moved out, this big house has plenty of room. But I guess that wouldn't be right with her as the hired nurse for Daddy and with a son to take care of, too, huh?"

Becky's words struck a nerve, his senses vibrating. Why hadn't he thought of this?

James turned the corner in the vineyard and approached the main house, intent on finding Sara and asking if she'd made any headway. To his surprise, she was arm-in-arm with his father, the two slowly traversing the pathway near the pinewood forest. His dad was bundled up in a thick winter coat, the black Stetson on his head noticeable. His walker was nowhere in sight, the man's intentional steps slow and steady with noticeable improvement.

He smiled and picked up his pace. "Hey!" he hollered.

Sara and Roy looked his way in unison, his dad's grin infectious. "I thought I might see you out here, son. How's the vineyard looking?"

James grinned. "Looking good, Dad. Hey, Sara."

"Hi." Her smile held shyness as she firmly held Roy's arm.

Immediate heat surged up the back of James's neck. He wanted so badly to hug her. To slide his finger across the random strand of auburn hair fluttering against her cheek in the cold breeze and tuck it over her ear. He wanted to hold her hand, lead her inside the warm kitchen, and vocalize the idea he'd formed since his conversation with Becks.

"We were just about to head back inside for some hot

tea. Care to join us?" His father's blue-gray eyes held mirth. Could he feel the attraction brewing between them?

James eyed Sara. "Would it be okay with you?"

"Of course," she said.

The three of them ambled toward the stairs. Their feet crunched atop the thick layer of pine needles, dredging up the scent of evergreen and earth. He was surprised when Sara urged Roy up each step of the stairway leading to the back door of the kitchen without the aid of a cane or walker. His father had come a long way in the past month under Sara's care, and he was grateful.

"Way to go, Dad," he congratulated.

"Whew! I'm tuckered out," Roy panted once he crested the last stair.

Inside the mud room, Sara helped him off with his coat and hat. "Would you rather I bring your tea to the bedroom where you can rest?"

"I think that might be better." He patted her on the shoulder as she unfolded his walker tucked in the corner and set it in front of him.

"I'll be there in a few."

"Take your time, darlin'." He shuffled out of the space using his walking aid like a champ.

James grinned, overcome with a sense of relief at how far his dad had come. "I can't believe he climbed those stairs like that."

Sara unwrapped her scarf from around her neck and hung it up. "We've been working hard. All the physical therapy is finally paying off, and he's gotten stronger. The staircase is the latest hurdle he's conquered. He's making new strides daily. Your dad's a good patient."

"Well, you're a good nurse."

She dipped her head and suppressed a grin.

"I haven't seen you in a while. How's the house-hunting situation going?" he asked.

"It's definitely a situation," she laughed nervously.

The two entered the kitchen, where a note from Becky lay on the island, letting everyone know she was at the market. Sara filled the tea kettle and turned on the stove.

"Speaking of my situation, I'm taking time off from the clinic today to look at a few places."

James grabbed three mugs from the cupboard and set them on the counter. "Oh? You want some company?"

Her hands stilled, her focus suddenly on him. "You'd... wanna come with me to look at houses?"

"I'd love to. I know the lay of this land and could be a great help to you."

Sara shook her head with chagrin. "You've already helped me way too much."

James approached her and lightly pressed his hand against her arm. "It's always my pleasure to help you, Sara. And to be perfectly honest, I've missed you. We could look at some houses and catch up while we're at it. You know, kill two birds with one stone."

"Two birds. One stone," she repeated. "Why not?"

"Exactly," he laughed.

---

By the third house, Sara had turned unusually quiet. The inventory on the realtor's list was nothing but run-down dwellings in disrepair. They stood on the dilapidated front porch of a country house in the middle of nowhere, the front door pinned with a bold black and red warning sign, "Keep Out."

"Seriously, this is the best your realtor has to offer?"

James questioned. He was beginning to think they were being punked.

"You should've seen the two I looked at last weekend. One was a double-wide trailer down by the river. The other was a converted barn loft with no central heating or air conditioning."

James grimaced and kicked an acorn off the weathered porch boards with the pointy tip of his cowboy boot. "This is bullshit."

"There you go again, inserting your favorite word into the equation," Sara sniggered.

"I'm being serious."

She sighed. "So am I."

She looked tired, her hair tussled around her shoulders from being outside in the breeze, the lapel of her winter coat wrinkled with travel, one of the big buttons missing. He realized he wanted to walk with her through the rows and rows of vine trellises and Christmas trees as the sun set, where it was quiet enough to hear the way their boots crunched along the thawing earth. Where leaves and pine needles might tangle in their clothes and hair, and they could fill their lungs with the clean, crisp mountain air. He wanted to make tea with her in the main house, take Noah and the big dogs for a ride in the ATVs, and watch them frolic in the fields.

He wanted to help her the only way he knew how.

"You could always move in with me." His voice was deep with conviction.

"What?"

"You said it yourself. Your life has been very unconventional. So why not? You and Noah can move into the carriage house with me."

"James, I…,"

"—think about it," he interrupted. "I have two extra rooms. You could take the one you stayed in the night of the party, and we could move the gym equipment out of the other so Noah could have his own space. You'd be on the property and wouldn't have a morning commute anymore. And you wouldn't have to live out of a suitcase in a tiny motel room by the highway."

He slowly approached her and palmed her shoulders. "I know you're looking for a place to call your own, but it could take some time. Until then, move in with me. Give your boy and yourself some space to stretch out."

Sara's smile tipped up into something beautiful. "How do you do it?" she asked.

"Do what?" he grinned back. The combination of Sara's sweet perfume and the heat emanating off her skin soothed him. Without thinking, he pulled her in for a hug.

"How do you make it impossible for me to say no?"

James breathed in her scent and smiled. Pulling back from their embrace, he licked his bottom lip, his gaze mapping her beautiful face. Her eyes were bright with hope as she smiled back at him.

He wasn't sure why she showed this side of herself to him, but he knew he needed to move forward with care. Sara was way more sensitive than she let on, her wounds running deep, her entire motherhood spent trying to escape from the ghosts of her past.

"So, is that a yes? You'll move out of the motel room and into the carriage house with me?"

"Maybe."

"Maybe?" He pouted with an over-exaggerated lip, making her giggle.

"First, I have something I need to tell you. It's something I haven't told anyone."

"What is it?" He frowned, hoping she wasn't about to tell him she was being transferred.

"It's about Russell."

"Oh, shit…"

"He's dead, James." Her words hung in the air like a dark cloud, cold and thick.

"I found out several days ago when I looked him up online. That's one of the main reasons I've decided to stay and put down roots. He's… he's gone. He died in January." Her voice cracked with emotion.

"Come here." James pulled her into his arms again and squeezed. "I'm sorry this grieves you. I get it. But you have to look at the other side of this now. You can turn the page, Sara," he whispered into her ear, hoping against hope she was tracking with him. "You can move on with your life without ever looking over your shoulder again. You *can* put down roots."

She nodded into his neck. "I know. And I want to stay in Langston Falls. I do."

When she pulled back, their eyes met, something searing and downright vulnerable passing between them. She looked so pretty his heart physically hurt.

James watched her, trying to remember every detail: The sweep of her lashes. The golden shimmer of sunlight against her reddish-brown hair. Her muddled eyes flaring with heat.

He'd known the first day they met when she walked outside to confront him, there was a certain chemistry between them. The atmosphere changed instantly, his life suddenly morphing into something better. Something he never had with Sam. And he knew that now.

Fast forward, and the revolutionary words coming out of her lush mouth instantly impacted his life.

"I want to stay… with you."

# Chapter Seventeen

## SARA

"We don't have much time, James. Crystal will be here any minute." Sara fluffed the pillows on her son's made-up bed before clicking on the side lamp. She was surprised they'd managed to unpack his room in record time.

"I'm on it!" James hollered from the other room.

Crystal's assignment was to meet Noah at the bus stop near the motel and bring him directly to Bennett Farms. Sara wanted this to be a surprise and hadn't told him about their new living arrangement.

With the help of James and his brothers Teddy and Walt, they were able to load everything from her motel room and storage unit into two pickup trucks. Thank God she had some muscle carrying everything up the stairs into James's home. Usually, it was just her and Noah handling the arduous process themselves.

She would forever be indebted to the Bennett boys and their sister. Becky kept the big dogs sequestered inside the main house and even took Roy to his cardiology appoint-

129

ment that morning, allowing Sara the extra time she needed to get things done.

Coming out of Noah's bedroom, she surveyed the main living space and watched James shove leftover packing paper into an empty box. Too bad the rest of the carriage house was in shambles, including her new bedroom.

Stacked cardboard and small pieces of furniture wrapped in thick pads crowded the home, evidence of her unexpected move surrounding them. But there'd be time to unpack her personal items later. She was excited to see her son's reaction to his new bedroom.

"She's here!" Sara exclaimed when her phone pinged with a text message from Crystal.

James shut the door to Noah's new room and tossed the box full of paper into his bedroom. He looked devastatingly handsome in his navy thermal shirt, his hands resting on his hips, accentuating his muscular physique.

"How do you think he's going to react?"

Sara grinned from ear to ear. "He'll be blown away. He hasn't seen his bedding or most of his books and toys for weeks."

She threw her arms around his neck and kissed his cheek. "Thank you for this. Thank you, thank you, *thank* you!"

James chuckled. "Anything for you, darlin'."

She inhaled a deep breath and squealed with excitement. Throwing open the front door and standing at the top of the steps, she yelled, "*Surprise!*"

"Oh my, Lord! You scared the bejesus out of me!" Crystal yelped, clutching her hand at her throat, the other holding a yipping Tinkerbelle as they ascended the stairs. She was at least a foot taller than Sara with her heeled booties and blonde hair piled high on top of her head.

"Mom? What's going on?" Noah scowled from behind his glasses, looking around the living space crowded with familiar marked boxes, some in his childish penmanship.

Sara knelt to his level, slid the backpack off his shoulders, and unzipped his coat. "I wanted to surprise you, snuggle bunny. Welcome home."

"Home?" He took a few tentative steps inside before looking right at her, confusion marring his youthful face. "Why are some of our boxes here in Mr. James's house?"

"Because you and your mom are moving in with me," James explained.

Noah was wide-eyed, looking up at him. "We are?"

Sara cupped her son's chin and nodded with glee. "We sure are. And guess what?"

"What?"

"You have your very own bedroom. You wanna see it?"

"Duh!"

Sara held his hand and pulled him through the maze of chaos toward his closed bedroom door.

"Now, before you go in there, I want you to know I'm still looking at houses for us. But for now…" She looked over at James and smiled. "For now, Mr. James has graciously allowed us to move in with him, so we don't have to live out of our suitcases anymore."

Crystal set Tink on the floor and slipped off her winter coat, draping it over her arm. "This was a good decision, even though I'm going to miss our lobby happy hours." She pouted. "And James?"

He jerked his head to look right at her. "Yes, ma'am?"

"You're a real-life superhero for taking them in like this."

"It's the least I could do after everything Sara's done for my dad."

Sara gripped the doorknob to Noah's new room. "You ready?"

"Yes!" He jumped up and down and clapped his hands.

"One… two… *three*!" She flung open the door. "Welcome home, Noah."

Her little boy scampered into the tiny bedroom, mesmerized by all his familiar possessions unpacked and on full display. His toy chest was filled with cars and trucks. Favorite books lined up alphabetically on the skinny shelf she'd painted blue when he was just a baby. His clothes and shoes tucked away in the dresser drawers and closet, and his favorite Teddy bear sitting smack dab in the middle of the bed.

"*Franklin*!" he yelled, clambering over the side of the mattress and grasping his beloved stuffed animal against his chest. "I thought we lost him in the last move?"

"Nope." Sara beamed. "James found him shoved in the wicker laundry basket with your pillows when we pulled it out of storage. Franklin must've snuck in there somehow."

"Silly bear," he giggled. Tinkerbelle hopped up onto the mattress and settled against his pillow.

The three adults watched Noah fall back against his bed and hug the stuffed animal, broad smiles on all their faces. To experience her son's unmitigated joy was everything she'd ever hoped for. She leaned her head against James's shoulder, grateful he was instrumental in helping with this epic surprise.

"He seems happy," he mumbled out of the side of his mouth.

"Mmhm. He sure does."

"What about you, mama. Are you happy?"

She looked up at him, the perpetual smile on her face hard to contain. "I haven't been this happy in a long time."

He winked, sending a pleasurable zing straight to her basement.

"Well, I should get going unless you need more help unpacking," Crystal offered. "Come on, Tink."

"Please stay," Sara begged. She rushed over to her friend and held both her bejeweled hands. "Becky insisted on a 'welcome home' meal tonight. Can you join us?"

Crystal looked over at James, who smiled and nodded. "You're welcome to stay, CC. I'm sure my dad would love to see you."

The woman blushed and coyly touched her hair. "Oh. Well, I, uh… I'd love to. But I'll need to call my evening employee and let him know I'll be gone a little longer than expected."

"You do that. And then you can help me rearrange my closet," Sara teased. "We're not eating until six, so we have some time."

---

Dinner in the Bennett home was delightful. The entire family, Becky's boyfriend, Glen, Sara, Noah, and Crystal, all sat around the big farmhouse table filled with good food, flickering candles, and wine. The only couple missing was Hank and Ella Mae, who were on a tour bus somewhere headed to their next show.

Becky made a simple, kid-friendly meal of baked chicken, green beans, and decadent macaroni and cheese. When Noah asked for seconds, the entire table erupted in heartfelt laughter.

"I'm so glad you like my cooking, Noah," Becky beamed. She sat beside him and happily dished out another serving on his plate.

Sara looked on, the immense gratitude she felt close to overwhelming. It was amazing James and his loving family had opened their doors and welcomed her and Noah into their fold.

She felt James press his hand against her thigh under the table. "Did you get enough?"

"Plenty. Everything is so good."

He nodded and poured her another glass of family wine. And then he surprised her by dinging his knife against his glass. Clearing his throat, he stood.

"I'd like to thank Becky and her team for this delicious meal."

"Here, here," male and female voices replied.

"And I'd like to officially welcome Sara and Noah to Bennett Farms." He looked at her and tapped his glass against hers. "Welcome home."

"Welcome home," the dinner guests echoed.

Sara blushed and cleared her throat. She stood next to James and palmed Noah's shoulder, looking around the table at everyone present.

"Thanks for making this transition go so smoothly today. And as much as I'm going to miss my good friend Crystal at her motel, I won't miss living out of a suitcase. Sorry, girl." She puckered her lips in a mock kiss, thankful for her friend.

"Aw, honey, you know you can't get rid of me," Crystal teased. "You and I will always be unfinished business. Just like Mr. Bennett here." She'd been sitting next to Roy the entire meal, their heads close together in friendly conversation. It was nice seeing the patriarch of the family light up in her presence, Sara wondering about their history.

"You got that right, CC," Roy chuckled. The old man looked happy. Smitten by the bubbly blonde bombshell.

"Noah, sweetie, would you like to say something?" Sara encouraged.

Her son pushed his glasses up his nose, remnants of cheese sauce surrounding his mouth. "Thank you for my new room. I love it. And I can't wait to have Jaxson and Delia have sleepovers with me."

The family laughed as Sara shook her head, unsure if her son should be sharing his bed with two big dogs. But he'd never had a pet before, let alone two. And James assured her they'd be just fine.

When the hubbub died down, she added, "And special thanks to James for giving up a big chunk of his home to accommodate us, especially his workout room."

"He never used it anyway," Walt chortled. Elyse giggled next to him, slapping him on the arm.

"Yeah. Guess who had to take all those dusty weights down the steep stairs and into the garage?" Teddy added, fisting a hand and flexing his bulging arm muscle. Robyn kissed his bearded cheek as another wave of laughter permeated the room.

Pure joy infiltrated Sara's system. The laughter. The family teasing. The apparent love they all had for one another.

She and James sat, and she spoke near his ear for only him to hear. "Thanks for finding Franklin."

"Thanks for moving in with me," he whispered.

"Thanks for asking."

Their eyes met, something sweet and playful passing between them. Between the delicious meal and flickering candlelight, the wine, and the overwhelming sense of family, Sara was feeling it all.

James slung his arm across her shoulders and gave her a

side hug. The two sipped from their glasses and took in the controlled chaos surrounding the table. And that's when it hit her.

This right here was what it felt like to be wanted. *This* was family.

# Chapter Eighteen

### JAMES

"And why does a bed need a skirt?" James asked.

He stood in Sara's new bedroom and watched her finish making up the queen-sized bed with precision.

"A bed skirt helps conceal the box spring and all the clothing containers I'll store underneath."

"Hmmm. Makes sense."

She sat on the edge of the mattress and blew a puff of air from her mouth. "There. That's all I can handle for today."

"What about those smaller boxes against the wall?"

She waved him off. "I'll probably store those in the closet. It's some keepsake items from my childhood. You know, yearbooks and a few trophies."

James sat beside her, causing the mattresses to dip from his weight. "Congratulations. What sport did you play?"

"What do you mean?"

"You said 'trophies'. Did you play volleyball? Basketball? No, I've got it—you won in tennis, right?"

Sara rolled her eyes. "No sports. I was in choir and drama club."

"Oh." He was taken aback and confused. "They give out trophies in choir and drama club?"

"Yes, silly. I won best supporting actress in a play and was in an award-winning show choir my sophomore year in high school. It was an elite a cappella group. The girls wore matching black polyester gowns, and the guys wore tuxes. We were so chic," she laughed.

James reciprocated with a deep chuckle. "Tell me more."

"We won the state choral championship. And yes, everyone in the group received a trophy."

"Cool. You and my brother, Hank, will get along real good. He sang in our high school choir for one semester."

"Only one?"

James nodded with chagrin, his admission juvenile and embarrassing. "Yeah. Poor thing. He quit because me and my brothers teased him about it. We called him 'nerd' and 'geek.' We shouldn't have done it, but we were young and immature. We were into all the sports. And don't get me wrong, Hank was a good baseball player. But he was an even *better* musician. And look at him now. He's gone and made it in the world of country music. He's freakin' engaged to superstar Travis Miller's songwriting sister, Ella Mae."

"Yeah, shame on you boys. Look who gets the last laugh now," Sara snickered. "By the way, when is their wedding? Have they set a date?"

"Not officially. They're on tour for the next few months. He mentioned they'd like to shoot for sometime this summer if they can work it out."

"I was sorry to hear about Travis Miller's death. He was so young."

"And talented," James added. "It was a sad situation all around. But Hank and Ella are carrying on Travis's legacy, performing his hit songs nationwide. Travis was Hank's music idol when he was a little boy. He's the reason Hank wanted to pursue music."

"Wow." Sara fumbled with her hands in her lap. "I didn't know that. I'll bet it was hard on them both losing Travis."

"It was."

She started to stand, but James grabbed her by the wrist and pulled her back onto the mattress.

"What?"

"I want to know how you're doing. You know, since you found out about Russell's death."

Sara turned rigid sitting next to him and shook her head. "I haven't had time to process it because we've been so busy moving."

James tucked her hair over her ear with tenderness. "I'm here for you if you ever want to talk about it, okay?"

She snuck a glance at his face and meekly smiled. "Okay."

Looking around the room, she relaxed a bit. "Is it weird that I'm here?"

"Weird? No. I'm glad you're here."

"You are?" Her heated blue eyes watched him with intensity.

"Mmhmm. And truth be told, I've been eyeing those lips of yours all day long."

Sara's mouth turned up into a sly smile. "Oh, really?"

"Yes. We haven't kissed in a long time."

"So that's why you asked me to move in with you, right? Free kisses?"

"Dang it, you figured me out, darlin'," he chuckled.

She held on to his shoulder and leaned her body so she could see into the living room as if making sure Noah was out of sight. The boy hadn't come out of his new room in over an hour, playing with his toys as the big dogs looked on.

"Is the coast clear?" James whispered.

Sara nodded and locked eyes with him. He swept her hair back and held her face in his hands. When his lips melded with hers, immediate heat and contentment pulsed through his veins.

He was a man grateful for the chance to help a mother and her son. Thankful for family gatherings, a home-cooked meal, big dogs, and the taste of wine made from grapes grown on the hillside right outside his bedroom window. He was grateful for the chance to love on everyone around him.

And right now, he wanted to love on Sara. She pushed at his seams, time spent with her something he wanted more of. The sound of her laugh, the smell of her hair, the taste of her kiss.

Screw the dating rules. They'd moved right into cohabitation without a second thought.

He groaned and crushed his lips against hers again and again, their kiss becoming passionate as his thick cock ached between his legs.

"Damn, girl," he whispered, nipping at her ear. His voice was raw with arousal. "You taste so sweet and good."

"So do you." They were quiet, studying their fingers locked together, fatigue setting in from the long move-in day.

"James?"

"Hmm?"

"What are we doing?"

"What do you mean?"

She let go of his hand and looked right at him. "Are we playing house? Are we a couple now?"

"*Mom?*" Noah interrupted, calling from his room.

She clumsily fumbled away from James and stood. "Yes?"

"Where are my pajamas?"

"I'll show you," she hollered back. Pausing, she pressed her fingertips to the underside of James's chin. "I'd like to show you something later too."

"Oh?" He was intrigued, her blue eyes boring into his like a hot gas flame.

"It'll have to wait until Noah is asleep."

"I can wait." He was wide-eyed, staring up at her; his breathing turned shallow with desire.

She smiled and bopped the tip of his nose before she sashayed out of the room, her hips swinging with pleasure. James scrubbed a hand down his jaw and shifted in his seat, his raging boner outlined in denim.

"Down, boy," he muttered with humor.

Jaxson's collar jingled as the big dog trotted into Sara's bedroom and cocked his head.

"Not you, Jax," James laughed. He stood and roughed up the dog's fur around his neck. And then he adjusted himself into a more comfortable position, the evidence of Sara's kisses lingering with pulsating heat between his legs.

Exhaling a long, steady breath, he shook his head. He didn't have a chance to answer her question and wasn't sure what to say.

Were they playing house? Did she want to be his official

girlfriend? Where were they headed in this unexpected situation?

The only thing he knew for sure was that Sara Larson wanted to show him something. And he had a good feeling he knew exactly what it was.

———————

"Are your eyes closed?" Sara asked.

James scrunched his face and pressed his eyes together, anxious to get this little show on the road. He'd been patiently waiting to have her all to himself so he could kiss her. Touch her. Possibly love on her into the next morning.

Seated on her bed, he was thankful Noah and the dogs were down for the night in their first official sleepover. But he knew he and the single mom couldn't do *everything* he wanted. Making love to Sara would have to be meticulously planned when they could truly be alone. For now, he'd take what he could get, even if it was only a few passionate kisses.

"Yes. My eyes are closed." He felt her weight press into the mattress and waited.

"Okay. You can open them now."

James blinked and looked at her sitting next to him, so sure he would find her wearing a sexy nightgown, ready to continue their dangerous liaison with her son sound asleep in the next room. And she was sexy, but not in a slinky nightgown kind of way. She wore one of his old T-shirts he used to keep in the spare dresser until she moved in. He could tell she was bra-less, and her bare legs peeked out from under the long hem of the shirt, leaving him wondering if she had anything on underneath.

His eyes roamed her figure until he realized she was holding something in her hands. "What do you have there?"

"It's my great-great-grandfather's stethoscope. I told you I had something to show you. Isn't it marvelous?"

James frowned. This wasn't the kind of show-and-tell he had in mind.

"I don't bring this out when Noah's around because it's hard for him to be gentle with it. I found it when I was unpacking. See?" She held the instrument delicately between her splayed hands. "The earpieces are made out of real ivory."

He tried not to show disappointment and cleared his throat, angling his head to get a better look. "You must have a long line of doctors and nurses in your family, huh?"

Sara carefully put the piece back into a velvet satchel. "My great-great-grandfather was the only doctor in the family that I knew of, and I was the only nurse."

"Tell me more about your family. You mentioned your grandmother raised you, correct?"

She stood and set the satchel on the dresser before settling beside him on the bed with her hands in her lap. "Yes. My grandmother raised me."

James frowned. "What happened to your parents?"

"Well, my mother gave birth to me when she was a teenager and didn't want the responsibility, so my grandmother took over. I saw my mother occasionally while growing up, but she was never really there for me. And she never talked about my biological father."

James was shocked by this news as he stared into Sara's eyes. They were the color of an impending storm, her family history rocking him to his core.

It suddenly dawned on him she was part of a generational cycle, with no mother and an absent father. He was glad she had her grandmother who raised her, but still, her household had to have been dysfunctional. Distressing. Even heart-breaking.

Sara never knew her father, and unfortunately, her son would never know his.

She suddenly smiled wide. "Grandma Ginny was wonderful. She's the one who encouraged me to go to nursing school. Being a nurse had never been on my radar until she suggested it. And it turns out, I'm a *good* nurse. I like taking care of people."

"You're a great nurse. And you want to know what I think?"

"Sure."

"I think you like taking care of people because it heals the part of you that needed someone to take care of you."

Sara mulled over his words. "Wow. That hits hard. I never thought about it like that before."

James understood her need to take care of people. Wasn't he doing the same with her and Noah? They were more alike than he realized.

"I'm sorry about your parents," he stated with empathy.

"I'm not." She yawned, shutting their conversation down. "It's been a long day, James. I think I'm going to turn in for the night. Thanks again for moving us in. I don't know how I can ever repay you."

"You owe me nothing, Sara. I hope you and Noah enjoy living here with me. This is your home as much as it is mine for as long as you want it to be."

"I appreciate it. It means a lot to us. And you've made things pretty cozy here at Bennett Farms." She tapped her index finger into his chest.

He grabbed her finger and kissed the tip. "I sure hope you feel welcome."

"I do. I feel… happy. It's a good feeling."

"Good." He gathered her into his arms for a final hug, his voice low and directed into her ear.

"And to answer your question from before, I'm not playing house or any games with you. But I think we missed a very important step in this equation."

"Oh? What?"

He pulled back from her and grinned. "We've never even been on a first date. So how about it? Will you go out with me, Sara Larson?"

Her smile said it all.

"I'd love to go on a date with you Mr. Bennett."

# Chapter Nineteen

### SARA

Sara and James fell into a steady routine living together in the carriage house. After she'd said yes to going out with him, they experienced their first official date in the middle of the pine tree forest on Bennett Farms during lunchtime before her afternoon clinic shift. The March sun was high and bright, the trees secluding them from the day laborers and cold mountain breezes.

There was something romantic about eating outside with him while they sat on a plaid blanket and sipped hot apple cider from a thermos. He'd packed a wicker picnic basket with cut up fruit, vegetables, cheese, crackers, and little bites of chocolate brownies she was sure his sister had made. They talked and laughed and ate to their heart's content, James telling her repeatedly how happy he was having her and Noah living under the same roof with him.

Stretched out across the blanket, he tipped his cowboy hat back and said, "I woke up this morning and had a thought."

"What kind of thought?" she'd replied, popping a grape into her mouth.

Holding her hand, he pressed his lips to her knuckles, his eyes never leaving hers. "The only thing that'd make this date any better would be having you as my girlfriend. What do you say? Can we make it official?"

A huge grin unfurled from her lips, and when he kissed her among the wild scent of evergreen and budding grapevines, she replied, "Yes."

Apart from their first date and agreeing to be girlfriend and boyfriend, her favorite part of her day was after supper, when it was just her, Noah, the big dogs, and James in the carriage house.

She'd often indulge in a fantasy where they were their own little family unit living quietly at the farm. And what if they became more than just girlfriend and boyfriend? What if they became a real-life family? It could happen. Their attraction to each other was apparent, their flirty banter and stolen hugs and kisses something she looked forward to after a lengthy workday.

What if she belonged to him, and he belonged to her? What would it be like to let go of her past, love this man, and be loved in return?

Her heart swelled with longing, wanting it to be so. But then the little devil on her shoulder reminded her of the brutal facts in her life:

Her mother abandoned her.

She never knew her father.

Her grandmother died unexpectedly.

Her son's father didn't want children; therefore, he didn't want her.

Everyone she was destined to love left or didn't want her in the end. On the flip side, maybe they left because she wasn't capable of love. But she knew she was. My God, she loved Noah with her entire being. She'd take a bullet or walk through fire before she'd let her son feel like he was nothing.

Perhaps everyone she loved left because *she* was the problem. Maybe she was unlovable? But there again, she knew her son adored her. Even James seemed smitten by her presence, especially living under the same roof and announcing to his family she was his girlfriend.

But the common denominator in her life up until now remained the same: everyone left.

This is why she never put down roots or allowed herself to get close to people, her fear of abandonment a source of PTSD that would often rear its ugly head. She wanted to call the shots and leave before she got hurt—before another fault line splintered her heart all over again. She couldn't fathom going through another rejection, the wasted years running from Russell nearly destroying her.

Sara moved away from the bedroom window, the last colors of the sunset fading beyond the mountain peaks. Standing tall on her own two feet, she readied herself for the evening. She wanted to talk to James about something important—something she'd been mulling over since she learned of Russell's passing.

Releasing a breath, she walked into the empty family room and looked around. The carriage house was quiet and homey, the boxes all unpacked and pieces of her furniture fitting nicely with James's, even with the obnoxious deer head on the wall, minus the beads of course.

Their blend of her shabby chic and his cowboy charm worked well together. Leather and throw pillows. A recently watered spider plant on a skinny stand. A bar cart stocked with family wine and whiskey. An ancient record player in a corner unit with colorful albums lined up neatly under-neath. The home felt lived in and well-loved—like an actual family resided there.

And wasn't that what they were for the time being? Some wonderful and unconventional form of a family?

Even though they agreed to be romantically involved as boyfriend and girlfriend, they still hadn't had sex. Of course, they talked about it, but having an eight-year-old living within the same thin walls complicated things. They agreed to stay in their separate bedrooms for the time being, the future of their relationship unfolding slowly and steadily.

Like the time he fondled her breasts in the barn loft, the two of them dangerously close to making love in the hay. Or when Noah was engrossed in a movie and James led her into his bathroom to conveniently show her something. He'd clicked the door shut and held his index finger over his mouth indicating to be quiet. He'd wanted to kiss her and touch her for a few brief seconds in private, shocked when she knelt in front of him, yanked his sweats down around his ankles, and wrapped her lips around his thick cock, giving him a little prelude of things to come, pun intended.

But keeping their libidos sequestered was a whole lot harder than she ever imagined.

"Hey," James said, startling Sara out of her thoughts.

"Hey."

He'd come out of his bedroom, sat on the sofa, and released a satiated sigh. His hair was damp from a recent shower, the air smelling of clean soap and manly deodorant. Patting the empty space beside him, he asked, "How was your day?"

"Good." She sat next to him.

"Where's Noah?"

"Probably finishing up his homework."

"Why on earth would a second grader have homework?"

Sara smirked. "I don't think it's really homework. He checked out a new book from the school library today and was anxious to dive in."

"Good for him," he chuckled. Grabbing the remote, he clicked on the television. "Anything on tonight?"

She snuck a sideways glance at James. She could never tire of his handsome looks. He was tall and lean with broad shoulders and warm brown eyes the color of melted chocolate. She liked how his muscles bulged in his long-sleeved thermal shirts and how his dark hair magically fell into place after he ran his hands through it.

Never had a man looked so strong, so steady to her before. She knew she could trust him and needed his trust after what she'd been through.

"Can we pause with the TV for a minute? I'd like to run something by you."

James clicked off the television and gave her his undivided attention. That was one of the things she liked most about him. He made her feel seen.

"What is it?" His brow furrowed, dark eyes pinning her with focus.

"I, uh… I want to do some research on Noah's biological father."

"Russell?"

"Mmhm." That he remembered his name was impressive.

Gently, he slipped his hand into hers and squeezed. "What kind of information, darlin'?"

Sara swallowed hard and squeezed back. "I need to find out if Russell has any surviving relatives."

His frown deepened. "Why would you want to know that now? You're free and clear of the man after eight long years."

Bowing her head, she decided to be brutally honest. "Keeping Noah's paternity a secret has been hard. I know there've been consequences to my decision. He's asked me over the years what happened to his father, just like I used to ask my grandmother about mine."

"And what have you told him?"

She locked eyes with James and confessed her lie. "I told him I didn't know where he was and that it wasn't his fault he had an absent father."

"But in reality, he *wasn't* an absent father. The man didn't know Noah existed."

Sara nodded, her guilt consuming her. "And now it's too late for Russell. But if his parents are still alive, it wouldn't be too late for them."

"Why the change of heart?"

His question was fair, and she tried to control her feelings. "I'm not sure. Being around Bennett Farms with you and your family made me realize how selfish I've been all these years. I should've told Russell I was having his baby with or without his consent. But I was young, and I was scared. When I first told him I was pregnant, he got angry and was adamant I not go through it. I idolized him because he held power in the hospital system. And I feared he'd retaliate if I went against his wishes. He could've filed a professional misconduct charge against me with his authority, and I would've lost my nursing license. I couldn't risk waiting around for his wrath. That's why I ran."

"So you could keep your baby and live your life on your own terms. I get it, Sara." He paused and stole a quick glance at Noah's closed bedroom door.

"But are you sure you want to go down this road now? Noah seems perfectly happy and content. Are you sure you want to mess that up, bringing strangers into his life? And on the flip side, you might want to consider something else."

"Something else? Like what?"

"If Russell does have surviving family members, they might see this as you going after inheritance rights or looking for financial support from his estate. Things could get ugly."

Sara vehemently shook her head. "I have no desire for *any* part of Russell's estate. I have plenty of my own money. And I don't even know if I would have the guts to reach out to one of his relatives. Right now, I'm just curious to see if there are any."

James nodded as if tracking with her. "Sheriff Jenkins is a good friend of our family. I could pay him a visit and have him do some digging on your behalf."

"Could you?" Her heart blipped in her chest.

"Of course. But I need you to do me a favor first."

"What?"

"I want you to sleep on this. You know, make sure this is absolutely something you want to pursue."

"I can do that."

James had a point, his final comment on the matter a definite consideration.

"Because once you open up this can of worms, you might get more trouble than you bargained for."

# Chapter Twenty

## JAMES

With Sara's permission, James called Sheriff Jenkins and agreed to meet during lunch the following day.

The inside of the station was like stepping onto a television set for a 1980s crime drama. Several oversized desks were lined up with computer and telephone cords snaking over the sides. Worn chairs with ripped, mauve-colored seatbacks lined the walls—the same ones he'd once sat on when Teddy was booked after his unfortunate fight with Glen Kirby at the Harvest Hoedown two years ago. The painful memory made him grimace.

From behind a glass partition of a large corner office, the middle-aged sheriff in full uniform waved James in. The pungent scent of raw onions and Italian dressing hung in the air as the sheriff pushed his half-eaten sub-sandwich to the wayside and thrust his hand across the desk for a shake.

"James Bennett. Good to see you, man."

"Yeah, it's been a while. Sorry for interrupting your lunch." James nodded toward the sandwich.

Sheriff Jenkins waved him off. "Have a seat. How's

Samantha doing these days? I haven't seen her around these parts in ages."

Immediate heat surged up the back of James's neck. It felt odd knowing he hadn't considered Samantha in months, his thoughts focused on his new girlfriend and her son.

"Oh, you haven't heard the news?"

"What news?"

"Sam's been training at the FBI Academy in Quantico, Virginia."

"Are you shittin' me?" His high-pitched tone and wide eyes indicated he was surprised.

"It's true."

The sheriff interlocked his hands together on his desk. "I swear Sam has always been a go-getter. Good for her. How's the long-distance relationship working out for you two?"

James licked his lips and avoided the sheriff's stare. "It's not. We broke up mid-February, right before she left."

"Aw, man, that's too bad. I was rootin' for y'all, especially after hitting it off when she was your brother's parole officer and everything she did to get him acquitted. Samantha was team Bennett for sure."

"Yeah… well, not anymore." He shrugged, the memories of Sam leaving him uncomfortable and empty.

"So, what brings you by the station today?"

James shifted in the worn wooden chair, thankful he'd changed the subject. "I'm trying to get some information about a deceased man's family."

"Oh?"

"Yes." He pulled a print-out of Russell's obituary from the *Valdosta Herald* Sara had given him and passed it off.

"I need to contact one of Mr. Chamber's living relatives. My… friend has something his family might be interested in. Can you help me find a contact number or address of someone in his family?"

He wasn't about to discuss his new girlfriend being the reason for his research. He needed to keep things vague and casual.

Sheriff Jenkins scanned the article and nodded. "Sure. Easy-peasy. I can run a background check on the guy and search public records. I'm sure we can drum up some information. Shouldn't take long."

"Cool."

"Why don't you grab a bite and return in an hour or so. I should have something for you by then." The sheriff stood, and James followed suit.

"That'd be great."

Ten minutes later, he sat at a table in the local coffee shop and ordered a sandwich and black coffee. It was odd eating alone away from the farm. But his circumstances were short-lived when he noticed Glen Kirby enter the establishment.

"Glen!" he hollered, waving the man over.

His smile was broad from behind his thick beard. "Hey, James. What brings you into town?"

"I was just about to ask you the same thing. Have a seat."

As he shrugged off his heavy coat and cowboy hat, a waitress greeted him by first name.

"Hey, Glen. How's it going today?"

"Good, Sherry. How are you?"

"Real good. You want the usual?"

"That'd be great. Thanks."

"Not a problem." She turned toward James. "You still doing okay? Need anything else?"

"No. I'm fine, thank you."

She nodded and walked away.

"You come here a lot? She knows your name and order. I thought that only happened in the movies," James teased.

Glen shrugged. "I come here at least twice a week when I'm in town for my AA meetings."

James was struck by his commitment, thankful the man was living his life on the right track. "Good for you, man."

"What about you? Why are you in town?"

He wasn't sure how to answer the question. And how odd that he'd just come from the sheriff's office, which held horrible memories when it came to Glen and his family. But that was all in the past. Knowing he was the only one who knew about Sara's plight, James kept his answer vague.

"I'm doing research on a project."

The waitress dropped off a decadent coffee drink topped with whipped cream in front of Glen. His beaming smile was immediate. "Thanks, Sherry," he offered.

"Enjoy," she replied.

James watched him stab the whipped cream mountain with a straw and lean forward for a generous sip.

"What kind of research?" he asked, smacking his lips.

"I'm not at liberty to discuss it. Hope you don't mind."

"I don't mind at all, as long as it has nothing to do with me."

He chuckled. "Nothing to do with you, Glen, I promise."

"Whew! Thank God."

The two were silent for a beat, and Glen focused on his drink.

"How's Becks been treating you?" James asked.

The brawny man's entire face softened at the mere mention of Becky's nickname. "She's awesome. Truth be told, she's the joy of my life." His heartfelt admission was moving.

"Glen, I want you to know I'm glad for you and Becky. It wasn't easy getting to this place, but I see how her face lights up when she's around you. You make her happy, and that's all I want for her. I hope you realize that."

He wiped remnants of cream from his whiskers with a paper napkin he pulled from the table dispenser. "I appreciate your kind words. And for what it's worth, she makes me happy too."

Glen hesitated before he asked, "Can you do me a favor?"

"Sure." James leaned back in the booth, unsure what he would ask him. "Fire away."

Heaving a deep sigh, he nodded. "I love your sister. I do. I've never loved another woman besides my mother in my entire life. I hope you know I would never, *ever* do anything to upset or hurt her."

"Go on."

"I'm doing some renovations on my house. You know, updating some things inside and adding a back porch to the outside. We don't officially live together yet while Becky helps your father recover. But a back porch is something she told me she wants in her future home, and I want to give it to her."

James was taken aback. Glen was constructing Becky's dream house?

"Wow. That's… great."

"Your sister pays close attention to detail. She has these… visions in her mind of exactly how she wants things. I've already painted the house white and the shutters yellow, and I plan on tilling a huge section of the yard near the kitchen window where she can plant her dream garden. But

I'm having trouble picking out the railing style for the back porch. There are so many to choose from. Do you think you could pick her brain and get back to me? I want to surprise her with this."

Glen was animated, his joy and happiness contagious. James was glad for him and his sister. They were the epitome of opposites attract, their love story emerging from the ashes of pain and heartache involving their family history. But both parties had moved on with reconciliation and forgiveness. And now James was experiencing a delightful and unexpected encounter with his sister's beau.

"I'd be happy to help you, Glen."

He nodded with glee. "I appreciate it."

"Are you, uh, planning on proposing any time soon?"

James dared to ask the question everyone in his family had once been concerned about. But everyone knew it was inevitable. Might as well ask while they were discussing dream homes and gardens, right?

Glen dipped his head with chagrin, his cheeks lighting up with color. "We've talked about it some. But we're in no hurry. I want to finish buying back my property from Walt and getting the house updated first."

James and his brother, Walt, talked daily while working in the vineyard, his brother excited to finally hand back the reins of the Kirby property to its rightful owner, Glen. Thanks to a bountiful apple harvest and the projected commissions he'd receive from selling their new apple-infused wine they created together named *Rebecca Rose*, he was sure to have full ownership in the next month or two. And the best part about it? Glen insisted he do this independently, even after Becky offered to help him financially with earnings from her lucrative YouTube monetizations.

James was proud of him, thankful for his dedication to

getting clean and sober and for making his little sister happy. For her to have her dream home created by the hands of this man who used to be his archenemy was something he would've never thought could happen in a million years.

"I heard you're close."

"Yup. Super close. I've got my eye on the prize."

James offered him a genuine smile. "Would you do me a favor in return?"

"Sure."

"Let me know when you're close to a proposal. I'd love to help any way I can to make it something special she'll never forget."

The two men eyed each other from across the table, their love for the same woman palpable.

"You got a deal." Glen stretched out his hand, and they firmly shook on it.

James's phone buzzed. "Excuse me, Glen. I gotta get this."

"No problem." He happily dove back into his coffee, the big man's pleasure in the decadent drink comical.

Pulling the phone from his pocket, James eyed the text message on the screen from Sheriff Jenkins and nodded.

*Got the deets you wanted. Come on back to the station when you're ready.*

# Chapter Twenty-One

## SARA

"Billy's mom will pick the boys up from school today and bring them back here tomorrow before lunch. It's Noah's first sleepover, so I hope tonight goes well."

Sara came out of the bathroom carrying her toiletry bag and set it on the dresser, eyeing James with concern. "Are you sure you can handle them tomorrow on your own while I'm in Valdosta?"

"We'll be fine. I'm planning on taking them fishing at Langston Falls. We'll stop in town and pick up some sandwiches, just like my dad used to do with me and my brothers when we were their age."

Sara grinned and sat next to him on the bed. "I'll only be gone for one night."

"I know."

Sheriff Jenkins had come through with a phone number and an address for Russell's mother, Betty Sue Chambers. She was his only surviving relative and lived in an upscale retirement community near the Valdosta Country Club, a few miles from Russ's old home. That she had no family left in her retirement years left Sara feeling gutted, her guilt rising to the surface.

Over the last week, she thought about calling and introducing herself but changed her mind. She needed to see the woman in the flesh and decide once and for all if telling her she was Noah's biological grandmother was worth it. She insisted she wanted to do this alone, claiming she needed to figure out some kind of closure.

Sweet James agreed to keep an eye on her son and his friend Billy while she traveled the six-hour drive and spent the night in a hotel, turning his weekend into the ultimate little boy adventure. The boys were in good hands.

"Have I told you lately how much I appreciate you?"

"Every single day." His chocolate irises latched onto hers for a few beats. She expected him to chuckle, but he stared at her as if waiting for something more.

Leaning forward, she lightly grazed her lips against his mouth. "It's true, you know."

"I appreciate you too. But instead of telling you, I'd like to show you."

Her brow cocked. "Oh, show me? What did you have in mind, Mr. Shit?"

"I have plenty of ideas." His voice was thick with arousal as he captured her lips in another soft kiss.

Free-falling into bliss, she realized part of her wanted to draw out their coveted alone time together. But the other part felt like they might never get another chance if she didn't take advantage of their situation in the moment. With her son gone, she was uninhibited and free.

She enjoyed spending the morning with James after dropping Noah off at school. It was nice returning to the farm with hot coffee in to-go cups from the local café and extra weekend muffins from the Langston Falls bakery in a cute purple box closed tight on the kitchen counter. The big dogs lounging across their beds, and James's work hat hanging on a hook by the door. It was nice being alone with him for the first time in forever, his dedication to her and Noah pulling her deeper into his world. His work ethic and loyalty to his family. His attention to detail when it came to her. His quiet caretaking and generous heart.

Her eyes scrolled his features, and she wondered if he had the same thing on his mind: sex.

Leaning forward to where they were nose to nose, she pressed her lips against his again, immediate heat pouring into her.

"Mmmm, Sara?" he mumbled.

She continued, not letting him speak, her tongue licking and lips nibbling against his as she boldly straddled his lap. She reveled in the feel of his smooth skin against her jaw. The pressure of his mouth against hers and the heat he was pouring into her.

Coming up for air, she let her fingers trace his full lower lip, tendrils of warmth peppering her skin. Desire washed over her so powerfully that she swayed against his thighs.

"We're finally alone," he exhaled breathily. "And I have nothing pressing to get to on the farm."

He kissed the center of her palm, the action so unexpected, so chivalrous and endearing, she knew she was falling hard.

"I told your dad I'd be late this morning. What shall we do?" She wiggled her eyebrows and smirked.

"I can think of a whole lotta things we can do, darlin'."

Sara nodded and stood, understanding the assignment.

James watched her slowly lift her sweater over her head and fling it to the side. As she reached around her back and unhooked her bra, he grasped her by the hips and trapped her between his muscular legs.

"Let down your hair," he uttered, eyes fixated on her face.

With her bra hanging off her shoulders, she unfastened her claw clip, causing her hair to tumble around her shoulders. James slid his hands up her stomach and underneath the lace of her bra, squeezing her breasts.

"You're so beautiful."

Standing half naked in front of him, blood pounded in her ears. She was unaccustomed to such a compliment. Not used to receiving seductive attention from a man like James Bennett.

"You should know I haven't been with anyone since Russell," she nervously confessed.

His dark eyes shot to hers, vast and wild. He was sexy as sin, pinning her with his feral stare.

"We can go nice and slow. We've got all the time in the world."

She nodded and slipped off her bra, anxious to feel his hot mouth on her pebbled nipples. The moment his tongue flicked across her twin peaks, she gasped with immediate pleasure.

"Oh, James."

He was bold and untied her work pants, yanking them down her legs. She held onto his shoulder and toed her shoes off, allowing him to undress her. When he edged his hand against the fabric of her panties, her gasp was audible as he tunneled his index finger under the elastic.

"So wet," he groaned.

"Don't stop," she panted. She was definitely turned on, thick warmth surging around his fingertip.

James pulled her panties down her legs, and she kicked them off, giving him full access.

"Shut the door and lock it," she demanded.

"But we're the only ones here."

"The dogs."

He chuckled and stumbled into a standing position, quickly locking the door. She watched him lower himself to his knees, about to dive into the apex of her thighs, when she stopped him.

"Take off your shirt."

Quickly, he tugged at his thermal and peeled the fabric off his hard body, his chest rising and falling with wanton lust, hair tousled and sexy.

Sara eyed him with pleasure and ran her hand down the ripples of his abs. She knew the man was good-looking with clothes on. But shirtless? Good gracious, he was some kind of Greek God or airbrushed hallucination.

Leaned back with flexed arms and hands, she steadied herself. James watched her, heat flaring in his eyes as she purposefully spread her legs wide. She arched her back and neck, anticipating all the sensory feels of pleasure, something she'd denied herself for years.

James licked his lips as her sweet scent permeated the room. Her moan was low and husky when he slipped his hand between her legs, warmth lighting up her cheeks. A single touch of his fingers set fire to her insides, surges of intense pleasure filling her with sensation.

And at the first sweep of his tongue tracing her seam straight up her center, she yelped. She was unashamed of the powerful sexual tension and pressure building and writhed euphorically in front of him.

"I'm almost there," she panted frantically. "Oh, God. It feels so good. It's happening so fast. I'm gonna come…"

"I want you to," he growled, coming up for air.

His fingers pressed into her bare ass like he owned her. And when she gave in to the rush, spiraling higher and higher, she careened off the edge.

Her entire world was reduced to this one blissful moment as she trembled in his arms. She'd completely let go and come undone.

"Shit!" she exhaled.

"Hey, that's my word," James chuckled.

She watched him retrieve a condom from his pocket and hold it between his teeth as he shucked off his jeans, his commando disposition underneath immediately revving up her insides for round two.

"Are you always this prepared?" she giggled.

"Only prepared for you, darlin'."

A surge of heat flooded her core again. She liked the way he took charge. She'd felt an unexplainable pull toward him since their first meeting. But it was worse now. Deeper. More intense. And it wasn't because they were having sex for the first time.

Kneeling between her legs, he rolled the condom on. His actions were seductive and practical in the moment. There wasn't any awkwardness or fumbling like it'd been with Russell, his complaints the entire time about having to wear a rubber ruining the moment. Granted, Russ was an overworked, grumpy doctor, perturbed she wasn't on the pill. But looking back, she was positive he screwed any girl he pleased wherever and whenever he wanted and was glad they'd used protection.

Until that one time, they didn't.

And Russ was nothing compared to the man in front of her now. James was mature and confident in his own skin. He was rugged and strong. Everything about him exuded manliness, from his six-pack abs and a smattering of hair on his chest to his muscular arms and thick, hard cock.

Her vision blurred, and she struggled for her next breath as he slid his length inside her. He kissed her long and hard and deep, the thrusting of his tongue matching the rhythm of his hips. She was drunk on the scent of his skin and the way his weight felt between her thighs.

Running her hands down his back, she gripped his round ass, pulling him deeper. He groaned and crushed his lips against hers again before he moved faster. She clung to his hard body, and he pumped her hard and fast, grinding against her.

Sara concentrated on the heat and friction, their sweaty bodies becoming one. James had gotten crazy with his hands, unabashed in the bed. He was verbal and playful, calling out her name and ensuring she liked everything he did. It was the kind of thing you wouldn't guess just by looking at him, with his chiseled face, perfect manners, and rugged cowboy physique. She liked that.

This was about desire and chemistry, their two worlds exploding in unison between ragged breaths. They gave in to the rush together, shattering together in a ripple of shared bliss.

Afterward, they lay on their sides staring at each other, legs tangled atop the twisted bedding on Sara's mattress. They were hot. Sweaty. Panting. That's when she heard him say something out of the blue.

"What?" she whispered. She struggled to hear him over her thundering heart.

"I don't want you to leave me." He pushed her hair back from her face.

"But I'll only be gone for one night."

"I know. But I don't want what's waiting for you in Valdosta to make you change your mind."

# Chapter Twenty-Two

## JAMES

James was wound up when the two of them reconvened at the carriage house after the long workday. He couldn't get the woman out of his head.

Her back was to him, her sexy sweater falling off one creamy shoulder as she worked at the kitchen stove browning ground beef in a skillet. She insisted she make him a simple supper, the leftovers something he and Noah could eat while she was away. Almost all the counter space was occupied with various pots and kitchen utensils, and he noticed a mason jar perched on the windowsill crowded with a handful of daffodils.

She looked happy. Domestic with errant hair pieces beginning to slip out of her lopsided ponytail. She appeared deliciously relaxed, a vision of loveliness from across the room. And the only thing on his mind was giving her more pleasure late into the evening.

James shoved the urge away as she gazed at him with a half-smile curved across her luscious lips.

"Do you want me to open a bottle of wine?" he asked.

"Of course. And turn on some music. Maybe one of your favorite albums from your record collection?"

"Great idea."

James uncorked a bottle of Bennett Farm's wine at the bar cart to let it breathe and knelt next to the ancient record player in a corner unit, his colorful album collection lined up below. Perusing the eclectic musical catalog of his youth, he landed on The Young Rascals LP and grinned.

Firing up the stereo, he carefully pulled the black vinyl from the jacket and placed it on the turntable. Lifting the long arm attached to the stylus, he put the needle on the spinning disc on the wanted song. After a few pops and crackles of sound through the speakers, the soulful music echoed in the room, the song "Groovin" humming through his blood.

He felt like dirty dancing.

"Oh, I love this song," Sara remarked, leaning her head back from the counter so she could see him.

"Come here, beautiful." He held his hand out and comically wiggled his hips, shimmying closer to her.

She seemed to track with his cue and giggled, turning off the stove and taking several rhythmic steps toward him. Their fingers engaged, and James jerked her flush against his body into a dirty dancing hold: right hip glued to her right hip with his right leg between her legs.

Sara moved her hands around his neck, his hands trailing down her hips and around her ample rear end, squeezing with pleasure. They were loose, moving to the sexy rhythm of the song, both of them going all in with their impromptu dance and grinding against each other.

James deviated from their pose and slightly turned, helping her into a dramatic dip, her back arching and her ponytail cascading in a waterfall down her back as her laughter peeled like a church bell. His lips landed on her throat and made a path to her mouth, the seductive kiss throwing him off kilter.

Angling her body to where she faced out from him, she squealed, and he pressed himself against her back. He groped her thighs and hips with splayed hands, and she moaned, lifting her arms high to circle his neck.

"You're a good dancer," she said, grinding her butt against his raging boner.

"So are you."

His fingers continued tracing her body along her hips and over her tummy until they slid up to her breasts. She angled her head to where he had full access to her neck, her sweater dangerously close to falling off her shoulder and exposing her chest. Peppering her skin with several licks and kisses, he felt her hands cover his over her bosom.

James closed his eyes. He wanted to bottle up this moment with Sara groovin' to the music without a care in the world.

It was heaven spending all morning with her, naked in bed with her hair falling all around her face. Pink lighting up her cheeks after their first time making love. It was nice sitting at the kitchen table with hot coffee in their mugs and remnants of muffin crumbs dusting their lips as they stared into each other's eyes. The big dogs lounging across their beds, and Sara's nurse clogs discarded by the door. It was nice seeing her come down the hall after the long afternoon apart, hair still damp from a shower, sweater hanging off one shoulder, her blue eyes lighting up at the sight of him. It was heaven being pressed against her feminine body soft and sweet, grinding to the steady rhythm matching his beating heart.

As the music faded, the two of them stilled, and James

swore she could feel his thickness pulsating against her lower back.

"Wine?" he uttered close to her ear.

"Mmhmm."

He disengaged from her as another tune began. Turning the volume down, he poured two tumblers of red wine and willed his boner to settle. The dogs looked on, nonplussed by his behavior, lazily lounging on their beds.

"Here you go."

"Thanks." Sara clinked her glass with his and took a slow sip. Looking up at him through her lashes, she said, "The sauce is simmering for a little bit. Can I make a request?"

James licked his lips, the earthy overtones in the wine leaving him satisfied. "Sure, darlin'. What did you have in mind?"

She dipped her head, the apples of her cheeks ripening with color. Peony pink, like the sky right before the sun went down over the Langston River.

"Slow dance with me?"

His chest rose in a deep intake of air, and he nodded. "I've got the perfect song."

He set his glass on a side table and was quick with an album change, finding Neil Young's "Harvest Moon." Turning it up a notch, he stood tall and gallantly approached her, offering his hand. She took it, and he pulled her close in a classic dance pose.

They were cheek-to-cheek and swayed to the old-fashioned rhythm. More than once, he turned them in a slow circle in front of the windows, the night sky splattered with a million twinkling stars. A delicious heat unfurled between his legs, singing through his blood until he turned rock hard.

He breathed heavily against her neck, nibbling at her ear more than once.

He loved their cloistered little life in the carriage house, but the reality of her world held unfinished business. Things he couldn't even imagine because he'd lived in a bubble for so long. He'd fallen hard and fast and wasn't sure what the future had in store for them.

Sara pulled back, her come hither stare lulling him into a trance. She led him to her bedroom and locked the door. A lamp was turned on, and their clothes were suddenly in a pile, the two of them naked and panting with a feral need. She pushed him against the mattress, and he abided, scooting across the sheets in awe when she straddled him.

He watched with bated breath as she pulled her glorious auburn hair over one shoulder and rested her palms against his bare chest. Sliding her hands lower, she grasped his penis with her mouth wide open. At the first touch of her lips on his hot skin, his eyes rolled back into his head. She sucked him and massaged his balls, the feeling so intense he thought he might pass out.

And just as he was about to peak in the moment, she stopped and lined up his unsheathed, hard-as-steel cock to her soaked center.

"I need... a condom...," he stuttered in heavy breaths.

Sara shook her head. "It's fine. You can pull out."

Sliding into her heat, he gave up all control as she moved slowly above him. The combination of Sara's deep heat and her sweet smell soothed him. Forever, the scent of this woman would live in his memory, tucked away with his ancestor's pine forest and fresh grapes plucked from the vine. Something beautiful that would haunt him in unexpected moments.

He dragged the tips of his fingers across Sara's cheek

and offered a lustful smile. "You feel so good." His voice was raw and provocative.

She leaned her forearms along his sweaty chest, their mouths hovering inches apart, breath hot and full of lust.

"Do you like me on top?"

"Oh, yes," he hissed.

Their passion was intense. Making love to her was incredible, but this was something different. It was driven by wanton desire as much as gentle lovemaking. But he felt like what they had together would end before it even began. It felt like fucking goodbye. And what if it was?

He flipped her over and pumped her hard and fast, pulling her tight against his body and grinding like they had during their earlier dirty dance. His vision blurred, and he struggled for his next breath as an orgasm completely took control of him.

He couldn't speak, paralyzed from the rapture exploding through him as hot bursts of pleasure pumped into her. He was completely and utterly astounded. An out-of-body experience.

As his soul slowly crept back into his body, he realized he hadn't pulled out in time, shocked he'd been so careless.

"Shit, Sara. I didn't pull out." He sat up, sweat trickling from his furrowed brow.

"I told you, it's fine. I like knowing there's still a part of you inside me." Her smile said it all.

James relaxed and lay beside her, his head pressed against his forearm. Tracing her lips with the tip of his finger, he asked, "Did you come?"

She shook her head.

"Well, damn, darlin'. I need to take care of you."

Straddling her, he flipped the sheet over his head and winked before he disappeared underneath. Sara spread her legs, her intoxicating scent making him rock hard again.

But this time, it wasn't about him.

"Don't move a muscle," he growled.

This time, it was all about driving the woman underneath him crazy with his nimble fingers and salivating mouth. He was ready, willing, and able to bring her to the edge of desire.

And watch her freefall into bliss.

# Chapter Twenty-Three

## SARA

Sara blinked open her eyes against the first soft slants of light coming in through the window. James lay asleep next to her, his head turned the other way, quiet snuffles pressed against his pillow. She smiled and quietly peeled the sheet back to rise.

Immediately, a calloused, warm hand pressed against her bare back. "Don't go."

Sara turned to see his drowsy gaze fixated on hers, his bare, muscular upper body hard not to notice in the romantic light of the new day.

"Good morning," she said.

"Morning." His seductive mouth kicked up at the corners into a wide grin. "I guess we had our own little sleepover last night, huh?"

"You could say that again."

He flung open the sheet, revealing the continuation of his gloriously naked body underneath. "Come here."

Sara slipped into the lingering warmth where she'd slept

and snuggled against his hard morning composition. "I need to get going. I want to get an early start."

"I know you do." He spoke into her hair, his hot breath making it very hard to concentrate. "But the sun's just starting to rise. You can spare another thirty minutes."

She melted into him and relaxed, her smile satiated and horny. "You're making it extremely hard to stick to my schedule."

"The word 'hard' being the correct term in this context, darlin'," he chuckled. Pressing his length against her bottom, he brought his hand around her waist and stroked her soft mound.

Sara's eyes rolled back into her head, and she sighed. "I could get used to this."

"Waking up in the same bed?"

"Yes. And your amazing hands touching me like you are now." He dipped his fingers into her saturated seam, and she squeaked, tensing for a millisecond.

"Relax. I want to send you off with something to remember me by."

Exhaling a steady breath, she replied, "Another orgasm?"

"Several." He flipped her over onto her back and straddled her, his manly figure shadowing her features.

She gripped his boner and felt him tense as she lined it up against her center.

"Hold on. I need to grab a condom."

"No, you don't."

He gripped his hands over hers causing her to still, his brow furrowed in confusion.

"We need to play it safe, Sara. I was careless last night. I don't want you to end up pregnant from the get-go."

She smiled and teased herself with his tip, his features

twisting with controlled lust. "I'm not worried about that. Remember when I told you I suffered from female problems? The chances of me getting pregnant a second time are zero to none. It'd be like getting struck by lightning again with the same bolt."

James pressed his top teeth into his lower lip, mulling over her words. He was clearly turned on, his manhood rock-hard with veins bulging.

"You sure about that?"

"Yes." She urged him forward. "Make love to me, James Bennett. Feel me. *All* of me."

The strong column of his throat moved in a substantial swallow before he made up his mind. With palms pressed on either side of her head, his arm muscles flexed as he hovered over her, his dick a slow impale into her center. His movements were halting and shallow, as if he couldn't believe there was no protection between them.

"I'm still going to pull out," he growled.

She nodded, all feeling and sensation dive-bombing to the hard nub pulsating between her legs. Delicious heat unfurled and swam through her blood until she was limp beneath him, panting against his neck.

And then he plunged in so deep it hurt, yet she desperately wished she could take him even deeper. Wished she didn't have to leave for Valdosta. Wished she could stop time and stay wrapped up in him this way, skin on skin. Profound and penetrating to her core.

Even as they raced to the finish line, their bodies had a mind of their own, unwilling to slow down and make the moment last. She begged him not to stop, his ragged breathing and the violent way he moved inside her indicating he was close to release.

They gave in to the rush together, James pulling out at

the last minute in a flood of pleasure spewing across her tummy. It was a rush like no other, surges so intense she felt like she was floating through space.

"Holy shit!" James collapsed next to her, his chest rising and falling in deep breaths.

Eyeing him through sweaty strands of hair that had fallen in front of her face, she ran her finger across the swell of his cheek. She wanted to remember this moment, his body hard and masculine on top of the sheets, the sounds of the outside world waking up around them. Sunlight flicking through the window, and floorboards creaking underneath the big dogs pacing in the hallway. His thick warmth across her tummy, pooling in her belly button.

Right then, she knew exactly what she wanted. But she knew it was selfish to want it.

"Let me grab a towel," James muttered. His tight ass flexed when he stood.

She lay there in the aftermath, her auburn hair spread across the white pillows like spilled dark honey and one hand cupping her breast. She felt like a modern-day Botticelli painting depicting the *Birth of Venus*, the goddess of love and beauty.

"Sorry about that." He'd put on sweatpants and sat next to her, running a warm washcloth against her belly. He was tender in his actions, his entire focus pinpointed on her naked body.

She was immobile, satisfied from their lovemaking and reveling in his attention. He truly cared about her, his thoughtful heart an important trait she looked for in a man. Well, when she was looking. For him to sit beside her and take care of her in this way was special.

"There you go." He held the bunched-up cloth in his hand.

His face held a smattering of scruff in the early hour, and his hair was disheveled in a sexy lover kind of way. Her heart had been lonely, and she knew his had been too. But they'd taken things to a different level now, and she was sure this was only the beginning.

Sara had always dreamed of finding her forever someday. That James showed up out of the blue was a legit miracle. He loved his family and made her and Noah feel they were already a part of his large brood. The selfless man took them into his home and made her feel like she hung the moon even on her worst days.

Since Russell, she looked more single every weekend, every month, every year that passed by. She pined for a man to jumpstart her heart again, and James had been right there to do it.

He was the right kiss. The right words in a song. The right man to come along and sweep her off her feet. It couldn't have been just anyone. It *had* to be James. It was the way he smiled and said her name, their meet-cute so original and unforgettable she knew she'd never be the same again.

James was like a fine wine, and she knew to her core he would get better with age. And she wanted to be there to witness it. To take care of him like he took care of her. To sit with him in their elderly years on the back porch and watch every sunrise until their last sunset. She didn't know what she was missing until he showed up. She longed for a great love to spend her life with, and from the moment they first met, she was pretty sure she'd found her forever.

"You want some coffee or breakfast before you go?"

When she didn't answer, he leaned lower and kissed her cheek. "Earth to Sara," he chuckled.

She blinked several times, her cheeks heating with

embarrassment. Lifting the sheet to cover her naked body, she offered James a timid smile.

"I'm sorry. What did you say?"

He tucked her hair over her ear. "I asked if you wanted some coffee or breakfast before you go. We still have some of those muffins left over from yesterday."

The purple bakery box came to mind, the assortment of muffins with crumbly tops they'd picked up for the weekend immediately making her mouth water. She smiled, her loving gaze tracing James's handsome features.

"I could eat."

"Good." He hopped up from the bed and started for the door. "Why don't you shower, and I'll get the dogs fed and the coffee started."

"James?"

"Yeah?" He turned around as if ready to accommodate her every whim.

"I'll be back tomorrow."

"I know."

"Maybe then we can tell Noah together."

James frowned. "Tell Noah what?"

Sara grinned, the lovelight in her eyes shining like the noonday sun.

"We can finally tell him we're together."

# Chapter Twenty-Four

## JAMES

"I can hear the waterfall!" Noah exclaimed. He ran ahead of James, his school pal, Billy, struggling to keep up.

"Careful, Noah. This trail can be challenging. Watch your step."

James shifted the heavy backpack he carried on his shoulders, his hands holding several rods and reels. He'd taken the boys to the fishing hole his dad used to take him and his brothers to near Langston Falls.

The falls dropped ninety feet into a twelve-mile-long gorge with cliffs towering above the Langston River. The trails weren't too strenuous, and there were several view-points along the one-mile hike. The hardest part was nearest the river, with a few steep steps taking them down to the water's edge.

But the reward was worth it, with close-up views of the rock cliffs and plenty of giant boulders for little boys to cast a line from. He planned on serving them a picnic after some fishing and looked forward to a bit of relaxation among the soothing sounds of the waterfall.

"Sara would love this," he muttered to himself.

The boys had stopped on the trail before him, kneeling on the hard-packed dirt to watch a box turtle scuttle toward the water.

"Look, Mr. James." Noah pointed at the reptile, his eyes wide with wonder from behind his glasses.

"Cool." He grinned, kneeling next to him. "We need to leave him be. We're guests in his territory. Y'all need to respect him and everything else around here. Got it?"

"Yes, sir." They nodded in unison, mesmerized by the turtle. When it slipped into the frigid waters of the river, they cheered, sharing high-fives.

James had already tied lures and skinny bobbers onto the fishing lines so the boys wouldn't be bored while watching him do this task. Earlier, they'd practiced casting their lines in the front yard of Bennett Farms with casting plugs before they headed out for their adventure. James had unfurled a plastic mat for them to aim at repeatedly. Each time they hit their target, they squealed with delight, the practice rounds helping with their technique without messy bait or hooks.

The sun was high, the sky the perfect cornflower blue. James breathed a sigh of relief once the boys settled on a big rock, their overhead casts just like they practiced, making him proud. They focused on the shimmering water and waited patiently for the exciting tap-tap of a fish.

Thirty minutes went by, and James could tell they were growing disappointed. "Not feeling anything?" he asked.

"No," Noah lamented. His shoulders sagged with a disappointed sigh.

"Well, sometimes the fish don't bite. It's part of the game. We could go ahead and eat our picnic if you'd like." His comment perked them up.

"I'm hungry," Noah admitted.

"Me too!" Billy added.

James quickly divvied out thick sandwiches and bags of chips, the boys scarfing down their lunch like they hadn't eaten in days. As he ate his own sandwich, he squinted in the bright sunshine and remembered a story his PawPaw Bennett used to tell him when he was growing up.

"Ya'll want to hear a story?"

"Yes!" They replied enthusiastically. He had their undivided attention now, their rods parked against the side of the big rock.

James tossed them homemade cookies Becky had packed in the picnic basket before he crisscrossed his legs and rested his elbows on his knees.

"Once upon a time..."

"—ah, geez. Is this some kind of baby story?" Billy interrupted.

"Yeah, Mr. James. We're not babies. You can tell us a scary story if you want to."

"Yeah!" Billy exclaimed animatedly.

James hid his immediate smile and ran a hand down his scruffy chin. The way these two fearless little boys had their chests puffed out with gumption had him chuckling.

"Okay, okay. I hear ya. But my story isn't scary. It's more of a mystery. And I promise I'll tell it like I'm talking to one of my brothers. Deal?"

Noah's eyes grew wide from behind his glasses. "As long as you don't say the 'S' word."

"No worries. I promise." He popped the last bite of cookie into his mouth and chewed.

"Have you ever heard the story about the lost treasure in North Georgia?" He cocked his head and waited for their response.

"Lost treasure? What kind?" Billy asked.

"Hey, we live in Georgia!" Noah exclaimed.

"That's right, we sure do," James grinned. "To answer your question, Billy, this story is the legend of the one thousand bars of lost Confederate gold."

"One thousand bars? How did it get lost?" Noah asked.

James shifted on the hard rock. "Well, legend has it that back in 1865, two wagon trains filled with gold bars were robbed. The gold was supposed to be returned to France, who had loaned the money to support the Confederacy in the Civil War. But don't worry about that part. You'll learn more about America and its history in school." He shifted on the hard surface and glanced at the limp fishing lines in the water.

"Toward the end of the war, a Navy captain and a group of volunteers brought the gold from Virginia to South Carolina by train. From there, they took it by wagon, hoping to get it to a port in Savannah, a city in Georgia by the Atlantic Ocean. Their goal was to load the gold onto a waiting ship and return it to France. But that never happened."

"Then where did the gold end up?" Billy asked, riveted by the story.

James leaned in for dramatic effect. "Folks say the gold was hidden for safekeeping in a cave in the mountains somewhere around here." He waved his hand into the air, the boys looking around at the craggy rock face on either side of the river.

"There are tons of caves in this region, and folks have searched and searched. And still, over one hundred years later, no one has ever found the gold."

"Wouldn't the people who stole it know which cave it's

in?" Noah asked. He was such a quizzical and intelligent little boy.

"You'd think so. But apparently, the entrance to the cave was destroyed in the war, and no one's been able to find it since."

"I'll bet we could find it," Billy announced.

"Yeah, we could go on a treasure hunt and find it. Then we'd be rich!" Noah fist-pumped his hand into the air.

James laughed. "Don't you think everyone in America has been trying to find the lost gold after all these years? Heck, me and my brothers thought the same thing when we were your age. My grandfather even pointed us toward an area near our house, where the cave is rumored to be hidden. We hiked all over that mountain, which has tons of caves. But exploring them can be very dangerous. There was this one we came across that looked promising. It had a small opening the size of a basketball."

"Did you squeeze into it?" Billy asked, his eyes filled with wonder.

"We shined our flashlight inside and saw a huge snake, so we didn't stick around to check it out after that. But I often wonder what we might've found if the snake hadn't been there."

Noah stood, his shadow slanting across James's face. "Do you think you could find this cave again? Maybe you could show us, and we could look inside."

"Like I said, caving is extremely risky, especially if you don't know what you're doing. I think I'd feel better if I took you to some of the more popular tourist caves first to give you a sense of what they're like."

Before Noah could respond, he squealed at the sight of his reel and grabbed it before it slipped into the water. "What the…?"

James scrambled to his feet. "You got a hit, Noah!"

His friend, Billy, was vocal, coaching him like a fishing pro. "Come on, Noah! You got this!"

Noah grunted and flexed his little arms, struggling to get the fish out of the water. James stayed back, knowing this was a precious moment in the young boy's life.

"Keep her steady."

A gorgeous rainbow trout appeared at the end of his line, the speckled black spots on its bluish-green back and pink stripe on the sides of its body shimmering in the sunlight. James helped Noah net the fish and explained how to hold it for a photo-op.

"Be gentle, buddy. It's best to control a trout with a hand around the tail like this." He showed Noah and had him do it. "But don't squeeze too hard. Hold his body horizontally with your hand underneath to support his weight."

Noah giggled the entire time, enthralled with his first catch as he pulled out his phone and snapped pictures of the boy posing proudly with his healthy two-pounder.

"Billy? Can you take a picture of the two of us, and then I'll get one of you boys together."

"Okay."

James handed off his phone and posed proudly with his arm stretched across the boy's shoulder. He reciprocated and took a few shots of Noah and his friend cutting up and making goofy faces for the camera.

"Can you send those to my mom? Please?" The grin on his youthful face was contagious.

"Of course. She's going to be so excited for you." Tucking the phone into his pocket, he asked, "You ready to release this beauty back into the water?"

The two boys stared at the fish, Billy using his index finger to touch the slimy scales. James carefully used needle-nose pliers to get the hook out of the fish's mouth before lowering it back into the net.

"Nice and easy. Lower the net gently and give him a second. That's it. Move the net back and forth to force water through its gills."

Noah followed instructions like a champ, the fish returning to life and disappearing underneath the dark water in a flash.

With his hands resting on his hips, James sighed with pleasure. "Congratulations on your first catch, Noah."

"Thanks, Mr. James. My mom's not going to believe it."

In his mind, he knew Sara would be thrilled for her son. And he was too.

# Chapter Twenty-Five

## SARA

The regular six-hour drive to Valdosta took an extra forty-five minutes due to the congested Atlanta by-pass around the city and a big-rig accident further south near Cordele, Georgia.

Finally exiting the highway, Sara breathed a sigh of relief when the route went from four lanes to two. Her directions took her under the familiar canopy of Spanish moss hanging from Live Oak trees lining the streets, the conjured memories of her time spent in the small college town flitting through her mind like a camera reel.

Passing the Spanish Mission architecture of the university buildings, the pretty campus filled with red terra cotta roofs was peppered with picturesque landscaping. The beauty of the palms, tall Georgia pines, numerous azaleas, camellias, and a mix of other flowering plants made her smile. She rolled down the windows, the air unseasonably warm with a gentle breeze.

Her GPS directions continued through town to the south side, where she arrived at her destination. Taking in the charming aqua-colored façade of the senior living facility, her face fell as she read the large sign out front: Azalea Grove Assisted Living and Memory Care.

"Oh, no," she muttered out loud.

She thought she'd be walking into an upscale retirement community, not a place where elderly folks with Alzheimer's, dementia, and other debilitating mental diseases lived. She shook her head and chastised herself for not calling and asking more questions. But her guilt overruled, the need to lay eyes on Noah's biological grandmother urging her forward with the surprise visit.

Slamming the car door, she stretched her back and eyed the structure with trepidation. It would be so easy to skip a potential meeting with Betty Sue Chambers, return to her hotel, and sleep through the night. Or should she get in her car and head back to the only place where she felt comfortable? A place where a handsome vintner and her precious son waited for her—the place she was ready to call home.

But she'd made it this far, the old saying "curiosity killed the cat," nagging at her subconscious and competing with a warning bell dinging in her overly inquisitive mind.

Was it wise to bother the woman and tell her she was a grandmother? And what if she was in the last stages of her disease and incoherent? She didn't know if Betty Sue had limitations regarding her health or if she could even answer questions in the first place. Perhaps there was nothing valuable or beneficial in traveling all this way, and she'd made a terrible mistake?

Sara was all about privacy and setting boundaries. And if Betty Sue was coherent and talkative, she needed to be mindful of her limitations and what she was willing to share. She needed to be prepared to accept she might not find the answers she searched for—especially from an elderly patient suffering from a mental disease.

Still, she'd come all this way, the need to see this woman in the flesh with her own eyes propelling her forward. She needed to muster the strength to find closure for herself and her son.

"May I help you?" A young African-American woman asked. She was seated behind the check-in desk of the facility, her warm eyes and tiny gold cross hanging around her neck strangely comforting.

"Yes. I'm here to see Betty Sue Chambers." Sara stood tall and shifted her purse over her shoulder.

"Is she expecting you?"

"Um, no, ma'am. She's not. I'm traveling through town and wanted to stop by and pay my condolences. I was a... friend of her late son, Dr. Russell Chambers."

She shot Sara an empathetic gaze and nodded. "I see. Let me check real quick and see where she might be."

The keyboard clicked with her fast fingers as she stared at a large screen. In a matter of seconds, she nodded again.

"Miss Sue, as we all call her around here, should be in the atrium having supper about now. Would you like me to show you the way?"

Sara swallowed hard. "Yes. Please."

"And by the way, my name is Renora."

"It's nice to meet you, Renora. I'm Sara."

"Sign in on the clipboard, Sara, and I'll come around the counter and take you to Miss Sue myself."

"I appreciate it."

Once she was checked in, Renora strode next to her and pointed out some of the amenities of the recently updated facility. Sara was amazed by the beautiful planters filled with live foliage and the giant atrium with skylights highlighting the dining area near an impressive water feature.

It was apparent Russell had spared no expense for his mom, the thought making her heart clench.

"See the woman sitting at the corner table beside the nurse wearing pink scrubs?"

Sara homed in on where Renora pointed and nodded. Betty Sue Chambers was a petite woman with hair as white as snow, her shoulders hunched over a plate of food.

"I know Miss Sue will be thrilled to see you. All she ever talks about is her son, Dr. Chambers. Did you know he donated a substantial amount of money to this facility for the latest renovations? His philanthropy helped his mother and all the other patients benefit here at Azalea Grove."

Sara pressed her top teeth into her lower lip to avoid saying anything negative about Russell. If Renora only knew.

"I'll let Miss Sue know you're here. When the wait staff comes by the table, please help yourself to something to eat or drink. We pride ourselves on Chef Rosemary's menu." The woman grinned, obviously proud of where she worked.

"Thank you very much."

"Now, be aware Miss Sue has substantial memory loss due to her condition. And she can get confused at times. But she can carry on a conversation, especially if you bring up her son. He's one of her favorite topics." She winked.

"Does she know he's dead?"

"She does. But again, sometimes she forgets, and we have to gently remind her. I suggest you let her drive the bus on your conversation so you can gauge how things are going today."

"Good idea."

Renora patted her arm and walked over to Miss Sue's table. They talked for a beat as her caregiver stood and moved over to an empty table within sight of her patient. When she waved Sara over, Betty Sue grinned from ear to ear.

"Hello, Sara. How nice of you to come and visit me."

"Hello." Sara's voice vaporized in her throat, the uncanny resemblance of the woman's eyes to Noah's unmistakable.

"Please, have a seat. I was just enjoying Chef Rosemary's famous chicken and dumplings. Would you like some?" As if on cue, a female waitress approached the table.

"No food, but maybe some iced tea?" The waitress nodded, and a tall glass was set in front of Sara before her butt hit the chair.

"Renora said you knew my Russell."

Sara nearly choked on her first sip, the tea so sweet it made her teeth hurt. Dabbing a napkin against her lips, she nodded, relieved Mrs. Chambers used past tense.

"Yes, ma'am. A long time ago, I was a nurse in the same hospital where Dr. Chambers practiced."

The joy on her face was apparent. "Isn't that special? I've met several of Russell's work friends since his passing. Did you stop by to pay your condolences?"

Sara was surprised Miss Sue was unemotional asking such a question. "Yes. I'm sorry for your loss."

Her chest rose in a deep intake of air. "Thank you, dear. I begged Russell to go to the doctor for years and years, but he was too stubborn. And I'm sure you know this because you work with doctors. Don't they make the worst patients?"

"You're right about that." They both laughed, the lighthearted comment adding some levity to their odd conversation.

"He was a good son up until the very end. He made sure I was taken care of, and the staff here has been wonderful."

"I'm glad for you."

Picking up her fork, Betty Sue swiped it across a piece of what appeared to be lemon cake parked next to her dinner. "Did you and Russell ever date?"

"Yes, ma'am. We did."

"Where did he take you?"

Sara knew the woman was trying to make small talk, but memories of their handful of dates bombarded her with force. A candlelight dinner at the Valdosta Country Club. Sitting under the twinkle lights of an outdoor patio and sampling beer at the Georgia Beer Company. Singing along to the musical *Mamma Mia*, performed by the Peach State Summer Theatre cast on the college campus. Slurping oysters from the half-shell and listening to live acoustic music at the Salty Snapper.

But as quickly as those favorable memories played out in her mind, she was also struck by the bad ones. His anger when she told him she was pregnant. The way he threw around his money and clout as an egocentric doctor. His threatening tone badgering her to get rid of Noah.

Clearing her throat, Sara was short and straightforward with her words. "We had dinner at the club. It was a very nice date." She smiled sweetly and put a lid on her erupting feelings.

"The club is nice." Miss Sue chewed another bite of cake and stared off into space. "Russell is taking me there this weekend."

Sara frowned, taken aback. "Excuse me?"

"I said, Russell is taking me to the club this weekend. I always wear my string of pearls when we go." She palmed her empty neck. "He gave them to me for Christmas the year he graduated from medical school. I adore my pearls. They go with everything."

Glancing nervously at the caregiver sitting at the next table, Sara was thankful for her presence. Maybe it was time to shut this conversation down.

"Well, it was lovely to meet you, Miss Sue. I'm so glad you were here so I could stop by and... say hello."

"I'm glad you did, my dear. And when you see Russell, please tell him to call his mama." Her eyes shimmered with unshed tears as she looked at Sara.

She didn't know if it was the memories coming at her full force or the guilt of knowing this woman would never know she had a grandson, but Sara did something unexpected. It was as if a supernatural power entered her soul and caused her next fumbled move.

She pulled a photo of Noah from her purse and handed it to the woman. "Miss Sue, I'd like for you to have this."

Betty Sue Chambers lifted the reading glasses hanging from around her neck and settled them across her eyes. Scrolling the picture, her lips trembled into a fractured smile.

"My sweet boy," she softly spoke. Pressing the photo against her chest in a hug, she eyed Sara with gratitude. "Thank you for this."

"It's my pleasure, Miss Sue." Her voice was weak, tainted with emotion.

She watched the woman stare at the photo again, her wrinkled hands holding the edge. Betty Sue Chambers seemed lost in a recollection of a grinning little boy with glasses, her demented memory taking her back to a happier time with her only son.

It was obvious she thought the childhood photo was Russell.

Sara stood and said nothing else, leaving Betty Sue in her own world. As she made her way to the facility entrance, she could hear her speak to her caregiver about the picture.

"This is my son when he was a youngster. Isn't he the most precious little boy you've ever seen?"

Swiping hot tears from her face, Sara was a dichotomy of emotions: glad Mrs. Chambers had a fleeting moment to bask in the memories of her beloved son and sad she'd never know the real boy behind the smile in the photo.

"That was fast," Renora said with a hospitable smile.

"Yes." Sara steeled her emotions and signed out on the clipboard. Fumbling for her business card, she handed it to the friendly receptionist.

"Can you please keep my contact information in Miss Sue's file and let me know how she's doing from time to time? I know I'm not immediate family, but…"

Renora's gaze was sympathetic, and she nodded. It was as if she knew exactly what was happening, even though Sara knew she didn't.

"Of course."

"Thank you very much."

Her lungs threatened to burst from holding her breath to keep her tears at bay. She marched through the parking lot toward her car and slammed herself inside. Gripping the steering wheel, she finally allowed herself to hang her head and release her pent-up emotions in deep sobs.

She had no regrets. Meeting Betty Sue Chambers in the

flesh was something she had to do. Something she *wanted* to do, her fearless love for her son coaxing her forward.

And knowing Noah's grandmother held his picture in her hands was a comforting consolation—even if the woman would never get to hold him in real-time.

# Chapter Twenty-Six

## SARA

"How am I supposed to concentrate on anything when my brain is full of nothing but you?" James asked.

Sara shifted across the hotel room bed and sighed. "Your brain is full of me, huh?"

"Yes. I miss you, darlin'."

"I miss you too. I miss Noah. How is he?"

James chuckled. "He's basking in the glow of his first catch. He talked my dad's ear off while showing him the pictures. God, I wish you could've seen him pull that fish out of the water. It was incredible."

The photo image of her baby boy's contagious smile immediately came to mind, her motherly instincts aching to hug him.

"Thank you for being there to witness it. And thank you for sending me those pictures. I'm gonna have to frame the one of you two together."

"Oh yeah?" His words held the lilt of a smile.

"Yeah."

They were quiet for a beat.

"You okay? You sound tired. Are you going to bed soon so you can get an early start and come home to us?"

The word "us" hung in the air like a promise. A pledge. A bridegroom's oath to love and to cherish until death, or something like that.

"I haven't eaten much all day. I think I'll go to the restaurant next door and grab a bite before bed. And don't worry. I was already planning on getting an early start."

"Good." He paused, his next words a soothing salve to her hurting heart.

"Hey. I'm sorry things went sideways today. My mama used to tell me everything happens for a reason. And there's a reason you felt the need to drive to Valdosta and speak to Mrs. Chambers. You may not understand the why right now, but eventually you will. You followed your heart, and that's a good thing. You're a great mom, and your son loves and adores you. Trust me, that little boy would do anything for you."

"Thanks, James. Seriously. Your words mean a lot to me right now."

"I'm glad. And I'd like to add, I adore you too."

A rush of heat spiraled through her system, her earlier angst uncoiling and letting go. She was taking her life into her own hands, ready to return to what was most important to her—Noah, James, and her newfound Langston Falls home.

"Go get some food, darlin'. And text me goodnight when you get back to your room so I won't worry."

"Okay. And James?"

"Yes?"

"I adore you too."

A chain restaurant was conveniently located near Sara's interstate hotel. She walked across the parking lot and breathed in the fresh scent of magnolia flowers permeating the air.

Looking around, she noticed the large tree growing near the building, branches peppered with pretty white blooms. The fragrant flowers were a herald reminding her of warmer weather soon to come in the mountains. Plucking one of the lower flowers from a gnarled limb, she inhaled the sweet scent from the unfurled cup-like petals.

Sara was ready for spring. New beginnings for her and Noah. She didn't know what that looked like exactly but held on to the hope of a quintessential spring day. To feel the warmth in the breeze that wasn't there before. To bask in lighter and brighter days. She compared herself to a bud upon an optimistic branch, brave enough to finally open and tilt her face toward the sunshine.

The restaurant was packed, local college students and tourists out for an affordable meal on a Saturday night. Opting not to wait for a table for one, she headed to the bar and hoisted herself onto an empty stool while twirling the magnolia flower in her hand.

"You want a cup for that?" The middle-aged female bartender noticed her as she was busy filling glasses from a soda gun.

"Sure."

"And what would you like to drink?"

"A glass of your house Chardonnay would be great. And a menu when you have a minute."

"No problem."

Sara glanced at the televisions surrounding the bar, various sports channels blinking and flashing with basketball games and commentators. It was hard not to notice all the families with loud little ones in the restaurant and a few couples out on dates.

How she wished James could've accompanied her. But she shot that idea down from the get-go, claiming she needed to do this on her own.

And now? Now she realized she was tired of doing everything alone and ready to take things to the next level.

"Here you go. One Chardonnay, a menu, a glass of ice water, and another paper cup for your pretty flower."

Sara grinned and tenderly placed the magnolia into the water. "Thank you."

"Draft beer and house wines are two for one tonight until ten, so let me know when you need a refill. My name is Rita, and I'll be back soon to take your order once you've looked over the menu."

"I appreciate it."

Rita nodded, working furiously to stay out of the weeds on the busy Saturday night.

As Sara scanned the menu, a female voice behind her asked, "Is this seat taken?"

Angling her neck to look at the woman, she was shocked to see Renora from the Azalea Grove Assisted Living and Memory Care facility. Her red lipstick smile was bold, her gold cross shining against her dark skin.

"Renora?"

"Hey, Sara. I thought that was you. Is this seat taken?"

"No. Be my guest."

Renora sat and placed her tiny purse on the bar top, gaining Rita's attention.

"What'll it be?" she asked.

"White tequila on the rocks with a lime, please."

"You got it."

Sara smiled. "That's hardcore."

Renora laughed. "I'm priming the pump for my hot date."

"You're on a date?"

"I will be in…," She glanced at her cell phone parked beside her purse. "Thirty minutes."

Rita dropped off her drink in record time. Renora lifted her glass, and Sara reciprocated, the two clinking in a toast.

"Cheers, he's not a dud. You never know with these dating apps nowadays."

"I'll drink to that," Sara laughed.

They settled in and ordered an appetizer to share, their chit-chat a welcome reprieve from the long day. Another round of drinks was ordered, and Sara finally felt her shoulders relax—until Renora broached the subject of Miss Sue.

"You used to date her son, right?"

"Yes. A few dates. Nothing serious."

"And you never met Miss Sue while you dated?"

"Nope." She took a long pull of her wine.

"Is the kid in the photo really Dr. Chambers?"

"She showed you?"

Renora laughed. "Of course. She showed everyone in the facility."

Sara licked her lips, unsure if she should open up her can of worms. But Renora was sweet and fun, her friendly nature daring her to confide in another female.

"The child in the photo is my son, Noah. He's eight years old."

"Mmmhmm." Renora's red lips pursed as she hummed with quiet surprise and gave Sara the side-eye.

"What?" she giggled nervously.

Renora waggled her finger at her. "You've got a soap opera story you're not telling me."

"I do?"

"Yes, you do. Come on now. Spill the tea."

Sara laughed, the funny banter between them and the alcohol giving her loose lips.

"What do you suppose my soap opera story is?"

Taking a sip from her second glass of tequila, Renora thought for a moment and sucked on a lime wedge. Smacking her lips, she looked right at her.

"I think the boy in the photo is you and Dr. Chamber's love child."

Heat billowed across Sara's cheeks. Or maybe it was the wine. She swallowed hard and boldly said, "Maybe it is?"

Renora's eyes bugged, and she leaned in closer. "Girl! Tell me everything."

Draining her glass of wine, Sara filled her new friend in on the soap opera that was her life. Renora listened intently and immediately seemed to understand when she told her about Russell's reaction to her pregnancy.

"Of course, he couldn't be bothered. A big, important doctor like him? Good for you for standing up for yourself and having your baby boy on your own terms."

"But I didn't stand up to him. I lied to him. I told him it was a false alarm, and then I ran."

"You ran?"

"Yes. For years, I've been a travel nurse. I've never settled down. I've never given my son a proper home because I've been scared of running into Russell at a hospital again. Everything got away from me. Looking back, I know I was naïve and stupid…"

"—you're not stupid," she interrupted. "You were and still are a mama bear protecting her child."

"Yes, but in the end, Russ deserved to know. I made a mistake by not telling him. I should've told him the truth."

"So, when you found out he died, you thought telling Miss Sue might be the next best thing, right?"

"Yes. And look how that turned out."

"You know Miss Sue would never be able to wrap her head around something this big in her condition. And you did the right thing by not correcting her and telling her the boy in the photo was your son, not hers." Renora squeezed Sara's arm. "Being a nurse, you've heard of time-shifting in patients, right?"

"Yes. It's when a dementia patient has delusions of being in another time and place."

"Exactly. Miss Sue goes in and out of time-shifting all the time. Some days are worse than others. She'll experience a different reality than us. Sometimes, she believes her son is still alive, and there will be other times when she knows he's dead. Pointing out mistakes to a person with dementia who has time-shifted can be very upsetting to them. And when you handed her the photo of your son, she was transported back to when Dr. Chambers was his age. And it made her so happy."

Renora's smile was wide with reassurance.

"And isn't that what we want for them in their last days? A happy patient content with their sweet memories?"

Sara nodded, thankful for her wise words.

"Where is home for you now?" she asked, changing the subject.

"I'm living in Langston Falls, Georgia, at a family farm with my new boyfriend."

"Oh, a hunky farmer? Now that sounds promising."

"Very promising. He's the shit."

Renora laughed out loud before noticing her phone light up with a text message.

"Oh, Lord. He's here."

"Who's here?"

"My date!"

The two glanced at the hostess station and noticed a tall, dark, handsome man waiting alone.

"He's cute," Sara admitted.

"And he's *not* a doctor," she stressed. Pulling out her lipstick, she reapplied and fluffed her hair. "How do I look?"

"Hmm. You're beautiful, but you're missing something."

"What?"

Sara pulled the white magnolia flower from the paper cup and wiped off the drippy end. Carefully, she tucked it into Renora's dark hair and leaned back with satisfaction.

"Now you're perfect."

Renora's eyes sparkled. "Quick. Give me your phone."

Sara handed off her cell and watched her new confidant fill in her contact number before calling herself. "Now we can keep in touch."

"I'd like that."

Renora stood and gently touched the bold white bloom in her hair, her excitement contagious. "Well, there's no turning back now. Wish me luck."

"You don't need any luck."

"You got that right." She laughed again before her features turned softer. She laid some money on the bar and asked, "Are you going to be okay, Sara?"

"I'll be fine. Don't worry about me. Keep in touch and let me know how tonight goes with your hot date."

"Oh, I will." She posed with one hand on her hip, looking like a lady boss, her confidence beguiling.

With a wink of her flirty lashes, she turned and sashayed her hips in a confident swagger toward her handsome date.

And in her wake, the sweet scent of magnolia flowers lingered in the air—reminding Sara of spring.

# Chapter Twenty-Seven

## JAMES

Standing on the front porch, James's grin was in full tilt as he waved at the giant black Prevost tour bus with classic chrome paneling heading up the drive. It was just like his little brother, Hank, to surprise the family with an unannounced visit. Their dad was going to be ecstatic.

Jaxson and Delia bounded over the grassy knoll toward the large vehicle and barked a welcome. Noah paused mid-throw holding a tennis ball to take in the marvelous piece of machinery with mouth agape.

"Whoa," he muttered. His eyes bugged out from behind his glasses. "Who is that?"

James approached the boy and palmed his shoulder. "That's my brother, Hank-ster. He's a musician."

Noah looked up at him, squinting in the bright light of the late afternoon. "Is he famous?"

"Sure is. You're going to love him and his fiancée, Ella Mae. Come on."

The two trotted to where the bus parked in an easy graveled turn-around. James saluted the portly, middle-aged driver seated behind the wheel when the twin glider door opened outward from the hull.

"Hey, Lenny. How's it going?"

Before he could respond, Hank flew out of the vehicle and straight into James's arms, nearly knocking him to the ground. His well-worn cowboy hat flicked off his dark head, revealing thick, unruly hair.

"Dude! I'm so glad to see you!"

James's laugh was hearty as he slapped his brother on the back, not realizing how much he'd missed him. "Why didn't you tell us you were coming home?"

"Because we wanted it to be a surprise," Ella Mae said, coming down the bus stairs.

She was casually dressed in jeans and boots, the sweater she wore the color of burnt orange. A thick braid hung over one shoulder, her pretty expression filled with joy.

James opened his arms wide and hugged his future sister-in-law with delight. He was glad his brother had found his special someone, the two of them a famous singing duo climbing the charts in the world of country music. For them to make a pit stop at Bennett Farms was a dang miracle with their busy touring schedule.

"Hey, little dude. What's your name," Hank asked, kneeling to pick up his wayward hat and to be at eye-level with Noah.

James watched him shove his glasses against his nose and confidently say, "My name is Noah Larson."

"Well, howdy, Noah Larson. My name is Hank, and this here pretty lady is my fiancée, Miss Ella Mae Miller."

Ella smiled. "Pleased to meet you, Noah."

"Hi," he replied, shuffling his feet against the gravel.

"And the man operating this fine piece of machinery is our bus driver, Lenny. Say hello, Lenny."

"Hello, son." His low voice was raspy with age. "You want to come on up and take a look-see inside?"

Noah jerked his head toward James for permission. "Can I? Please?"

"Of course. Mr. Lenny will give you the grand tour." James ruffled the boy's hair.

"Cool!" He scampered up the steps, his little voice bombarding the driver with dozens of immediate questions.

James chuckled and didn't realize Hank and Ella were staring at him.

"What?"

"Nothing, bro. Daddy told us all about your new living arrangement. You're a damn natural with that boy," Hank said.

Ella Mae looped her arm around Hank's bicep as the three ambled toward the main house. "It's very sweet."

James felt heat surge across the back of his neck. "Yeah? Well, Noah's mama, Sara, is sweeter than Becky's iced tea in the summertime. You'll get to meet her soon. She's on her way back from Valdosta."

"So, you've been babysitting her kid?" Hank asked.

"I've been looking after him, is all. I took him and his friend, Billy, fishing yesterday at Langston Falls, and then they had a sleepover in the carriage house. Billy's mom picked him up about an hour ago. We're just biding our time until Sara gets home."

James stopped, opened the front door, and immediately noticed the peculiar grin on his brother's face. "*What?*"

"Fatherhood looks good on you," Hank teased. "Don't you think so, Ella?" He turned and eyed his fiancé.

"Absolutely." Her smile was warm without a hint of sarcasm.

"Yeah, well… now I have a newfound appreciation for what we put Mama and Daddy through."

"I'll bet," Hank guffawed.

"Yeah, yeah." He slapped his brother on the back and ushered Ella over the threshold. "Ya'll get inside and surprise Daddy and Becks. Teddy and Walt are off today and at home on the Morgan compound. You'll have to call and let them know y'all are here. I'll come in after Noah gets his bus tour."

"Cool," Hank replied.

The door clicked shut, and James could hear Becky's outburst of happiness from inside, sure their baby sister was as surprised as he was.

He patted Delia's panting muzzle and stood at the edge of the front porch, thankful for his brother's unexpected visit. When Noah reappeared at the top of the bus stairs, his face lit up at the sight of him, and he scampered happily toward the house with energy.

The boy hadn't stopped smiling since he moved in at Bennett Farms. This gave James much satisfaction and an uncanny instinct to protect, comfort, and commit. Day or night. Biological son or not.

He knew full well Sara was a buy one, get one more deal. And the life-changing decision he made was a no-brainer.

He chose *both* of them.

"Well, what did you think?"

"It was so cool!" In an instant, he switched gears. "Can I throw the balls for the dogs again?"

"Sure thing. But stay in the front yard. Your mama should be home any time."

"Okay."

Noah took off running with the dogs following closely

behind, the scene in front of him reminding him of those days long ago when he was just a boy. The only difference? He was blessed with a mother *and* a father, loved on by two adoring parents since day one.

Could he become a father figure to Noah? Could he love, care, and support a little boy who wasn't blood-related, through good and bad times—forever?

Forever was a mighty long time, the life-changing decision one he didn't take lightly. But the answer came to him immediately in joyful laughter and the flash of a little boy's smile.

Yes. James was willing and able to step up in every sense of the word, the title "stepfather" a word of honor and in a category all its own.

Now, if he could only get Sara to agree with him.

───────────

"God Almighty, I'm glad you're home."

James inhaled the scent of Sara's flowery hair, tucking his nose into the space where it was strongest. "I missed you," he whispered across the shell of her ear.

"I missed you too." She kissed his cheek. "Where's Noah? Where's my baby boy?"

James held her by the hand and led her inside the main house, the interior bustling with family and big dogs like a celebration was happening in real-time.

"Noah!" he shouted, gaining the boy's attention.

His head popped up from behind the kitchen island. He shrieked, scurrying to get to his mama as fast as his little legs could take him. Sara picked her son up like he was light as a feather, peppering his face with kisses.

"Mom!" He admonished, running his hand across his

cheek as if annoyed. But James knew Noah was a mama's boy, secretly thrilled and relieved to see her again.

"I know it's only been twenty-four hours, but I swear you've gone and grown up on me."

"I have?" he grinned.

"Yes. I missed you."

"Me too." They rubbed noses, and she set him down.

"Mom, you've got to go inside Hank's tour bus. It's so cool."

Sara ran her fingers through her son's hair, her motherly gaze transfixed on her only child. When her blue irises shifted to James, they latched onto his for a few beats, and he expected her to smile, but she just stared at him.

He knew she'd been through an emotional wringer taking a trip to Valdosta in hopes of connecting with her son's biological grandmother. From the outside, she looked like she was happy to be home. But he knew internally she was fragile from her deep blue "need you" eyes.

"Let me introduce you to Hank and Ella Mae real quick, then we can head back to the carriage house."

She nodded, and as he introduced her to his brother and his fiancé, he stood a little taller, pride bubbling up from his center as Hank and Ella glowingly sang her praises for all to hear.

"It's very nice to finally meet you, Hank."

"Nice to meet you too. I can't even begin to thank you for all you've done to help our father regain some sense of normalcy. You've done an amazing job. And let's not forget about this goofy smile you've tattooed on my brother's face." He playfully patted James on the cheek.

Sara giggled. "Your brother's been amazing helping us settle here on the farm. Noah absolutely adores him. I'm kind of partial to the man myself." She leaned into him, noticeable heat infiltrating his system.

Hank chuckled. "Well, James is the best of all us Bennetts rolled into one. We're happy he found you."

"What a nice thing to say, bro," James said.

"Well, it's true."

Sara's lashes fluttered. Her smile was pure, filled with glowing happiness, much like a spring flower opening on a sunny day. It came from deep within, lighting up her eyes and spreading into every part of her. He could hear it in her voice and her choice of words and knew it was genuine by how she finally relaxed.

"Seriously, I'm the one who's happy," she said.

And she was beautiful.

# Chapter Twenty-Eight

## SARA

Sara loved getting to know Ella Mae and Hank during their extended stay at Bennett Farms.

They ate dinner together almost every night. Took long, slow walks through the pine forest with Roy, showing off how far he'd come since being under her care. But her favorite moments were watching the sunset on the back porch while listening to Hank and Ella render a few tunes among the gentle strum of an acoustic guitar.

By Friday, the Bennett women had joined forces, insisting she come with them on a girl's night out on the town before the country music couple hit the road again in their giant tour bus. The inclusion was something she'd longed for, the feeling of belonging to a family, a heady dose of contentment.

"Have fun," James said, adjusting the collar of Sara's coat.

"I think I will," she replied, thankful he was once again keeping an eye on her son for a few hours. Grateful to be included in the circle of Bennett women.

"Make sure Noah wears his jacket tonight. Once the sun sets, the temperature takes a nosedive, and he'll get cold, whether he realizes it or not."

"I know, darlin'. I've got this."

"I know you do." She stood on her tiptoes and kissed him long and hard. When she pulled back, she sighed. "Have I told you lately how much I appreciate you?"

"Every single day."

"Well, I do. You're my handsome boyfriend."

"And you're my gorgeous girl."

Earlier in the week, the pair had sat Noah down and explained their romantic intentions of being a legitimate couple. The boy rolled his eyes and remarked, "Does this mean you're going to kiss in front of me now?"

Sara looked at James and grinned before she leaned in and gave him a deliberate peck on the lips.

"Ew!" Noah groaned, making them laugh.

The entire Bennett clan was next, their announcement at dinner resulting in a poignant toast from Roy himself about new beginnings. Life on the farm was happiness, pure and simple. And Sara savored this new chapter...

James pulled her in for a final hug. "Stay out as late as you want. Don't worry about me and Noah. We're doing manly things tonight. You know, grilling meat and hanging around the fire pit telling stories with the rest of the boys."

"Oh, manly things, huh?" She leaned against his chest and swooned.

James grunted for effect. "Oh, yes." He chuckled. "And later, maybe you and I can do a little dirty dancing to some more records in the living room." He swiveled his hips, making Sara laugh. She was inexplicably happy.

"I love that Noah and Hank have hit it off," she said.

"I know. He promised to show him how to strum a

few chords on the guitar. I'm hoping they can have one last night of fun before he and Ella have to leave tomorrow."

"I know. Their visit flew by way too fast. I've loved getting to know them too, and I look forward to spending time with Ella this evening before she leaves. You know, a regular girl's night out."

"Should I be concerned?"

"Concerned? Why?"

"You know... My hot girlfriend out on the town with all the pretty ladies? Maybe y'all need a chaperone?"

Sara waved him off. "Puh-lease. We're going to dinner. Nothing crazy."

James puckered his lips to the side. "Mmhmm. Says the beautiful woman who knocks my socks off every time I look at her."

"Really?" Her cheeks heated with a blush as she batted her lashes at him. She was intentionally baiting him for another compliment.

"Yup. You're my gorgeous girl." He cupped his hands around her neck and caressed her cheeks with his thumbs. "My advice? Stay close to Becks. She'll protect you."

Sara laughed. "I hardly think sweet Becky has it in her to fight off a local man with a stick, especially at a five-star restaurant."

"Five-star restaurant? I thought y'all were going to the local pub in town."

"No. Ella Mae insisted she treat us at one of her favorite places."

"Oh? Where?"

"The Speckled Trout."

James stepped back and was silent for a beat, his expression clouding. It was as if he'd seen a ghost.

"Not that great, huh?"

"It's alright. I left hungry the last time I was there. But that's ancient history."

"I'll be sure to order something substantial then. You know, so I won't end up starving before our dirty dancing session."

James offered her a meek smile. "I'm sure your experience will be much better than mine. And if you do end up hungry, I can always find a way to fill the void when you get home."

His hot lips pressed against hers again, and Sara knew there was more to his words than he was letting on, but she didn't have time to get into it now. The girls were waiting for her inside the main house.

Pulling back from him, her eyes scrolled his handsome face one last time before she adjusted her purse over her shoulder and hollered toward her son's bedroom.

"Noah, I'm leaving!"

"Bye, Mom!" he yelled, obviously too preoccupied with something.

Sara rolled her eyes even though she was secretly pleased Noah wasn't as clingy as he used to be since they'd moved to the farm. She chose to let him be, saving her motherly kisses for bedtime.

As if sensing her disappointment, James pulled her in for a final hug, his voice filled with reassurance.

"I've got him. Go have some fun tonight. You have nothing to worry about."

---

The five-star Speckled Trout Restaurant on the outskirts of Langston Falls was crowded, the interior intentionally dimmed to invoke a lovely candlelight glow. Couples stared lovingly from across their tables at each other, the vibe in the room thick with romance and euphoria, flirtation, and amore.

Sara frowned, knowing James had been here in the past, probably with his former girlfriend, Samantha. An unfamiliar and unexpected pang of jealousy hit her right between the eyes. She'd have to revisit this with him later and perhaps talk him into a do-over at the fancy eating establishment—with her.

She followed Robyn, Elyse, Becky, and Ella Mae through the bustling restaurant, wishing she was the one who could've shared this dining experience with James, not his former flame. As they stepped onto the expansive terrace beyond the large windows, the hostess showed them a cozy table near the mammoth outdoor fireplace crackling with orange flames.

The stunning backdrop of the mountains was highlighted in pale pink and violet, the onset of the early spring sunset sure to be spectacular with their fortunate seating. The vibe was everything she coveted for a date night with James, not a night out with the girls.

"This is incredible," Sara whispered to Ella Mae as they sat beside each other.

"It's one of my favorite places in Langston Falls. I wanted to treat my girls to something special tonight."

"This is special, all right," Robyn chimed in. "Teddy took me here right after we got engaged."

"That's so sweet," Becky said.

"Walter has some explaining to do," Elyse teased. She dramatically flicked her napkin open and rested the fabric in her lap, her mock attitude making the girls laugh.

"Walt has never brought you here before?" Robyn asked.

"Nope."

"Then he does have some explaining to do." Robyn turned toward Ella Mae. "And so do you. Why did you pick The Speckled Trout for our girl's night? This is fancy."

Ella held up her finger. "Hold that thought."

A waiter introduced himself and filled their water glasses as he explained the specials for the evening. When he asked for everyone's drink order, Ella Mae responded quickly and ordered for the entire table.

"We need a bottle of your best champagne, please."

"Coming right up," he grinned.

Becky leaned in with curiosity. "What are we celebrating? A new tour?"

"A new album in the making? A new song?" Elyse asked.

"I know," Robyn grinned. Her eyes glimmered with emotion. "You and Hank have finally set a date."

All eyes landed on Ella Mae, the pretty country music artist sitting erect in her chair like a proper lady at a debutante ball. She wore a tight black dress and thigh-high boots for the evening. Her dark hair spilled over her shoulders in sexy waves, and her engagement ring winked in the quixotic candlelight.

She radiated confidence and a certain star swagger, the woman used to commanding an audience of thousands when she performed with Hank out on tour. That she held the same mesmerizing power with the four of them left Sara holding her breath.

"Bingo," Ella replied.

The entire table erupted into girlish squeals of congratulations, the outdoor patrons joining in with hearty applause when Becky explained what was going on through happy tears.

And it was at that moment Sara realized her heart yearned to be in Ella Mae's boots.

# Chapter Twenty-Nine

## JAMES

"Your mama said you need to wear a coat when it gets dark," James explained.

"But it's not dark yet. I can still see the sun above the mountains," Noah complained.

Roy looked at their exchange and chuckled from his seated position in an Adirondack chair around the fire pit. "Let the boy run around a little bit longer without his coat. He's keeping warm playing with the dogs. It'll be dark soon enough."

James harrumphed. "Well, it'll be your fault if Sara comes home early and sees him coatless."

"Don't worry, son. I'll gladly take the blame."

Noah approached Roy and smiled. "Thanks, Mr. Bennett. Can you tell me about the gold story again? You tell it way better than Mr. James."

"Hey!" James lamented.

Teddy laughed. "Oh, boy. Here we go."

Hank looked at his brother and asked, "The story about the lost gold? The same story Paw-Paw used to tell us?"

Walt chimed in. "That's the one."

"Oh, this is a good one," Glen said.

"Go ahead, Dad. Tell it again in your special way. You've always been the world's greatest storyteller."

James patted the extra space in his chair and motioned for Noah to sit with him. The little boy nestled against his warmth as they listened to his father tell the familiar story.

By the time he finished, the sun had disappeared behind the mountain range, the sky a glorious burst of color, the chilly air around them nipping at their cheeks. Noah finally put on his coat without James having to remind him.

"I've always loved that story, Daddy," Hank said. "But you forgot the part about the cave glowing at dusk. In fact, I'll bet the outside of the lost cave up there in those mountains is glowing right about now, those thousand bars of gold reflecting the last light of day." He pointed toward the pine forest, where the trees eased up the mountainside in a carpet of dark evergreen.

"It glows?" Noah gasped, his focus pinpointed on the area of the forest Hank indicated.

"Sure does. Many explorers have waited until the golden hour to find the lost treasure, but no one's ever been able to locate it."

"That's right. People say they've seen a yellow shimmer in the mountains before. But no one has ever found the gold," Roy added.

"It's kind of like searching for the pot of gold at the end of a rainbow. It's a total mystery. But I believe it's out there." Hank's eyes had a definite twinkle, his boyish grin one James missed while his brother was away.

Noah nodded before he abruptly switched gears and focused on James. "Can I play hide and seek with the dogs?"

Hide and seek was a little game Noah had become fond of, darting in and out of the Christmas trees on the farm property with Jaxson and Delia hot on his trail. Sara loved it because it was a way for her son to expel the last bit of energy lingering in his body, the fresh air doing wonders for a good night's sleep.

"Sure. But only for a few minutes before it gets too dark," James replied.

Noah's smile was broad. "Thank you."

He took off running through the vineyard toward the forest with the big dogs bounding after him. Everyone around the fire chuckled as if remembering their boyhood games, hide and seek being a family favorite.

"He's a good kid," Walt said, tipping back his beer bottle.

"And his mama is a real sweetheart and a wonderful nurse," Roy chimed in.

"We love them both, James," Teddy admitted. "Right, Hank?"

James looked across the fire pit at his youngest brother; sad he and Ella Mae had to leave tomorrow but ready to hear his thoughts about his new girlfriend and her son.

"I think Sara and Noah are awesome. Congratulations, James."

"Thanks, brother."

"And since we're on the subject of Noah…"

James frowned, unsure of what he was getting at. "What about him?"

Hank's grin was unmistakable, the flames of the fire reflecting in his dark eyes. "He seems like a responsible kid. Do you think he could handle ring-bearer duties this summer?"

James pressed his teeth into his lower lip and excitedly

slapped his thigh. "Bro! You and Ella Mae finally picked a date?"

"Sure did. This August in Nashville. We want a small, private ceremony at Ella's farm. Family only."

That he included Sara and Noah under the "family only" umbrella meant the world to him.

"Congratulations, Hank," Glen said.

"Thanks."

James stood and walked around the blazing fire toward his little brother, his heart surging with warmth, knowing he approved of his relationship. And, of course, thrilled his official wedding date finally on the calendar.

"I think Noah would make a great ring-bearer." His eyes pricked with hot tears as Hank stood, and the two bear-hugged.

Having the entire family gathered for the special occasion was a long time coming and something he wouldn't miss for the world. Having Sara and Noah by his side was the icing on the proverbial wedding cake.

"Seriously, I'm so happy for you," James muttered into his ear.

"Thanks, bro. I'm happy for you too."

The guys replenished their drinks from a nearby cooler as Glen added another log to the fire. The wood crackled, sending sparks shooting into the air. James glanced at the darkening sky and noticed the first glimmer of stars.

Ambling toward the vineyard, he cupped his hands around his mouth and hollered, "*Noah*! Time to come home!"

He planted his hands on his hips, waiting for a boyish reply or a bark from one of his dogs. Glancing over his shoulder, he smiled at the sight of his brothers, Glen, and his father gathered around the fire pit in an animated discussion about their new apple-infused wine about to hit the market.

Flicking his head back toward the vineyard, he hollered again. "Noah! Come on back, buddy!"

He felt a hand palm his shoulder and turned to see Walt holding a fresh beer bottle. He offered it to him.

"Thanks."

"You're welcome. Pretty cool, they finally settled on a date for the wedding, huh?"

James took a swig of beer and swiped the back of his hand across his wet lips. "The best news I've had in a while."

"You think Noah will even want to play ring-bearer?"

"Of course. He and Hank hit it off this week big time. I think he'll be thrilled."

James took another sip of beer and stared at the entrance to the dark trail leading into the pine forest. There was no movement. No footfalls against brittle pine needles on the path. No big dogs panting and cantering toward him.

"Here. Can you hold this for a minute? I don't think Noah can hear me."

"Sure."

James marched between the trellises, his lips lifted in a smirk. This is what his father must've felt like coming after him and his brothers back in the day. But for Noah to blatantly disobey wasn't like him. In fact, he'd never seen him talk back or disrespect his mama or the family in any way. He was a rule follower through and through.

Noah was kind and loving, a "snuggle-bunny," as Sara liked to call him, sharing his bed with two big dogs and his teddy bear. He was inquisitive and smart, loved reading books and ogling tractors.

His young life had changed since he moved to the farm. He was free to roam the property and explore life in a way every little boy deserved. That James could give him any semblance of what he experienced as a child meant the world to him.

His boots crunched along the path, the scent of evergreen and musk heady in the twilight. That a little boy like Noah was brave enough to scour these trails on his own in the dark was impressive.

"*Noah*! Come on, it's time to go home!" Sticking two fingers between his lips, he whistled through his teeth for the dogs. "Jaxson! Delia! *Come*!"

James stopped and listened, the silence stretching on for several seconds. The hoot of a nearby owl startled him, causing his heart to plummet to his knees.

For his dogs to disobey was a whole other story. Something must've happened. Something bad.

Turning on his heels, he sprinted toward Walt, his breath coming out fast and frantic. "He's not answering when I call him. Neither are the dogs."

Walt scowled. "Well, let's go find them."

They sprinted toward the fire pit, all heads turning to see them stumble to a stop in front of the roaring flames. James set his beer bottle down, his stuttered words filled with panic and trepidation.

"He's not... answering," he gulped. "And the dogs won't come on my command."

The men stood and looked at one other as James's words resonated, the men quickly going into action.

"I'll go get the ATV," Walt said.

"I'll grab us some flashlights," Teddy offered. He took the steps up to the back door of the house two at a time.

Hank, Glen, and Roy surrounded James, his dad reassuringly pressing a hand against his shoulder.

"The dogs will protect him, son. He probably wandered off the path and is trying to find his way back in the dark. Jax and Delia will help lead him home. They know the way. I promise."

"You sure about that?" James was wide-eyed and stared at his father, heart hammering in his chest. "What the hell, Dad? One minute he was here, and the next…"

"—don't go there, bro," Hank interrupted.

"He couldn't have gone far," Glen added.

"All that talk about gold and glowing caves at dusk. He didn't want to play hide and seek. He wanted to search for treasure." James steeled himself with determination, trying to keep it together.

They should've known better than to fill his little head with dreams of striking it rich. They had to find him before Sara returned. They had to. She'd never forgive him if she discovered her son was lost in the woods.

The sound of an ATV cut through the tension as Walt skidded to a stop. Teddy was right behind him, flashlights blazing. James jumped into the front passenger seat as Ted climbed in the back.

"I'll stay here with Dad and Glen," Hank hollered.

"Text us when you find him," Roy shouted.

James nodded and held on as Walt jerked the vehicle into drive. He knew all that talk about gold treasure fascinated Noah. Hell, it enthralled him as a boy. Sara had told him that's all he talked about on their way to school in the mornings, the boy convinced he was the lucky one who would find the gold like a pirate finding lost treasure.

But what Noah didn't know was that the story was nothing

but an old wife's tale with no merit—a campfire story passed down from generations. It titillated James and his brothers when they were growing up. No doubt it did the same for Noah.

And now, here they were, searching for him after he wandered off the beaten path in search of the bogus treasure. That's what it had to be, or he would've been back by now.

James took a deep breath as they entered the trail under a canopy of gnarled branches and sharp needles, filling his lungs with the verdant scent of his homeland that defied description. The air was heavy with pine and the smell of wood smoke, thick with fear and trepidation. It was sensory overload between the ATV engine rumbling over the bumpy path and the roar of blood pulsating in his ears.

An unfamiliar coldness crept into his veins, a real fear rearing its ugly head. His lips quivered as he fisted his hands in his lap and offered a silent prayer to the heavens. He focused on the pinprick of illumination from the headlights, feeling the blackness surrounding him from all sides.

Swallowing him up like an unexpected storm.

# Chapter Thirty

## SARA

"You'll still be in Langston Falls this August, right? I mean, you don't have to move on to another assignment, do you?" Ella Mae asked Sara.

She looked around the table at the Bennett women, the flickering candlelight and glow from the fireplace accentuating the remarkable beauty surrounding her. These women welcomed her with open arms, their generous support for her and James's relationship giving her a new sense of belonging—of feeling wanted.

"I'm not planning on going anywhere," she said simply.

In fact, once her contract was completed with Mr. Bennett, she planned to work at the local clinic full-time. The owner had offered her the job a few days ago, and she was anxious to talk to James about it once their visit with Hank and Ella Mae was over.

"Well, I'd love for you to ask your son if he'd like to be our ring-bearer in the wedding ceremony. It was Walt's idea. I guess he and Noah have really hit it off. They're so cute together." She gripped Sara's forearm and frowned. "But only if you're okay with it."

"Oh, wow. It's fine with me." Visions of her son wearing a miniature tux came to mind, her grin contagious. "But I think you'll get a more exuberant answer if you or Walt ask him yourself. Sometimes moms aren't as cool as country music stars."

The girls all laughed, remnants of champagne and what was left of their dinner being cleared by the waiter. The chatter continued about wedding flowers and color schemes, the songstress telling them about a special melody she was working on for the ceremony.

Sara glanced at Becky from across the table and noticed her frown.

"What is it?"

All heads turned to look at the pretty Bennett sister. Her brown eyes were large when she looked up from her cell phone, her expression giving nothing away.

"I better get this. It's Daddy. He wouldn't call and interrupt our girl's night if it wasn't important."

Sara leaned forward, her mind going straight to possible scenarios. Had Mr. Bennett fallen? Was he feeling light-headed or experiencing pain? What if another cardiac arrest was looming while they sat and waited for decadent artery-clogging desserts?

But if he were in dire straits, he wouldn't be the one calling; one of his sons would.

Becky's eyes darted to Sara as she spoke softly to her father, making her shiver. She genuinely cared for Roy. For there to be an emergency after such a lovely celebration meal left her shaken.

"Well?" Robyn asked after Becky hung up.

"Everything is fine. Daddy is fine."

A resounding exhale of relief circled the table. But when Becky pinned Sara with her stare, she knew the phone call had nothing to do with Roy and everything to do with Noah.

"What happened?" Her voice felt stuck in her throat, scratched with unease.

"He wandered off, but don't worry, my brothers are out looking for him."

"*Looking for him?*" The legs of her chair scraped against the terrace floor as she stood with abruptness. "Can we please go? I need to get to my son. I want my son."

"Absolutely." Ella Mae waved their waiter over and took care of the check.

Becky approached Sara and helped her with her coat. "Daddy said he shouldn't have called, but he knew you'd be angry if he didn't."

"Of course, I'm angry. James was supposed to keep an eye on Noah. He's only eight." She couldn't help that her tone was short with his sister; her fear of losing her son always parked at the forefront of her mind.

"It's already pitch black outside. He hates the dark. He has a night light in his room. If anything happens to him…"

"—but nothing is going to happen. He's with Jaxson and Delia. They'll stay glued to his side and protect him until he's found," Becky soothed.

Robyn, Elyse, and Ella Mae surrounded her, the concerned looks on their faces ramping up Sara's angst. For a split second, she felt terrible they had to leave the celebration dinner; their plans ruined because James took his eyes off Noah for one second. But just as quickly as those feelings surfaced, they were trumped by a dark fear, turning her blood cold.

Noah was lost. In the dark. Alone on the mountain.

"Come on, let's go," Ella said, looping her arm with Sara's.

Her legs were weak, and she was thankful, leaning on Ella for support.

"I'm sorry about dessert," she muttered.

"Another time. I promise."

They walked swiftly through the crowded dining room, a few patrons eyeing and pointing out Ella Mae as if they recognized her celebrity. She took it in stride, undeterred and her grip on Sara's arm intensifying as they marched out of the restaurant and toward the car.

"We need to get you back to the farm. I'll bet the minute we get home, Noah and the guys will be sitting around the fire laughing and acting like nothing happened. You'll see."

---

The car barely rolled to a stop, and Sara was out, running toward the men surrounding the fire pit. Orange light flickered across Roy Bennett's weather-worn face as he removed his hat and welcomed her into his arms. Sara knew right then they hadn't found Noah.

"We've called the authorities. Sheriff Jenkins is on his way with a search and rescue team. I can't reach my boys, who are out looking for him. Cell service is crap in the woods."

Sara nodded, taking in every word and syllable Roy uttered as if her life depended on it. He guided her to a chair and motioned for her to sit.

"I can't sit. I… I don't know what I should do."

"Don't panic," Hank insisted. Ella Mae stood beside

him, her arm wrapped around his. "If anyone is going to find Noah, it's gonna be James, Teddy, and Walt. They know this mountain like the back of their hand."

"It's true," Glen chimed in. "They've traversed these trails since they could walk. When we used to go camping back in the day, I was never afraid because they always knew exactly how to find their way home."

Sara nodded, thankful for their words of encouragement. It still didn't stop her entire body from shivering with fear. Becky seemed to notice.

"You want something warm to drink? I could make us some hot apple cider or hot chocolate while we wait." Becky's tiny body pressed closely to Glen's, his strong arm protecting her as they waited for an answer.

"No. I don't need anything, thank you."

The group milled about the fire pit for several minutes, and when the sheriff arrived, followed by a Langston County Fire Department truck, Sara almost lost it.

Pulsating lights illuminated the sides of the barn and house, the severity of her son's situation driving a knife deep into her heart. Robyn immediately came to her side.

"Please, Sara. Sit down. This is all standard procedure. It doesn't mean anything bad has happened to Noah. They're just here to help."

All she could do was nod, her body trembling with fear. She sat in an empty chair and held on to Robyn's hand, her warm skin a lifeline preventing her from breaking down in front of everyone.

This wasn't supposed to happen. Noah was safe with James. She trusted him. He was a good man, a role model in her son's young life. She could see herself growing old with him, the two of them eventually marrying and watching her son morph into a fine young man, her past mistakes forgiven, and her future life blissful and happy.

But the fear she felt deep in her soul had returned. It started the moment she found out she was pregnant, her old habits and primal instinct to protect her only son scrambling to the forefront of her mind.

She went into default mode, the urge to pack up and escape the panic and anxiety that plagued her all these years coming at her full force. She wanted to flee with her son. Get in her car, rip off the rearview mirror, and never look back.

She'd made it this far as a single parent and was sure she could continue. It had worked fine before, her courage and mama bear instincts keeping them safe for the most part. That she'd let her guard down and trusted another man with her son was a mistake, her entire world crumbling in real-time.

"Miss Larson, I'm Sheriff Jenkins. I'm sorry we're meeting under these circumstances."

Sara nodded.

"I'd like to ask you a few questions and see if you might share a recent photo of your son from your cell phone."

Sara was numb, her clumsy fingers digging for her phone in her coat pocket. Firing up the device, the voices around her were nothing but white noise in the background. Her eyes filled with tears as she scrolled through her cameral roll, pictures of Noah and James, big dogs, and sunsets assaulting her senses.

She couldn't take it anymore and dropped the phone in her lap, hiding her face with her hands as she broke down and cried.

# Chapter Thirty-One

## JAMES

The high beams of the all-terrain vehicle shone bright along the craggy divots of the well-worn trail through the forest. Flashbacks of James and his brothers as boys traversing the familiar terrain kept his mind preoccupied for mere seconds, his thoughts scrolling through what might lie ahead.

Back in the day, their dad taught them at a young age how to read a map, use a compass, and remember landmarks that helped mark a destination just in case they went off the beaten path. James knew this was the scenario Noah was currently in. He'd wandered off and was lost, the black ink sky and overlay of thick trees and vegetation not helping matters.

He hoped the boy could stay calm, thankful his dogs Jaxson and Delia were by his side. Knowing his canine family surrounded Noah with unconditional love and protection gave him some semblance of composure.

But the growing dread of explaining things to Sara grew

exponentially with every yard the big wheels of the ATV traversed.

Walt slowed his driving, Teddy poking his head in between the two brothers in the front seat. "We need to holler and shine the flashlights into the woods," he said, handing one off to James. "Here."

He shone the beam of light through the trees, sweeping across the thick bark, branches, and spindly underbrush. A cold wind rustled through the pines among the scurrying of nocturnal animals. A large owl blinked back at him, doused in the spotlight, his yellow beak and piercing black eyes giving no clues as to where Noah and his dogs might be.

He couldn't fathom him wandering off the main path, the growth beneath the tall pines almost as tall as him. Something spectacular must've beckoned him off the trail, like the flash of illumination when the sun dipped below the horizon, the twilight mistaken for gold.

"*Noah!*" he yelled repeatedly until he was hoarse. His brothers joined in, Teddy sweeping his light through the trees from the opposite side as Walt drove at a snail's pace.

James's senses were on high alert, every sound, every whoosh of cold mountain air reminding him that a little boy's life was in danger because of *his* irresponsibility. He should've kept a better eye on him. He shouldn't have let him play hide and seek so close to sundown. He should've glued himself to the boy's side and never let him out of sight.

A large deer darted in front of the vehicle, causing Walt to slam on the brakes. The impressive antlers protruded from his fully muscled neck, the animal's chest and shoulders deep and strong.

"Look at him!" Walt hollered. "He's at least a 10-point buck."

The male deer's nostrils flared before he loped off into the dark forest, leaving the brothers dazed with amazement. They hadn't seen a deer that size in a long time. The rustling and crunching of leaves led James to believe there were more deer in the area, and he was surprised when he laid eyes on Delia.

"*D!*" he shouted, anxious to get off the ATV and greet his yellow lab.

His heart leaped with joy. If Delia heard them, it meant Jaxson and Noah were somewhere nearby.

The dog panted, tail wagging as if she were happy to see him. James patted and stroked the animal, assessing if she was all right.

"Girl, you okay? Where's Noah? Where's Jax?" His hands trembled as he ran his thick fingers across Delia's coarse fur.

She barked once, and he watched her trot confidently to the trail's edge before turning back around as if making sure James was following.

"Do you think she can lead us to them?" Teddy asked.

"Fuck, yeah!" Walt exclaimed.

"Good girl!" James shouted. Adrenaline pumped through his veins, and his breathing turned staggered, wanting to cry with relief. This nightmare was about to be over.

"Take me to them, D. You got this!"

James shone the flashlight ahead of him as he swept errant branches away from his face, his focus pinpointed on his trusty companion as his brothers followed from behind. The old trail was thick with overgrown vegetation, tree roots, and vines, making him stumble more than once.

In the distance, the distinct sound of Jaxson's bark

perked his ears. And then he heard a child's voice, the tone desperate, yet excited, happy to have been found.

"*Help! We're over here!*"

James ran as if his life depended on it, Delia picking up her pace before abruptly stopping. He slid to a halt, dangerously close to falling over the edge of a steep cliff into a ravine. Shining his flashlight beyond the tips of his boots hanging over the precarious ledge, loose rocks and pebbles showered Noah and Jaxson, who were safely perched on a bolder jutting out several feet below.

"Holy shit," Walt muttered, coming up alongside James and peering down at them.

Noah blinked against the bright light beam before shielding his tear-stained face from the glare. Jaxson whined and spun in a circle around the boy, happy to see his master.

"Jaxson, sit!" James commanded. The dog obediently sat next to Noah, two pairs of hopeful eyes staring up at him from below.

"Noah, stay real still. We're gonna get y'all off the ledge."

He nodded, stifling a sob and holding onto Jaxson's neck.

The brothers went into action, James handing off his flashlight to Walt and holding onto Teddy's sturdy bicep as he was slowly lowered onto the boulder. Carefully. One slip and there was no telling how far he might fall into the black abyss.

With his boots firmly planted on the solid rock after a four-foot jump, James was taken aback when Noah rushed into his arms and buried his face into his chest, overcome with emotion.

He lowered to his knees and held him close, his silent prayers of gratitude causing a torrent of tears to stream down his face. He'd never been so relieved in his entire life.

The mountain air surrounding them was thick with love and consolation, comfort and happiness. An overpowering paternal instinct took over, not just for an eight-year-old boy but for his black lab too.

"Shhh, it's okay, buddy. I've got you. You're okay."

Jaxson pushed his muzzle into James's neck, and he ruffed up the animal's fur. "Good boy, Jax. You're such a good boy."

"Be careful, Jimmy. That drop-off is mere inches from Jaxson's hind legs." Teddy warned.

James pulled Noah and his dog closer and held onto them with a firm grip. He was never letting go.

"I've got them," he reassured.

"How do you want to do this?" Walt asked.

"I want to lift Noah onto my shoulders, and you grab him."

"Got it."

James swiped his thumb across Noah's wet cheeks and gently stroked his hair back, assessing his cherub face. His glasses were cracked in the corner of one lens, and a bright red scratch was noticeable on one of his cheeks, probably from the underbrush off the beaten path. He must've been scared out of his mind.

"Are you mad?" His little voice stuttered.

"I'm not mad at all. I've never been so happy to see you in my entire life." His smile was broad as Noah lunged and hugged him again.

James spoke near the boy's ear. "I need you to climb onto my shoulders and lift your arms high so Walt and Teddy can hoist you up onto the ridge. Can you be brave and do that for me?"

"Yes, sir." He sniffled and broke their connection, ready to do whatever James asked.

Carefully shifting his large body in the small space, he faced the craggy side of the ravine, back toward the blackness of the drop-off. He lifted Noah to his shoulders and firmly gripped his legs. There was no way he'd let him fall.

"That's it, Noah. We got you!" Walt encouraged.

James continued to lift Noah above his head like an acrobat performing with a partner perched upon his shoulders. Pure relief surged through him when his brothers easily pulled him to solid ground.

"Atta boy!" Teddy congratulated.

"What about Jaxson?" Noah asked, his tone turned panicked as he stared down at them on the precarious precipice.

"Same thing, boys. I'm gonna lift him into the air, and y'all grab him by the collar." James kneeled and scooped up the big dog into his arms, whispering words of comfort as the animal whined in his throat.

Delia cocked her head from above and barked as if giving Jaxson a pep talk. And when James lifted the one-hundred-pound animal with brute strength above his head, his boots slipped on the loose pebbles, causing his knees to buckle. He pulled Jaxson to his chest and fell hard on his ass, not letting go.

"*James!*" Walt shouted, the fear in his voice real.

"I'm alright. We're okay." His breathing turned ragged, his arms feeling like wet noodles after expending so much energy. Jaxson was a lot heavier than Noah.

"Give me a minute, and we'll try this again."

He heard the boy softly crying again. There was nothing James could do but watch as his brother Teddy tried to comfort him.

"Text Daddy and let him know we found him," James instructed as he rested for a beat.

"On it," Walt replied, pulling his phone from his coat pocket. A few seconds later, he cursed. "*Fuck*! There's no service out here."

"Language, Walter!" James admonished.

"Sorry."

Teddy lowered himself to the ground and laid flat on his belly. "Walt, hold onto my ankles."

"Got it."

James nodded, watching his brothers, and understanding the assignment. He stood and palmed his lower back, the dull ache in his backside reminding him of when he fell off a horse at their neighbor's farm. He knew he'd be black and blue before the night was over, but it was all worth it to see Noah and his dog safe on solid land.

Teddy hung off the edge of the cliff with strong, outstretched hands. James hoisted Jaxson into his arms again and used all his strength to hand him off to his brother. Walt grunted loudly and pulled Teddy's legs with all his might, sliding him to safety as Jaxson scrambled to higher ground.

Loose dirt and rocks pummeled James. He used his arms to shield himself from the avalanche of falling debris.

"Come on, Jimmy. I've got you," Ted encouraged.

He stretched his arm out again, James linking his forearms with his. His boots scraped against the side of the ravine, and he practically walked up the rock wall by the force of his brother's brute strength.

Once on solid ground, he slapped Teddy's back in a bear hug and unexpectedly laughed. "Well, that was no fun."

Jaxson and Delia crowded around his legs, pawing at his

jeans. James patted the dogs and roughed up their fur, giving them praise and the promise of delicious treats when they got home.

Noah stood nearby holding one of the flashlights, his expression of remorse. James's lips cocked in a half-smile of empathy, knowing the boy had been scared out of his mind.

Opening his arms wide, he was surprised when Noah flung his body against his again. He hoisted him onto his hip to where they were nose to nose.

"You ready to go?"

Jaxson barked what he supposed was a resounding yes in doggie language, making Noah grin.

"Yes, please."

He laid his head against his shoulder and aimed the flashlight toward the twisted trail, the group of men and dogs hiking toward safety.

Marching toward home.

# Chapter Thirty-Two

## SARA

The next few seconds were a blur of slow motion and sounds.

A beeping horn.

Dogs barking.

A little boy's voice cutting through the mayhem, screaming her name.

"*Mom!*"

Sara bolted upright from her seat to see Noah waving his hands in the air, his tiny body seated on James's lap in the front seat of an ATV.

"*Noah!*"

She ran toward the vehicle as if her life depended on it. And didn't it? Her hair came undone, causing her auburn tresses to tumble around her shoulders and fly wildly around her face. Noah's smile beamed with love, and she knew right then what it might feel like to enter the pearly gates of heaven.

The ATV came to a stop, and Sara plucked her boy out of James's arms and held him tight. She was laughing and crying simultaneously, palming the back of his head, and rocking him like a baby.

When their eyes locked, something touching and tender passed between them until she noticed the cracked lens of his glasses and the bright red scratch across his cheek.

Touching her finger against his wound, she was barely able to form a sentence. "Are. You. Okay?"

Noah nodded and wrapped his arms around her neck, squeezing with all his might. "I'm sorry, Mom. I'm sorry I broke my glasses."

His eyeglasses were the least of her worries. "You can wear your old ones until we get them fixed. It's okay, baby." She breathed in his familiar scent, utter exhaustion creeping into her being.

"Where were you?" she finally asked.

Noah leaned back in her arms and pushed his glasses snugly against his nose. "I was playing hide and seek with Jaxson and Delia. And then I saw a golden light over the mountain. I thought it was the lost treasure, you know, from the story? I was so excited I ran toward it. I didn't mean to go off the trail. I didn't mean to get lost and fall down the cliff onto a big rock. But Jaxson and D were there the whole time. Jaxson got stuck on the boulder with me, and I told Delia to get help. And she understood me, Mom! She did because she found James, and he *saved* me."

Sara was barely able to follow along with her son's rant, the words "fall down the cliff" and "stuck on a boulder" in the same sentence sending a shot of anxiety to her heart.

"Did James give you permission to play hide and seek?"

"Yes. But it wasn't dark yet. It's not his fault, Mom. I should've told him where I was going, but I didn't. I was too excited to find the gold."

Her eyes darted to the shadowy figure of James standing

stoically near the parked ATV next to his father, his brothers already reunited with their wives near the fire. She wasn't ready to talk to him yet. She needed time with her son. Time to think about her next calculated move.

Sheriff Jenkins approached them, his sigh audible. "Boy, are we glad to see you, Noah. How're you feeling?"

His eyes widened at the sight of the man in full uniform, gun holster noticeable on his hip. He turned to Sara and asked, "Mom, am I in trouble? Did I break the law?"

She shook her head. "No, sweetie. The sheriff and the fire department came to help find you. They're all here for you."

"The rescue team would like to check him out and ensure he's okay," Sheriff Jenkins said. "I know you're a competent nurse, but this has been quite a shock for you too. Let us assess him, and we'll be on our way."

"I appreciate it." She lowered her son to the ground.

Hank approached, overhearing the conversation. He kneeled in front of Noah, and they high fived.

"Dude, I'm so happy to see you. How're you feeling?"

"I'm fine." His voice was timid, not used to being around so many concerned adults.

Hank grinned and stood, shifting his focus to Sara. "I'm happy to take him over to the rescue team so they can check him out." He flicked his eyes toward his father and James. "I know a certain guy who'd *really* like to talk to you."

Sara tensed, knowing she needed to clear the air with James. But she wasn't about to leave her son's side for a millisecond.

"I appreciate it, Hank. But my first priority is my son. I need to take care of him right now."

"Oh. Yes, of course." Disappointment flashed across his face.

Sara held Noah's hand and dutifully followed the sheriff to the fire truck, where several staff lingered. Jaxson and Delia were never far from their side, the big dogs still in protection mode after her son's ordeal.

The friendly crew assessed her son thoroughly. Other than a few bumps, bruises, and a scratch on his cheek that was cleaned up and doused in antiseptic, Noah was given the green light. He waved as the big rig left the property, the driver turning on the bright lights and cranking up the siren one last time, much to his pleasure.

"You need to thank everyone for what they did for you tonight," Sara insisted.

Noah hesitated, his eyes roaming the fire pit area where the large Bennett family gathered.

"Go on." She gently pushed him forward and watched. Each member hugged him one by one and expressed their gratitude he was okay.

As she looked on from several yards away with arms folded against her chest, she noticed James moving toward her. She swallowed hard, unsure of what to say.

"You okay?" he asked. He was tentative, giving her space.

"What do you think?" she whispered.

His expression held sadness, the guilt he must've felt eating him up. "I'm sorry, Sara. I didn't think…"

"—no, you weren't thinking at all," she interrupted. "Why on earth would you allow a boy his age to traipse into the woods unaccompanied by an adult? I can't believe you let him out of your sight."

She didn't mean for her words to come out angry. "You had one job, James. One. Keep an eye on my son. And you failed miserably."

"I'm sorry. I… I messed up. But I found him, and I

brought him back safe and sound. Doesn't that count for something?"

The way he looked at her with pleading eyes while wringing his hands let her know he was absolutely apologetic for his actions. But she couldn't... she *wouldn't* allow herself to cave.

"I can't look at you right now," she muttered, eyes downcast and focused on the ground.

"What does that mean?"

"It means... I need time."

"*Time?*"

She forced herself to look at him again, the urge to wrap her arms around his neck and hug him very real. She knew he was sorry and never meant for Noah to get lost. But she needed a break to sort out her feelings. To come to terms with her unhealthy urge to run. But wasn't that precisely what she was doing?

"I think it's best if Noah and I spend the night at Crystal's place tonight."

He took a step toward her. "Sara..."

She held up her hand to stop him. "No. I need some time to think about what I'm doing. What we're doing."

James appeared crestfallen, the reflection of flames from the fire pit shimmering in his dark eyes. "I'm sorry this happened, Sara. If I could take it all back, I would." He motioned toward Noah, who giggled as Walt tickled his armpits.

"But this story has a happy ending, and I guaran-damn-tee you he'll never go wandering off again." His sigh was heavy. "Don't shut me out because of this. Please. I love Noah like he's my own son. I... I love you too, Sara."

Her lips trembled with emotion, shocked by his words. He loved her?

"Hear me loud and clear. The heart knows when the search is over. Not just tonight, but forever more."

Sara couldn't move, every nerve-ending in her body tingling with want and need, desire and love. She wanted to say it back to him. She wanted to tell him she loved him too.

They had a connection. A natural chemistry. She'd felt something big brewing beneath the surface between them for quite some time. For him to admit his feelings was a game-changer. They were, in fact, meant to be together. James walked into her heart like he always belonged there. He took down her walls and lit her soul on fire.

"I just need some space for one night, okay?" She nervously tucked her hair behind her ears.

His nostrils flared before he nodded. "Can I at least give you a hug before you leave? Please?" He opened his arms wide.

She shuffled toward him, the weight of her overwhelming feelings apparent in her sagging shoulders. To feel his solid warmth left her reeling, his following words piercing her heart.

"Our journey is far from over, Sara," he whispered. "But it's *our* journey, and I'll be here for you and Noah until the end. I love you."

Noah cried, watching Sara pack an overnight bag for them. She reassured him he'd be okay with one night away from the dogs—and James.

She wanted to cry too, her actions befuddling her. But she needed space to decompress and come to terms with almost losing her precious son. She also needed time to sit with James's love confession.

He stayed behind in the main house with his family and gave her and Noah space while she packed. Roy tried to convince her not to leave but understood her fragile feelings, needing a break from his large brood.

"I'll be back tomorrow," she promised.

When they pulled up to the economy motel on the outskirts of town, Crystal was waiting for them in the lobby.

"Lord have mercy," she lamented, opening her arms wide and hugging her hard. "Roy called and told me everything. But I want to hear it from the horse's mouth."

Tinkerbelle nipped at Noah's heels, the Chihuahua's butt wagging madly as if she were happy to see him again. He scooped her up into his arms and snuggled the animal with fondness.

Crystal ruffed up his hair with her pink nails. "You okay, little buddy? That must've been quite a fright being out there in the woods all by your lonesome, huh?"

"I wasn't alone. Jaxson and Delia were with me." He'd dozed off during the short car ride through town, the day's adrenaline finally catching up with his little body.

"I need to get him settled, and then we can talk," Sara said.

"Sounds good." Crystal handed off a room key and patted her dog on the head. "And Noah? Why don't you take Tink with you upstairs to keep you company? Okay? She's missed you like crazy."

"Okay."

"Take your time, Sara. I've got the hard seltzers iced down for some girl talk whenever you're ready."

It didn't take her long to get her son cleaned up and dressed for bed. Noah was out cold by the time she changed and washed her face. He quietly snuffled with his arms wrapped around his stuffed bear. Tinkerbelle lay beside him and raised her head as if to say, "I've got this."

Locking the door, Sara strode downstairs to the lobby where Crystal waited.

She hated feeling this way, hated the miserable flashbacks of her old life running from Russell. Her past nipped at her heels no matter how fast she tried to escape. And now that she'd finally turned the page and had some sense of closure, why did she *still* feel the need to run?

She was glad she had Crystal to talk to about it. And someone she could share her news with. News she was still grappling over.

James Bennett loved her.

She played his words in her head over and over again in a loop, waiting for them to seep in. And the way he said it, like it was a no-brainer, his words causing her out-of-control mind to come to a screeching halt.

"Hey, girl. You feelin' any better?"

"A little."

Crystal passed off a can of seltzer and leaned back against the lobby couch, her painted lips lifting in a genuine smile. "Take your time, sweetie. I've got all night."

Sara told her friend about the nice dinner with the Bennett ladies and then how Roy called telling them her son was missing. She shared how frantic she'd become, her feelings reminiscent of her past when it came to protecting her only child.

The men going after him. The bright lights of the fire engines with an additional team of search and rescue professionals on standby, ready to find her son. The relief when he was found and then the anger toward James for taking his eyes off him.

But the most poignant part of the evening wasn't when

she rocked Noah safely in her arms or realized he had always been a curious child and had wandered off on her too.

No.

It was when James told her point blank he loved her.

It came out of left field. Were his words perpetuated by the trauma of the evening? Did he say it to get her to stay?

Crystal allowed Sara to talk it out. When she finished, she crushed the now-empty can and sighed.

"I love him too, Crystal. I do."

"Did you tell him?"

She averted her gaze and forlornly shook her head. "No."

Crystal's bracelets jingled as she set her can on a side table. "You want to know what I think?"

Sara whipped her head to where she could look at her friend straight on. "Yes. Please."

She squeezed Sara's hand, the motherly gesture kind and loving. "You're scared of the unknown. But I want you to remember something important through all of this."

"What?" Sara focused on every word coming across Crystal's painted lips.

"You've been through a lot. But you are *not* the darkness you endured. That's in the past."

Sara scowled. "Then what am I?"

The woman's blue eyes underneath her thick lashes shown like precious jewels, her next sentence striking Sara to her core.

"You're a beautiful woman and a devoted mama worthy of all the love in the world. You, my friend, are a light that refuses to surrender."

# Chapter Thirty-Three

## JAMES

James lay awake in Sara's bed, the wrinkled sheets lingering with her scent after their weekend lovemaking.

He had every intention of stripping the bed and throwing the sheets into the laundry, so she'd have fresh linens to come home to. Instead, he took one look at the twisted bedding and the faint indent of her pillow and decided to call it a night.

He wanted to fall asleep in the last place he felt closest to her.

Laying on his side, he held her pillow in his arms and inhaled a deep breath, overcome with melancholy. He should've been holding her instead, running his hands up and down her fevered skin.

Sleep evaded him. Flustered, he flopped dramatically onto his bare back, eyes scrolling the ceiling, recalling their time spent together.

He didn't realize falling in love could be so simple. Coffee mugs in the sink, and yellow flowers blooming in a mason jar. Long, auburn hair between his fingers and woolly socks discarded at the foot of the bed. Album covers lying on the living room floor, and the faint melody of a sexy song thrumming through his body.

James had to blink at the pressure building behind his eyes. Until tonight, he'd felt like everything in his life was finally sliding into place. He was giving it his all. Settling into the happiness he'd found. But that was before he took his eyes off Noah.

Sara's behavior toward him after her son's ordeal in the woods was tinged with cautious control, flat and uncaring. He would've preferred her to scream at him. Punch him in the damn gut. Cry relentlessly in his arms. Not look at him like he was no one special. Not leaving him high and dry after the tumultuous search in the dark of night.

Her last words to him were lodged in his chest like poisonous arrows:

*"I need some time to think about what I'm doing. What we're doing."*

Scrubbing a hand down his face, he grimaced. Did she not hear the part where he told her he loved Noah like his own son? That he loved *her*?

Visions of the eerie forest haunted his thoughts, and no matter how tightly he pressed his eyes together, he couldn't shake them: gnarled branches. Wildlife in the shadows. Dangerous cliffs protruding over the river. If Sara had known the details of what Noah had gotten himself into, she'd be having nightmares too.

But he could protect her from that. He had to. He wanted to prove he would do anything to show his love, including risking his life for her child.

With a deep sigh, he lifted his heavy eyelids and stared

at the slits in the blinds covering the window. A tiny sliver of moonlight touched his skin. Harvest Moon. His mind reverted to a happier moment, their slow dance in the living room, unhurried and filled with promise. He loved her with all his heart, ready to give her his all.

And as his breathing finally calmed down, he closed his eyes, intent to dream the night away.

---

"James?"

He startled awake to find Sara sitting fully clothed on the edge of the bed. Dark circles were noticeable under her eyes, a sure sign she hadn't slept much of the night either.

"Wha... what are you doing? Where's Noah?"

Blood roared in his ears as he sat up and leaned back on his forearms. When their eyes locked, he glimpsed a spark of something beneath those heartbreaker pools of blue that sent heat roiling through his stomach.

"He's with Crystal. She took him to the Pancake House so we could talk in private." She smiled. "What are you doing sleeping in my bed?"

James didn't want to tell her the truth—that he pined for her all night long. That he felt closer to her, lying on the same sheets where her naked body had come undone beneath him.

"The dogs... there was mud... can you give me a minute?" He flipped back the sheet and swung his legs over the bed, hurrying toward his room in nothing but his boxers.

"Meet me in the family room," he hollered over his shoulder.

"Okay," she laughed.

Shutting the bathroom door, he splashed cold water on his face, his disheveled reflection in the mirror giving off hangover vibes with ashen skin and bloodshot eyes. He gripped the sides of the vanity and shook his head.

Sara's presence could only mean one of two things: she was sorry, or she was breaking things off with him.

Memories of Samantha and her breakup came flooding back, feelings he vowed he'd never come close to again. But what if he had no choice?

James brushed his teeth with force, finger-combed his hair, and shrugged on his discarded sweats and a hoodie. His bare feet padded along the hardwood floors as Jaxson and Delia met him in the hall with wagging tails. He noticed Sara sitting primly on the sofa, waiting for him.

"Let me feed them so they'll leave us be," he said.

"No problem."

The sound of dog food hit the metal bowls with a clang, a few random pieces flicking onto the kitchen floor. Jaxson vacuumed them right up with his tongue. After refilling their water bowls, James wiped his hands on his sweats and timidly entered the family room, ready to face the music.

"How are you?" He was bold and eased his tired body next to her. But he didn't dare reach out and touch her for fear of rejection.

"I'm… better. I've thought about what I want to say to you all night. And the truth is… I have a lot to say."

"Oh, boy."

"No," she smiled, reaching out and touching his arm. "It's nothing bad. Please, can you just listen for a few minutes? Can you do that for me?"

"Of course."

James snuck a glance at her, her beauty undeniable. She was confident with perfect posture and a warm smile with full lips like ripe cherries. He liked her strong, caring hands she twisted nervously in her lap, her long hair fashioned in an auburn braid hanging over one shoulder. The way her pretty brow crinkled between her eyes when she was thinking about something important.

Never had a woman looked so sure, so pretty. She was the woman he wanted to spend the rest of his life with—if she'd let him. At least she'd taken off her coat.

Her stare was heated as she released a deep breath. "I've always heard that love finds you when you least expect it." She paused and looked around the room.

He followed her gaze, landing on the deer head above her plant stand. The masculine decoration had been a source of contention between them at first. But now it made her smile.

"But I disagree with that statement. I think love finds you after you find yourself. And it's taken me a long time to slow down and just... be myself. Truthfully, I've never felt more like myself than when I'm with you."

His heart blipped with life. "Sara..."

"—Please, James. Let me finish."

"Sorry."

She reached for his hand and squeezed. "Since I came to Langston Falls, somewhere along the way, I decided not to settle or tolerate less than I deserve. I decided I wanted someone who made me a priority. Who sees only me in a large crowd and no one else. Someone who is 'Team Noah and Sara.'" Her lips trembled in a forced smile, her eyes welling with tears.

James listened, his thumb caressing the top of her hand. He knew she was talking about him.

"Someone kind and caring. An incredible romantic who's not afraid to show it. A man who's thoughtful and silly and who can always make me laugh. Someone who supports me and allows me to figure things out when I need to. Someone who's always up for an adventure and loves my son like I love him."

By this time, her tears overflowed and trickled down her cheeks, but she was undeterred.

"I've dreamt my whole life of finding someone who is the *shit* and makes it crystal clear that he cherishes me. Someone who brings joy into each and every day of my life." She ran her free hand under her nose and sniffled.

"James… I don't have to wonder anymore if I've found my person because every part of me knows exactly who he is."

She swallowed hard, her voice cracking with pent-up emotion. "It's you, James. Only you. And I couldn't wait to tell you when the realization hit me over the head like a hammer last night after I calmed down. The only reason I didn't get in my car and drive over here in the middle of the night was because Noah was sound asleep."

James could hardly contain himself and slid his hand around Sara's neck, pulling her forward, lips slamming against hers in a passionate kiss.

She laughed into his mouth, her fingers twisting into his damp hair as she tugged him closer. When they came up for air, they were forehead to forehead, her hands pressed against his cheeks.

"I love you, James. I'm sorry I didn't tell you last night."

"Say it again," he whispered.

He would never tire of those three little words—words that meant more to him than anything. Words that gave him the life he'd always dreamed of.

"I love you."

"One more time please."

"I love you, James."

"And I love you, Sara."

Her azure gaze sparkled behind a shimmer of happy tears. And when they embraced in the quiet of their shared home, all his fears and doubts were cast away knowing he held his forever in his arms.

# Chapter Thirty-Four

## SARA

The giant Prevost tour bus sat idling in front of the main house on Bennett Farms, Hank and Ella Mae offering hugs and goodbyes to the receiving line of family sending them off.

Sara stood next to James, whose hands clamped on Noah's shoulders as he leaned against his legs. Jaxson and Delia frolicked nearby, more interested in Crystal's little dog, Tinkerbelle, who sniffed around the grassy knoll. It was funny seeing the dichotomy of animal sizes, Tink acting more like a giant Mastiff or Rottweiler, her yips and yaps keeping the Bennett dogs at bay.

Crystal stood next to Roy, her arm curling around his bicep to keep him steady on his feet. But Sara had an inkling there was more to this mature friendship than they were letting on.

Hank kneeled before Noah and tipped his cowboy hat back, fist-bumping his little hand. "I'll see you soon, buddy, okay?"

"Okay," Noah pouted. He and Hank had a special bond —almost as special as James.

"And thanks for agreeing to be our ring-bearer this summer. You're gonna look so cool in a tux." Hank ruffled his hair before slinging his arm around Ella Mae's waist, the two grinning with love.

Turning his attention to James, he joked, "Keep an eye on this one. I'll see ya, bro."

"See you later, Hank-ster."

The two brothers hugged affectionately as Ella squeezed Sara tight. "I'm so happy for you two," she whispered in her ear.

"Me too."

The family waved at the accelerating bus picking up dust toward the main road, and Becky reminded everyone to stay for Sunday supper. James held Sara's hand, the two following Noah from behind as he threw random sticks to the dogs, much to their pleasure.

The peace walking hand in hand with the man she loved was everything she ever wished for, and then some.

"Do you need any help, Becky?" Sara asked.

Becky walked next to Glen, the other Bennett boys, and their wives, already climbing the stairs to go inside.

"Thanks, but no," she grinned. "I've got a roast in the crock pot. Easy-peasy. Supper will be ready in about thirty minutes."

"Gotcha."

They continued to meander across the pathway leading to the house when James stopped.

"I had a thought." He kicked a pebble with the pointy tip of his boot and nodded toward Noah, who chased Tink and the big dogs, his screeching laughter a testimony to his joy.

"Oh? What are you thinking about this time?" She leaned into him and laid her head against his shoulder.

"What if we got Noah a dog?"

She didn't see that coming. "What?"

"Hear me out. You said it yourself: he's always wanted a pet. I think having a dog of his own would be good for him. It'd teach him about responsibility and give him ownership over something important to him."

Sara mulled over his words, her gaze following her happy child, who acted like the Pied Piper, tempting the dogs with more sticks.

"I think he'd be blown away if we got him a dog. But what about Jaxson and Delia? Won't they be jealous?"

James laughed and pointed at Tinkerbelle chasing Jaxson along the fence line, the animals running wild and free. "Does that look like jealousy to you?"

They walked up the front porch steps and stood on the top stoop, Sara noticing Roy and Crystal slowly progressing along the pathway. It was evident by the way their heads were close together in animated conversation that their gait was slow on purpose, not because Roy was still in recovery mode.

"Tink is gonna be wiped out tonight," Crystal said, humor tingeing her voice. "She hasn't had this much fun in a long time." She focused on Roy and helped him up the last stair. "Easy does it, handsome fella."

He grunted and stood on the porch staring off at the horizon. The view at this time of day was breathtaking and the whole reason his ancestors built the main house on this spot to begin with. It had a vantage point that gave you a panoramic view of Bennett Farms—the Christmas tree forest, the vineyard, the big red barn. It was heavenly up here, the air itself pure and refreshing.

"Good job, Dad," James commended.

"Thanks, Jimmy." Locking his hand around Crystal's wrist, he squeezed. "And CC?"

"Yes, Roy?" She batted her false eyelashes at the man.

"You're welcome to bring Tinkerbelle over here anytime you'd like." He puffed his chest out with bravado and nodded.

James winked at Sara, the two stifling sly smiles, watching his father's friendship with Crystal Cavanaugh morph into a bona fide crush. And what if the Bennett patriarch started hanging out with her on a more regular basis? He was obviously out of crisis mode and feeling better with each passing day. And besides, folks his age deserved romance too.

Sara's phone buzzed in her pocket, and she stilled.

"Who is it?" James asked.

Peering at the screen, she said, "It's my friend, Renora, in Valdosta. I should get this."

"You go ahead. I'll make sure Noah gets washed up for supper. Take your time." He kissed her on the cheek and grinned. "And think about the dog idea. It's a good one."

"I will."

Walking to the edge of the porch, away from the chatter, she held her phone to her ear and answered. "Hello, Renora. How are you?"

"Hey, Sara. I'm good. How are you doing?"

"Real good. Are you still dating the guy from the restaurant? Oh my goodness, why can't I ever remember his name?" She snapped her fingers, trying to recall the tall, dark, and handsome man Renora had texted her about.

She laughed. "Benjamin. And yes, we've gone out a few more times. Taking things real slow."

"Fantastic." Her grin faded. "But I have a feeling you

didn't call me in the middle of a Sunday afternoon to dish about Ben." She could hear her friend sigh through the phone.

"You're right. Although, we do need to catch up sometime soon because I want to hear all about what's going on with you. But I'm calling you today to let you know… Miss Sue passed away in her sleep last night."

Sara froze and closed her eyes, tension grabbing hold of her muscles.

"Sara? You there?"

She cleared her throat. "Yes. I'm still here."

"Please know, she didn't suffer. She had a very peaceful passing and a long, good life."

"I just wish…"

"—don't go there, girl. It's all good."

"I know." She took in a deep lungful of air, working up the nerve to ask her next question.

"Can you send me the details about her funeral? I probably won't make it, but I'd like to send some flowers."

"Miss Sue didn't want people making a fuss, so the memorial is for her and Dr. Chambers close friends only. And instead of flowers, she requested folks donate to her garden club. She was always an advocate for keeping Valdosta beautiful."

"How lovely. Please send me the information, and I'll gladly donate."

"Sure thing. And I want you to hear this from me and not through the newspaper."

"What?"

"Miss Sue left her entire estate to her favorite charities and another substantial gift to the Azalea Grove facility under one condition. That the board rename the place to

'The Dr. Russell Chambers Assisted Living and Memory Care Center.'"

Sara's eyes went wide. "Wow, that's a mouthful."

"Tell me about it," Renora chuckled. "The board was unanimous and agreed. They don't care what the name of the building is as long as all that money goes to a good cause. I hope you're okay with it."

Sara frowned. "Why wouldn't I be okay? I told you this has never been about money."

"I know. I'm just… disappointed for you and your little boy, that's all."

"Please, don't be. We've never been better." And she meant it too.

"She left something for you. A few days ago, she said, and I quote, 'Please make sure pretty Sara gets my message.'" Renora changed her voice to sound like the Southern elderly woman, over-exaggerating her vowels.

"It's the picture of Noah, right?"

"Yes. And a little something else, but I don't think I can send it until everything goes through probate, which could take a few months."

Sara was curious but shrugged it off. "Send it when you can. I'm not going anywhere."

James whistled through his teeth, causing Noah and the dogs to run toward him. She watched him pick up her son and swing him around in a circle, the two a regular duo. And she knew moving forward, their relationship would only grow stronger. Her son would finally have a solid father figure to count on in his young life. And who better to help her raise him than James Bennett?

"I'll text you my home address when I get off the phone."

"Great."

Renora cleared her throat as if trying to find the right words. "I hope you can move on with some sense of closure now. I know your son never met Miss Sue, but you did. That has to count for something."

Sara continued to watch the guys in the front yard, enthralled by their interaction. It was natural, like they'd been related their whole lives.

James held Noah and dipped him up and down, his arms spread wide like wings, the dogs jumping and trying to lick his face. But James was too quick, flying him high in the air before their big tongues could make contact. Their little game was precious, causing her eyes to well with happy tears.

"I appreciate your concern, Renora. But I know I'm finally right where I'm supposed to be. And being here counts... for everything."

# Chapter Thirty-Five

## JAMES

Bennett Farms buzzed with excitement, the farmhands, Becky and her team, and James and his brothers gearing up for the first big event of the season.

The Honeybee Festival was the official kick-off to spring, the farm already hosting a variety of local food trucks on the property accompanying the wine tastings. And with their new *Rebecca Rose* label hitting the market, the season appeared promising.

James looked out over the blooming vineyard, the leaves of the seasonal bud break clinging to thick vines blowing in the breeze. The air held the faint aroma of sweet fruit among the earthiness of the farm, the barn doors open wide at the family-friendly establishment with tourists sipping and sampling wine made from the grapes grown right outside his and Sara's bedroom window.

Jaxson and Delia lay in the sun near the barn. Their ears perked with interest at the sound of a puppy barking a welcome. James planted his hands on his hips and watched with delight as Noah's Golden Retriever, Betty, ran with puppy fervor toward the two older dogs and belly-flopped right on top of Jaxson. The black Lab didn't seem fazed, growling playfully and wrestling with the puppy like they did most days since Betty joined the family.

Noah skipped happily from behind, tempting his new dog with a stick. Her little ears perked, and she stumbled into a run, going after it as if her life depended on it. The boy was a great doggie-daddy, and James and Sara were pleased with how he latched on to his responsibilities in taking care of her.

"You ready for the festival?"

James turned to see his father coming toward him, looking strong and hearty. The walker and cane were gone, although his gait was a bit slower since his health scare. But thanks to Sara, Crystal, and the entire family, Roy was given the all-clear, the gleam in his eye and jovial disposition intact just like before.

Only this time, he had a pretty lady by his side.

"Hey, Dad. Hey Crystal. Yes, I'm ready. How about y'all?"

"Ready as I'll ever be," Crystal replied.

She set Tinkerbelle on the ground, who took off toward the pack of dogs, yipping and yapping in a high pitch announcing her arrival. The three adults watched the canines, big smiles etched on their faces. Life was certainly good.

"Have you seen Sara? I need to ask her what she's wearing to the festival," Crystal asked.

James eyed the woman who had toned down her looks over the last several weeks since she and his dad started officially dating. Gone were the high-heels, bouffant hair, and her eye-popping décolletage.

Her hair appeared softer, hanging loose around her

shoulders with wispy bangs. Cowboy boots replaced the heels, more practical for those long walks around the farm with Roy, and she wore feminine, blousy shirts with hip-hugging blue jeans. If it hadn't been for her signature false eyelashes and bright pink nail polish, Crystal looked like she could pass as a mature model in a Ralph Lauren spring catalog.

"Sara's in the kitchen helping Becks," James replied.

"Okay." She turned to Roy. "You need anything while I'm up there, sweetie-pie?"

"Nope. I'm good."

James watched Crystal pucker Roy's mouth with her hand and kiss him on the lips. "I'll be right back."

The two men watched her ascend the stairs toward the back door of the kitchen, her hips intentionally swinging. When she coyly looked over her shoulder at Roy, she winked.

"Ain't she something?" He chuckled.

James looked away, his cheeks flushing with awkward-ness. "As long as you're happy, Dad."

The two started toward the barn but didn't get far, summoned by Crystal.

"James?" she shouted.

"Yeah?"

"Come on up here. Sara wants to show you something."

"Okay. I'll be right up." He turned to his father. "Can you please keep an eye on Noah and Betty? You know how excited those two can get. I don't need a repeat of the little lost boy in the woods."

Roy laughed. "Don't you worry, son? I'll keep my eye on 'em."

"Thanks."

James took the stairs two at a time, and when he entered the kitchen, he was confused seeing only Becks and CC inside.

"Where'd Sara go?"

"She's out on the front porch," Becky said, cocking her head toward the door.

He removed his cowboy hat and hung it on a peg by the front entrance. Stepping over the threshold, he looked around and noticed Sara sitting on the edge of the porch with her legs dangling. She was staring off into space.

"Sara?"

She swung her head to look at him, the love on her face noticeable. "Come here and sit with me."

James didn't say a word, unsure what was going on.

"I got something in the mail today from Renora. Remember when she called a while ago to tell me Miss Sue passed away?"

"Yes. Did she finally return the picture of Noah you gave to her?"

A breeze blew her hair back from her face as she looked down at the small, unopened package in her lap.

"I think there's a bit more in this package than a photo." Her blue irises latched on to his for a few beats, her expression holding trepidation. "I'm nervous."

"It's just a package, Sara. And you know the woman wasn't herself in her last days. Don't be surprised to find a lipstick tube or a grocery list in the box."

His comment induced a giggle from her pouty lips. "Don't tease me. This is serious, James."

"I'm sorry. I know it's serious." He nodded toward the package. "So why don't you go on and open it then?"

She paused before she ripped into the brown paper

covering the box. The first thing on top was a small white envelope. Running her finger across the seam, she opened it and pulled out two pictures.

The first was the familiar photo of Noah. Her smile was brief before she noticed the second photo behind it and gasped.

James's eyes went wide. Holding the photos side by side, it was uncanny, really. The photo of Noah looked exactly like the photo of Dr. Russell Chambers around the same age.

Flipping the second photo over, Sara read the tiny penciled cursive writing on the back. "Russell, age eight." The boyhood picture of the doctor held the same youthful smirk as Noah's from behind dark-rimmed glasses.

"Oh. My. God." Sara's hand shook as she pressed her fingers to her lips.

James took the matching photos from her grasp and eyed them intently. It was evident Noah was Dr. Chamber's biological son—they were the spitting image of each other.

"*She knew*," Sara exclaimed. "Miss Sue, with her deteriorating mind, *knew* that Noah was her grandson just by looking at his picture. In fact, she thought it was Russell at first, and I didn't have the heart to correct her. But in reality, she *knew*, and I didn't have to tell her a thing." Big, fat tears welled in her eyes as she expressed her revelation.

"Is there a note? Did she write you a letter?" he asked.

Sara quickly pilfered through the package, her hand landing on a faded red rectangular box that had seen better days. Inhaling a deep breath through her nose, she didn't open it and presented it to James.

"I can't. You do it."

"Me? But this is your package. Go on, darlin'. It's okay.

Whatever is in the box isn't going to change your life here with me."

"But it could change Noah's," she worriedly admitted.

"You've come this far. You can do this."

His pep-talk must've given her courage. Careful, she flipped open the lid, revealing a pearl necklace nestled inside. A sob tore through her throat and James was immediately taken aback.

"Sara, honey... it's just a necklace. A thoughtful gift from Miss Sue's estate, right?" He stroked the back of her hair, eyes tracing the necklace and the two photos resting in her lap.

Sara wouldn't let up, her tears concerning. He pulled her into his arms and hugged her tight.

"I'm... fine," she hiccuped, trying to overcome her emotions. "It's just that... I know the story behind these pearls."

"You do?"

She nodded and sat up, lifting the necklace from the box. "Can you please hook these around my neck?"

"Of course."

He was tender in his actions, looping the pearls over her head and clasping them at her nape. He watched her palm the jewelry against her chest and smile through her tears.

"Russell gifted this necklace to Miss Sue right after he graduated from med-school. She told me the story when we met. Told me she always wore her pearls when he took her to dinner at the country club because...," she didn't finish her sentence, another sob escaping her mouth, mixed with laughter.

His eyes scrolled her beautiful face, the joy behind her sorrow filtering like sunbeams through the clouds after a

terrible storm. Tucking her hair behind her ear, he leaned in
to catch her sparkling baby blues.

"Because why, darlin'?"

Her lips lifted into a half-smile, the delighted ping of her
laugh ending years of guilt.

"Because... pearls go with everything."

# Chapter Thirty-Six

## JAMES

### One Year Later

"Something old, something new, something *borrowed*, something blue…"

James watched as Sara slipped the pearl necklace around Crystal's neck and clasped it together. When the two women looked at their side-by-side reflection in the large oval mirror, their eyes held joy.

"Thank you, sweet girl." She palmed the pricey jewelry around her neck. "They're perfect."

"And you, my friend, are a *beautiful* bride," Sara added.

"You are CC," James agreed. "My dad will take one look at you and start boohooing. Don't worry. I made sure he had an extra hanky in his coat pocket."

"Thank you, Jimmy." Crystal walked right up to him and held his face between her hands. "If it hadn't been for you and Sara, none of this would've ever happened."

The two hugged with affection, James feeling thankful for her and the happiness she brought to his father's life.

"It's almost time. Are you ready to be the next Mrs. Bennett?" Sara asked.

Crystal laughed and took another look in the mirror. She ran her hands down her body-hugging lace gown, her French manicure showing off her incredible engagement ring, given to her by Roy less than six months after they officially started dating. She looked beautiful, her hair fashioned in a classic chignon, her aura radiating pure love.

"Sweetie, I was born ready. Are you ready for me to be your mother-in-law now?"

The three of them laughed, the thought outrageous but true. Crystal Cavanaugh-Bennett was about to officially become James and Sara's mother-in-law.

Love had definitely been in the air this last year at Bennett Farms. Hank and Ella Mae tied the knot in a beautiful ceremony in August at her home in Nashville, and Glen proposed to Becky on Halloween.

James was true to his word and helped Glen with the surprise, setting up four pumpkins with the words, "will you marry me" carved into them.

While the couple was on a date at the annual Halloween celebration on Main Street, James waited for his cue and lit the candles inside the pumpkins set up on the front door step and waited in the bushes. He captured the proposal on his camera, Becky laughing with joy, and Glen crying like a baby.

But they weren't the only ones celebrating love.

James and Sara were married in a quiet civil ceremony a month later at the Langston Falls courthouse decorated for Christmas with Noah by their side. And now, here they were, celebrating Roy and Crystal's wedding on a sunny spring Saturday, the farm and winery closed for the weekend for the family affair.

The area in front of the big red barn was transformed into a makeshift wedding aisle with seating on either side, the wildflowers and ribbons on the backs of the chairs floating in the pine-scented breeze. The barn interior held a buffet line with chairs and white-clothed tables decorated with mason jar candles, the simple aesthetic everything Roy and CC wanted for their celebration.

"God has been good to me," Roy had said to James and his siblings when he announced his intentions.

"It's not every day in your life that you're offered a second chance. And I'm not talking about my health. My heart may never completely heal from losing your mama. But I've discovered I'm still capable of loving again. And I love Crystal. I do. It's not the same love I had with your mama, and that's okay. I don't want it to be the same."

"We're happy for you, Dad," James reassured.

"Yes, Daddy. You, of all people, deserve all the happiness in the world." Becky cried.

They surrounded their father in a circle, arms linked in a group hug. And when Roy Bennett got down on one knee on the back porch as the sunset took over the sky in a dramatic show of glimmering gold, James knew his dad had found his treasure.

Sara palmed his shoulder, startling him out of his thoughts. "Do you want to check on Noah and make sure he's ready? We're supposed to start the processional in five minutes."

"Sure. He's with Hank and the dogs."

She shook her head. "Let's pray he hasn't completely dirtied his clothes before the ceremony."

James kissed her cheek and chuckled. "I'm sure Hank has everything under control." He turned to Crystal one last time before he exited the room. "CC?"

273

"Yes, sweetie?"

"Thanks for bringing the happy back into my Dad's life."

She nodded, eyes shimmering with joy. "Thanks for all you've done to make today so special."

James walked through the house and out the back door of the kitchen. Standing on the porch, he surveyed the guests already in their seats, the acoustic sounds of a string trio floating through the air. Palming his black cowboy hat on his head, he smiled as his brothers came around the corner, arms looped with their better halves.

"Hey, Jimmy. You look sharp," Walt said.

"You do too," he replied.

Crystal didn't want the Bennett boys in matching suits or tuxes. She told them to wear something nice they'd be comfortable in. Of course, they all opted for their Sunday best. Crisp, white dress shirts, pressed pants, spit-shined boots, and cowboy hats. There wasn't a shred of flannel fabric in sight. Even Glen Kirby was dressed up, his all-black choices reminding James of Johnny Cash.

"Is Crystal ready?" Becky asked. She wore a crown of daisies tied together in her blonde hair as an homage to their late mother.

"Yeah, she's ready. Sara will bring her out in a minute."

Noah and Hank rounded the corner and nearly collided with the dressed-up group.

"Whoa!" James hollered.

"Sorry!" Hank apologized with a boyish laugh. "The dogs are sequestered in the mud room until after the ceremony."

"Good," Teddy said. His arm rested across Robyn's shoulders. The new mother cradled their sleeping infant daughter. She'd come into the world on a snowy night in

February and was named Lilly, short for Lillian, their mother's namesake.

Noah pouted. "I still think we could put them on leashes, and they'd be fine walking down the aisle with all of us."

"We'll let them out for the party. They'll only be in doggie jail during the I do's." James motioned for Noah to come toward him and quickly patted his unruly hair back into place. It was crazy to think his dad and Crystal were grandparents. "This won't go long, I promise."

"Short and sweet like you and Mom's?" He pushed his glasses against his nose and looked up at him expectantly.

James had a flashback of him and Sara facing each other in the Langston Falls Courthouse in front of an appointed officiant. She wore the same pearls around her neck Crystal had on and a simple white dress, her auburn hair curling over her shoulders and her smile stunning him with legitimate joy. Noah held her hand, wide-eyed and excited, and Sheriff Jenkins agreed to be their witness.

The Bennett family knew they were serious and committed to each other, but as a couple, they didn't want to steal any of Becky and Glen's engagement thunder. The decision to go ahead with a quiet civil ceremony was made for insurance purposes, and wanting the legal part done sooner, especially with children involved.

Besides, Sara had no immediate family and preferred something quiet, opting for a Bennett dinner celebration after the holidays and when she was feeling better. They were, after all, the unconventional couple of the family.

James and Sara surprised everyone at Christmas with the news, Sara showing off her simple gold wedding band. Their reactions were happy, and the well-wishes they received added an extra layer of blessings to the holidays.

The family was supportive and loving, welcoming Sara and Noah into the fold as one of their own like they'd done since the very beginning.

"Short and sweet. I promise," James said to Noah.

The wedding planner instructed the couples to line up. When the processional music started, they walked carefully down the stairs toward the Bennett patriarch, who stood prominently next to the local preacher.

Roy was dashing in his dark suit and tie, his black Stetson hat making him look regal. His hands were clasped in front of him, and his lips quivered in an emotional smile as he winked at each couple as they got into place.

James, Sara, and Noah took up the rear and stood on the outer edge of the family line. As Roy and Crystal said their vows in front of everyone, James protectively circled his arm around his wife's growing waistline and watched Noah lean back against her protruding belly.

Sara's pregnancy was a shock to both of them, their months of unprotected sex resulting in lightning striking twice. Only this time, she had a devoted partner who was over the moon happy for their unplanned family. Hence the civil ceremony.

Sara told him the night he took her to the Speckled Trout. It was a do-over for them both, erasing bad memories of the nights they'd been there separately. When he was dumped, and her son went missing.

Only this night was a joyous occasion, James's reaction one of awestruck wonder.

It was hard not to tell his family immediately, especially his father. But once they were legally wed and the entire family was gathered together at Christmas, they presented their news as a gift, their love and commitment a precursor to their extraordinary future together.

"I now pronounce you husband and wife," the preacher announced.

James slapped his hands together, joining the rest of the crowd in hoots and hollers of joy.

"Look how happy they are," Sara proclaimed. Her face glowed with happiness and pregnancy hormones, her blue eyes glistening with tears.

James held her close and looked at his father, his new bride, and the audience of small-town friends gathered for the celebration.

His love for his extended family was palpable. His brothers and their wives. His sister and her fiancé. His infant niece, Lilly. His bonus son, Noah. And his miracle oops baby, a precious little boy.

Yes, James Bennett loved his family. But Sara would always be his home.

# Playlist

The Bennetts of Langston Falls

*Wanted* – Hunter Hayes
*Outskirts* – Sam Hunt
*Can't Have Mine* – Dylan Scott
*Next Thing You Know* – Jordan Davis
*More Than My Hometown* – Morgan Wallen
*Groovin'* – The Young Rascals
*Harvest Moon* – Bob Dylan
*The Good Ones* – Gabby Barrett
*Die A Happy Man* – Thomas Rhett
*Golden Hour* – JVKE
*Never Til Now* – Ashley Cooke. Brett Young

# Love's Refrain: Chapter One

"Oh, wow! Everything is...breathtaking."

Bathed in a wash of bright stage lighting, Kat Monroe palmed the front of her thick coat before running the tips of her fingers down the faux fur trim. Taking a few steps forward to the very edge of the stage, she tilted her head back and gazed at several impressive chandeliers gleaming from the old plaster ceiling above. The famous Art Deco interior of the Grand Theater had gone through countless renovations since constructed in the early 1900s, the most recent adding state of the art technical upgrades, enhancements to the modern sound and lighting systems, and new carpet.

"We're thrilled to have you back, Kat. To end your first national tour in your hometown has the entire Southeast scrambling to get tickets." The theater's general manager, and long-time family friend, Pete Alexander puffed his ample chest out with pride, making the buttons on his shirt strain to hold the fabric together. "I'm so glad you agreed to a two-weekend run. Local fans are chomping at the bit to see you."

Kat turned and offered Pete a sincere smile. "The only reason I agreed to a two-weekend run is because of my fans. They're the ones who got me on the map." Snaking her arm through his, they ambled under the intricate details of the proscenium enhanced by thick red curtains scalloped in perfect swaths framing the famous stage.

"It really is the perfect way to end this whirlwind tour. I couldn't be happier. You know what they say, there's no place like home." Even though her semi-permanent address was now a tiny studio apartment in Brooklyn, New York she'd barely stayed in the past couple of years due to her touring schedule, she was glad to be back. The town of Whitley, Georgia, where she grew up, felt like her true home.

Pete's robust chuckle was endearing, and he patted her hand while guiding her through the wings to the backstage area. "Whatever you need, just ask. Hospitality set up some refreshments in the Green Room, already anticipating your early arrival. Make yourself comfortable while the crew gets things set up for soundcheck." He gestured with his free hand for her to go ahead. "I've got a million messages waiting for me in the box office. It seems everyone in the state of Georgia wants a favor from me – a Kat Monroe concert ticket. And I've got a right mind to open up my own flower shop with all the special deliveries being made to the box office today. Opening night is sure to be a success."

Kat giggled and unbuttoned her coat. "Pete, I can't thank you enough for all you've done for me over the years. Ending the tour here, where I started, seems fitting." Standing on her tiptoes, she gave him a quick peck on the cheek. "Even though I don't technically live here anymore, and Mama and Daddy are gone, this is still my home."

His face turned ruddy as he nodded and swiped his chubby hand over his bald head. "Well, we all miss them terribly. I wish they were here to see how far you've come. We're all bursting at the seams with pride. Now, if you need anything, anything at all, just let me know. I'll look in on y'all at the soundcheck."

"Okay." She smiled and watched him bumble down the narrow hallway, his brown loafers clomping on the ancient floor with each step.

With a sated sigh, Kat pulled a black beret off her blonde head before shrugging off her coat and laying it over her arm. Surveying the Green Room, she was happy to spy a beverage cart arranged with an assortment of coffee and her favorite tea. Another table was artfully arranged with a massive crystal bowl of fruit, a tiered serving tray of trian-gular cut sandwiches, a veggie tray, and individual bags of chips. A candy dish filled with lemon drops beckoned her to sneak one into her mouth. She included the old-fashioned candy on the rider in her contracts, not because she had to have them but because she wanted to make sure the venues where she performed actually read her agreement which included the unusual request.

As she plucked a yellow candy from the dish and sucked, she set her coat and hat on a nearby chair. Crossing her arms at her chest, she walked the perimeter of the room, taking in the large familiar posters decorating the space. Performers from all over the world graced the walls dancing, singing, and acting their way across the famous stage, many of whom she enjoyed while growing up in the small Georgia community.

Pausing in front of her own poster from two years ago,

she took in the image of her younger self in mid-song posed under a bright spotlight. She marveled at how far she'd come. Who would have thought a Southern girl like her would have made it in the world of jazz music? Her gift for evocative songwriting paired with her charming lighter-than-air vocals blended old styles with the new and garnered the attention of NPR and other high-profile acts who insisted she open for them on their tours. Her debut album made it to the top ten on the Contemporary Jazz Chart, with the *New York Times* and *Boston Globe* dubbing her as "fresh as a floral bouquet" and congratulating her efforts as "an exceptional artist who embodies the spirit of the past while remaining unwaveringly au courant." To wrap up her first tour in Whitley and perform at the Grand was the ideal ending.

"Hey, you."

Startled out of her reminiscent thoughts, Kat turned and smiled at her long-time assistant and close friend, Sasha Manning.

"Hey. How's the dressing room set up? Is Charlie Chaplin's signature still legible in the far corner?"

Sasha grinned and sidled up to the food table to fill a plate. "Barely. They've covered it in some hard plastic and put a little plaque next to it for preservation. God, this place brings back so many memories! The last time we were here, you were just starting out."

"I know. Time flies. I feel like I've come full circle."

"Right?" Sasha agreed. "Oh, by the way, I had to move a bunch of flower arrangements and gifts to the floor to make room for your makeup and hair stuff. The entire room looks like someone came in and assembled a pop-up flower shop. I've hung all your dresses on the clothes rack, too. I'll steam them before tonight's show. I swear, Kat, wait till you see some of the enormous bouquets in there. This town is going crazy having you back."

Picking out a tea flavor from the beverage cart, Kat filled a mug with steaming water from a carafe before dunking the bag. "It feels good to end the tour here, don't you think? It'll be fun visiting my old stomping grounds on our off days, too."

Sasha nodded and spoke with a mouth full of sandwich. "I can't wait." Spotting Kat's coat and hat over the chair, she set her plate down. "You want me to hang up your coat for you?"

Kat waved her off. "Nope. I can do it later. You relax and grab a bite. I want to check out the lobby and backstage area to see what other renovations Pete convinced the Arts Council to complete."

"Okey dokey."

Posters continued down the narrow hallway along with a plethora of autographs taking over the white wall space, the scribbles of top-notch entertainers and musical casts from around the world hard not to notice. The Grand was centrally located in the state of Georgia, not far from Atlanta, a military base, and a major airport. Patrons from all over the Southeast quickly sold out the space, especially with some of the well-known acts Pete booked. Add the charming downtown area full of great restaurants, boutique hotels, and a more laid-back atmosphere than the bigger cities, and the southern town of Whitley was forever dubbed a unique destination getaway.

Using her shoulder to push a large metal door open, Kat entered a carpeted hallway leading to the iconic lobby. Her curiosity piqued as she paused by a door marked with a bronze plate that read, "Hall of Fame." The Grand had a rich history of entertainers who came through, including

Charlie Chaplin, Bob Hope, and Ray Charles. It was a well-known fact that 1920s illusionist and magician Harry Houdini was a featured player at the Grand back in its early heyday, with local lore claiming trap doors were installed in the stage floor specifically for his act. Several Broadway tours were booked in recent times, and it was home to the local Whitley Symphony Orchestra.

Interested, she sipped from her mug of tea and perused the room full of photographs, more posters, and memorabilia from days gone by. Antique furniture was artfully arranged in the room with curio cabinets and display cases holding vintage treasure. An old movie projector from the Grand's movie house days, a signed guitar from the Allman Brothers Band, a frayed showgirl costume from the vaudeville era, and numerous stage props with little information cards attached offered fascinating glimpses into the history of the beloved theater.

A massive mural with a local artist's rendition of stage performers posed with live animals from the infamous 1908 stage production of *Ben Hur* made her gawk. With one hand on her hip and the other holding her mug, she took a step back and cocked her head to take in the image of the giant spectacle depicted in the rendering. Reading from the information card, she learned this particular production required a stage capable of handling treadmills for a live chariot race with real horses. The New York production was legendary, Pete often boasting about the famous show folks still talked about over one hundred years later. And all this time, she thought he was pulling her leg.

"Well, I'll be," she whispered, impressed by the unique stage history.

Licking her lips, she turned and continued to take in her surroundings lazily. Her tastes were indeed of the vintage variety, and this little Hall of Fame was right up her alley. Over the last year, while on her tour, she loved exploring new cities when she had time off, getting lost in museums, or searching for classic clothing and accessories in consignment shops. Her style was eclectic with an old-fashioned vibe, effortlessly blending the old with the new, just like her music. Give her seam stockings, pinup-style heels, and red lips and nails every day, and she was a happy girl.

The sound of a piano tuner could be heard echoing through the hallways and made her pause. The monotonous one note at a time played over and over as an expert found the perfect pitch had her humming along. Her band would be there soon, and before long, they'd get down to business with their last sound check of the season.

Tucking a blonde curl over her ear, she took another sip of tea as her eyes landed on a portrait in the far corner. An LED wall-mounted display light highlighted the face of a handsome, smiling man making her breath hitch. Moving toward the photo in a slow daze, her brow creased as she took in his striking features. Too bad the picture was in black and white. His gray eyes seemed to stare back at her leaving her mystified and wondering if they were the color of green moss under an oak, the tawny gold of whisky, or the blue-gray waves of the sea.

As she stood there pondering the man's eye color, her skin unexpectedly prickled with goosebumps. She turned to look toward the door, her gaze roaming the entrance before she glanced up at the ceiling covered with square tiles of what looked like salvaged original tin from days gone by. Although she loved performing in historical theaters like the Grand, she was often easily spooked by the tall tales and shadowed surroundings.

"Weird," she muttered to herself. With wide eyes, she

was tentative as she turned to look at the black and white image of the man again and noticed a tiny nameplate below the portrait. Peering at the cursive letters, she read his name out loud.

"Phillip Gordon."

"Who?"

Kat whirled around again and exhaled loudly, her usually calm demeanor excited with jitters. "Don't sneak up on me like that, Sasha."

"What?" She grinned. "Has Pete been filling your head again with more ghost stories about this place?"

"Well, you know he insists the Grand is haunted."

Sasha scrunched her face and waved her off with a baby carrot. "Oh, pish-posh. You don't believe in that nonsense, right?"

Shaking her head with uncertainty, Kat smoothed her blouse with her nervous free hand. "Well, from the stories Pete has told me, you might want to rethink hanging around here after hours."

"Yeah, right," she guffawed, coming closer. "Who's the cute guy with the dimple in his chin?"

Kat thrust her face in the air and turned around to admire the portrait again. Locking eyes with the man's gaze in the photo, she sighed. "Someone named Phillip Gordon."

"Hmmm. Doesn't ring any bells. Was he a beloved hometown performer like you?"

Kat squinted and ran a finger across the nameplate hoping for more information, her crimson nails gleaming in the light. "I don't know. There isn't any more information about him – just his name and a date…"

"I'd kiss him," Sasha interrupted.

"Sasha!" Kat exclaimed, humored by her forward friend.

"Oh, come on. You would too. He's hot, in an old-fashioned chivalrous way. I mean, look at those dreamy eyes and that sharp jawline – and the dimple is adorbs. He's totally your type, too."

"My type? And what type is that?"

Sasha crunched the last of her carrot with a smirk. "The handsome-artist-with-a-dimple-type." She stood right next to Kat. "What's the date say?"

Kat leaned forward to peer at the tiny script again. "1987?"

Sasha leaned into Kat and squinted, pointing her finger at the date. "You mean *1947*, girlie. Seriously, I've been telling you to get your eyes checked. Now that the tour is almost over, I'll make you an appointment."

Her sigh was wistful as she stood tall with one hand on her hip. "Damn, he is a cutie-patootie. Too bad they don't make them like that anymore." She started for the door. "Come on. The soundcheck starts soon, and you've got a ton of cards and flowers to look through."

Sasha exited the room, and Kat started to follow, but felt an overwhelming urge to pause for a second more. Stopping in the threshold of the door, she dared to look over her shoulder one last time, her gaze lingering on the image of Phillip Gordon circa 1947.

With a meek smile, she had to agree with her friend. "Yeah, too bad they don't make them like that anymore."

# Love's Refrain: Chapter Two

By the time Kat hung up her coat, looked through the many cards of congratulations, admired the beautiful flower arrangements, answered several emails on her laptop, and fixed another mug of tea, her band had arrived and was finishing their set up on the stage.

"They're almost ready for you, Kit-Kat," Sasha announced through the open door. She pressed a clipboard against her chest, and she was wearing her horn-rimmed glasses, no doubt ticking off an endless to-do list before the concert.

"Great. I'll be there in a minute."

The bright bulbs surrounding the mirror in front of her seemed to enhance every freckle and imperfection on her pale face. She reached for the tube of lipstick Sasha had expertly laid out across a white towel with all her other makeup accessories and reapplied a light application before pressing her lips into a clean tissue. Energized being back in a place where she felt loved and appreciated, she knew the show tonight would be unforgettable.

Surrounded by various aromatic flowers in every color, she eyed her dress rack along the wall and mulled over which style she planned to wear that evening. Her New York costumer had an eye for detail, and many of her dresses had overlays of crystals or fringe, the vintage styles blending effortlessly with her music and brand.

The en suite bathroom was modern and sterile, but the dressing room itself was wrapped in pale green wallpaper edged with dark crown molding. A faded rose-colored Parisian tufted sofa was placed against the wall opposite the dress rack with a delicate round table next to it. An antique Tiffany lamp positioned on a lace doily glowed warmly on the table, and she knew it was Pete who added the framed picture of her late parents on the mahogany wood. They had always been her biggest supporters, and she was sure they would've loved all of this. Smiling at her reflection in the mirror, she smoothed a wayward strand of hair back from her face and winked at herself, pleased with her surroundings.

Flicking off the makeup mirror lights, she stood and started for the open door when she noticed a flash of reflective light. Preferring her door to remain open before sound-check, she hadn't noticed the large mirror positioned on the wall behind it. When she performed here two years ago, she'd been in a different dressing room across the hall.

Curious, she closed the door so she could take in the enormous, gilded piece on the wall that went from floor to ceiling, the ancient glass smoky and marred with age spots. The mirror's frame looked to be hand-carved, the golden curves intricate with dinged imperfections maiming the wood. Her reflection appeared to be in a sort of fog, and she thought to herself how mystical she looked posing from side to side. It wasn't creepy per se, but dream-like, as if she were coming out of the shadows and into the light.

"Fascinating," she mumbled.

There was no telling how old the piece was. That it mostly hid behind the door was disappointing. Perhaps it had been glued or cemented in place long ago, the history of the many faces of performers catching a glimpse of themselves before they took to the stage nothing but ancient silhouettes lingering in the past. Reaching toward the mirror, she was about to touch it when a sharp knock on the door startled her. Fisting her hand at her chest, Kat exhaled with surprise.

"You decent?" Sasha asked from the other side.

"Um, yes." Kat turned the knob and was face-to-face with her friend. "Did you see this incredible mirror behind the door?"

Sasha gripped the door frame to peek her head around to look, propping her glasses on top of her head. "Yes. Gotta love those fancy old mirrors. You ready?"

Kat shook her head with chagrin. She was the only one in her group who ever appreciated the charm of vintage pieces. "Yes. Lead the way."

The famous stage held a hubbub of activity, the tech crew busy taping down cables and making last-minute adjustments on some of the lighting. Her bass player, Cole Shannon, stood on a raised area and warmed up his large fingers playing scales on the beautiful upright instrument.

"Hey, Cole," she waved.

"Hey, Kat." His white teeth gleamed in a flash of a smile from beneath his bearded face.

Pausing at the drum riser, she wiggled her fingers in a wave to capture her drummer, Vance White's attention. He had on headphones and threw her a quick nod before concentrating on dialing up his click-track.

The piano tuner she'd heard earlier continued to work on the enormous grand piano positioned stage right of center. He was an older gentleman with white hair and glasses, his concentration intense among the clamor around him as he focused on each pluck of the tuning pins in the gilt harp. How his keen ear could tweak each note to perfection was a talent in its own right.

"How's it going, Kat?" Her accompanist and arranger, Spencer Bowman, stood patiently nearby the large instrument with his arms crossed, waiting for the man to finish. She and Spencer had a long history going back to their college days. They even gave it a go as a legitimate couple for a while. But after a few months and a handful of unwelcome fits of jealousy Spencer displayed in front of some fans, the two determined their first love was the music they arranged together and parted amicably as friends. Although on occasion, he still flirted with her after a few too many cocktails.

"Hey. It's going good – real good." She grinned and gave him a side hug. "Wow, I remember this piano from the last time we played here. It's exquisite."

The old man tuning popped his head up with glee, overhearing her comment. "Exquisite is an understatement. I've been tuning this piano for decades. Y'all won't find a more superb concert grand anywhere else in the Southeast. This particular Steinway is a delight to play." His gaze ran the length of the hand-crafted, ornate cabinetry of the piano.

Kat approached the man and offered her hand in a shake. "I'm Kat Monroe. I'm so sorry. I don't remember meeting you before."

Setting his tuner on the piano bench, he eagerly thrust

his hand into hers. "I'm James Blankenship, at your service. It's a pleasure to meet you finally. I'm a huge fan of your music."

"Thank you. Have you been working with the theater long?"

"Only his entire life," Spencer chimed in. "James is one of those rare piano connoisseurs who understands these valuable instruments. He's the in-house tuner, and his father held the position for decades before him."

"Really?"

James nodded with enthusiasm. "Oh, yes. I was an apprentice under my father when I was young. Back in those days, the Grand had endless acts coming through town, and before the addition of central air, the humidity would knock this baby out of tune every night."

The threesome chuckled. "Wow, you have been at this for a while." Kat loved hearing stories about the past, especially when they involved music or theater.

"It's a labor of love, really. The cherry on top is sitting in the audience and listening to the elegant, refined tone in this treasured, acoustic space." He lovingly ran his fingers in a quick, impressive scale across the black and white keys. "I'll only be another minute or so."

Kat palmed the ebony satin finish of the instrument. "Well, I'm certainly glad to have you on my team for the next two weekends." A thought crossed her mind. "Hey, I'd love it if you'd join us at the opening night party after the show tonight."

"Yes, Kat always throws the best parties with food, cocktails, and plenty of music," Spencer added.

The older man seemed smitten with the idea, grinning from ear to ear with his bushy white eyebrows rising above the frames of his glasses. "I'd be honored. Thank you very much."

"No, thank *you*, James. I'll see you tonight." Kat offered him a genuine smile and squeezed Spencer's arm as she walked around the enormous instrument toward center stage.

In her preferred position, a wooden stool held a water bottle and her setlist next to a cordless microphone clipped to a chrome stand. Kat picked up the paper and looked over the song choices. She liked to add classic jazz standards into the mix of her original music, sometimes changing her mind last minute if she so felt like it.

Everything seemed to be in order as she moved the items off the stool and sat. Scanning the dark cavern of the different levels of auditorium seating, she marveled at how far she'd come. Finishing her first headline tour was a dream come true in a space she loved, and she couldn't wait to greet the local fans.

———

The crowd noise was deafening as Kat took a second bow after her third encore and blew kisses to the attentive audience members with her gloved hand. The orbs of dazzling lights enhancing the Grand stage made her blink in astonishment, her chest rising and falling against the satin dip of her cleavage. A bead of sweat trickled down her rosy cheeks, the exertion of giving the show everything she had evident in her labored breath. Sweeping her arm toward her bandmates, they stood and bowed politely, looking ever so dashing in their matching tuxedos.

Pete Alexander appeared from stage left with an enormous bouquet of red roses in his hands and presented it to her, causing the audience to rise to their feet in succinct applause.

"Bravo, Kat. Bravo," he congratulated close to her ear. He, too, was dressed to the nines wearing a tuxedo and took a step back, slapping his chubby hands together.

"Oh, my goodness!" she exclaimed, waving at her fans in the balconies with her free hand. Her heart raced, about to burst through her chest with joy.

Several minutes later, after commending her band on a job well done and accepting numerous compliments from the tech crew backstage, Sasha and Pete escorted her to the dressing room where she sat on the Parisian couch with a delighted thump.

"You killed it," Sasha congratulated, settling the bouquet of roses on the makeup table before holding out her hands to take the long gloves Kat peeled off.

Pete stood by the open door with his hands on his hips, the bowtie of his tux askew. "You're the darling of Whitley, Georgia, my dear. I'm sure you'll make the front page of tomorrow's newspaper. Well done!"

"It really was magical, wasn't it?" Kat asked as if needing confirmation the show wasn't a dream. Every song choice and note played or sung was perfect, and her banter with the hometown crowd pure delight as she took them on a journey through her music.

"One of the best ever," Sasha reiterated. "Come on, let's get you ready. People are waiting for you to make your entrance at the opening night party."

Kat pressed her teeth into her bottom lip to thwart off a gigantic grin and shook her head. "You two go on ahead. I need a moment to take this all in and decompress. I'll be up shortly."

Sasha cocked an eyebrow. "You sure you don't need any help with your dress?"

Kat waved her off and stood. "No, I'm fine. You go on and enjoy yourself. It's been a long day. Show the band to the ballroom and enjoy the fruits of our labor. I know where it is. I'll be there as soon as I change and refresh."

Pete and Sasha excitedly shuffled out of the dressing room, and Kat closed the door with a click. Glancing at the gilded mirror behind the door, she paused and posed, looking like a character straight out of *The Great Gatsby* in the smoky reflections.

Elated, she sat at the lit-up makeup table, her brown eyes wide with happiness and the mirror lights highlighting the pinkish hue of her flushed cheeks. Using the pick of her comb, she fluffed her shoulder-length blonde hair and skirted her long bangs to the side. A touch of cherry to her lips and a quick dab of powder across her nose were all she needed before she changed into her party dress.

She chose a marigold floor-skimming gown in luxurious velvet, perfect for her opening night party at the beautiful Grand. The fitted bodice held flutter sleeves and a v-neckline, the open back topped with a slender tie. The dress was dramatic and required very few accessories. She opted for a pair of gold drop earrings and a faux diamond flower ring. Finishing off her outfit with glittery Mary Jane pumps she found online, she checked herself in the antique mirror by the door again, turning from side to side. Her hazy reflection was quintessential 1940s Hollywood, making her smile. Running her hands down her hips, she tilted her head and reveled in her happiness before grabbing her clutch and breezing out the doorway toward the ballroom where her party guests awaited.

The tinkling of glass and guffaws of folks enjoying

themselves grew louder as Kat carefully ascended the carpeted stairs from under the Art Deco sconces casting shadows across the intricate railing. At the top of the landing, a smiling young man holding a silver tray offered her a flute of champagne.

"No, thank you. I'll get some inside the ballroom after my meet and greet." Knowing she'd be inundated with VIP fans and friends when she made her entrance made her hold off on the bubbly. There'd be plenty of time to celebrate later. The waiter nodded and disappeared through a nearby swivel door next to the elevator.

The sounds of an improvised trumpet solo by Louis Armstrong over a speaker made her grin, and she hummed along. Smoothing the bodice of her dress one last time, she was about to enter the ballroom when she heard a warbled baritone voice call out to her from behind.

"*Katherine.*"

Turning with a smile, ready to greet the man she assumed was a fan, Kat paused. "Yes?"

An elderly gentleman moved toward her in an achingly slow shuffle with the help of a sturdy cane. When he reached for her with his free hand, she politely grasped it and was surprised when he slipped something into her palm.

"What is this?" she asked with a smile. It wasn't unusual for fans to treat her with little gifts. His grip turned firmer, preventing her from looking at the object wrapped in a white handkerchief. Peering at his weathered face, she noticed his lips tremble before he spoke.

"It belongs to you." His voice groveled. "Please, take it."

"What?" Her brow creased as she tried to take a step back, but the man held tightly to her hand, not letting go. His wrinkled skin was warm with noticeable age spots, his gumption perplexing. She'd met her fair share of star-struck fans but never one as old as the man standing before her, and never one who called her by her birth name.

A plaid scarf tied around his neck peeked from under his buttoned-up wool coat, and a dapper hat perched on top of his white head. When she looked directly into his gaze, she felt a flash of recognition but couldn't quite place him. Was he a friend of her parents? Perhaps he was a long-time board member whom Pete had introduced her to?

Searching his expression, his blue-gray eyes, the color of the deep sea crinkled into a melancholy smile before he reluctantly broke their connection and let go of her hand.

"Thank you for the music." He took off his hat and held it at his chest, his action chivalrous and endearing. "It was... breathtaking. *You* are breathtaking."

"Thank you," she replied simply, not able to tear her stare away from his while clutching the unknown object in her hand. "What is your name?"

Before the man could respond, Pete Alexander appeared next to her, diverting her attention. "Please, excuse the interruption." His slight nod toward the elderly man was polite. "Kat, I want to introduce you to a few of our VIP season ticket holders. I hope you don't mind taking a photo or two with them. They're extremely eager to meet you."

"Oh, yes. Of course. I don't mind at all."

Pete lightly grasped her by the elbow and turned her toward the party. She offered him a brief smile before she turned her attention back to the older man to bid him farewell. To her astonishment, the man had already walked away and was about to enter the open elevator.

"Wait!" Flustered, she broke free from Pete, her steps

brisk as she trotted across the carpet to catch up to him. "Please, wait! I don't even know your name."

As the doors closed with a ding, the stranger dipped his head in a short nod, his gaze a haunting expression of blue-gray melancholy.

Standing there with her hands fisted at her sides, flummoxed by his sudden disappearance, a flash of remembrance filtered through her memory – *the portrait.*

His expressive eyes were exact replicas of the photo in the Hall of Fame. They were the mature eyes of Phillip Gordon in full Technicolor.

# Love's Refrain: Chapter Three

Kat didn't mean to gulp her first flute of champagne after her meet and greet with the VIP folks, and her hand shook as she set the empty glass on the waiter's tray. Focused on calming down, she reached for another and lifted it to her lips, all the while Spencer eyed her conspicuously.

"Slow down, Kat, or you're gonna make yourself sick," he fretted, promptly taking the new glass out of her hands. His face clouded with concern. "Are you okay? You look like you saw a ghost."

"Most likely…," she mumbled. Gripping her clutch with the folded handkerchief tucked safely inside, she tried to make sense of her chance meeting with Phillip Gordon.

"You want me to fix you a plate of food?"

When she didn't answer, Spencer offered her some of the appetizers he'd been nibbling on from his small plate. "Here. Have some of mine. You need to eat something before all that bubbly goes straight to your pretty little head."

"Mmhmm." Unfocused, she appeased him and took a cheese straw off his plate, rolling it in between her fingers.

"Hello?" He attempted to garner her attention again and bent low to look her right in the eye. "Anyone home?"

When she met his gaze, she blinked, annoyed by his meddling in her current state. She knew Spencer was only trying to be nice, but it still bugged her.

"I'm fine, Spencer. I'm in deep thought. Please, don't worry about me."

"But I do worry."

"Why?"

Gripping her by the elbow, he led her to an empty table where they sat down. "You're in the home-stretch of your first epic tour. You've been traveling nonstop for the past year. This weekend was supposed to be the end, but then you agreed to add *another* weekend."

"So? I ran it by all of you, and everyone agreed to it," she huffed. "You'll get paid for the extra work. You always do."

"It's not about the extra work or getting paid. It's about you overdoing it time and time again. Kat Monroe, all work and no play." He gestured quotation marks above his head. "I mean, you haven't had much of a break since this whole thing started. You're tired. I can see it in your face and in the way you hold back on certain notes in your songs—"

"Gee, thanks Spencer," she interrupted with a hard glare. The last thing she wanted was to appear worn out in front of her fans, especially in her hometown.

Covering her hand with his strong, pianist fingers, he squeezed. "No one but me would notice, baby. The tour would've been finished this weekend if you hadn't agreed to three more shows. I just want you to take it easy. Relax and eat some food. You don't have to talk to every single person in this room. Make them come to you."

Kat stared at his hand cupping hers; irritated he'd called her, "baby." Once upon a time, she thought Spencer might be the one. Their friendship and tastes in music made them the perfect writing partners collaborating over the years and playing in every dive bar and jazz club in the Southeast that would have them. He was essential to her blossoming career, and when they crossed over from friends to lovers, she thought she'd hit the jackpot.

But Spencer was a jealous man, the throngs of male suitors clamoring for her attention as her career exploded, often setting him off. They had to come to an amicable agreement to remain friends and not date, or else the base of their friendship might implode. But even as "just friends," she'd seen his dark side emerge a time or two, his jealousy continuing to percolate under the surface.

"I appreciate your concern, Spencer," she sighed. "If you'd like to fix me a plate, I won't refuse."

His smile was immediate, and he patted her hand. "Good girl. I'll be right back."

She watched his handsome backside disappear into the crowd, thankful for a quiet moment alone. Opening her clutch, she pulled out the handkerchief and tenderly lifted the corners to reveal a heart-shaped locket. The gold was dented on one side, and there was a little hole where a chain must have once run through it. Inspecting the piece, she noticed a tiny hinge. Prying the edge with a red nail, her tongue poked out of her mouth as she tried to open it.

"Ms. Monroe?"

Her head jerked upward to meet James Blankenship's happy smile. The mature piano tuner was decked out in a dark suit and paisley tie.

"Hello, James," she greeted, quickly tucking the locket under her clutch and out of sight. "Please, have a seat."

James sat in the chair Spencer recently vacated. "Thank you. I just wanted to tell you how much I enjoyed your show."

Kat smiled. "Thank you, James. That means a lot to me. The piano sounded divine and added so much to the evening. What you do is very important for artists like me."

His wrinkled face dotted with color, and he chuckled with a bashful stutter. "W...well, you're very kind. Most musicians who come through town don't usually appreciate the behind-the-scenes efforts like you do."

"Are you kidding me? How rude. You could make or break a pianist with your efforts. They should be kissing the ground you walk on." She lifted her chin for dramatic flair.

"Thank you. You're a real gem in this business. You remind me a lot of someone else who used to perform here - and what a coincidence to see him tonight after all these years."

"Oh?" Her curiosity piqued. "Who?"

"You wouldn't know him. He performed here way before you were even born."

"Try me," Kat teased.

"Well, he was another hometown prodigy much like you; concert pianist Phillip Gordon."

Kat struggled to breathe. "Phillip Gordon?" she managed to vocalize.

"Yes," James continued. "I noticed him sitting alone in the box seat to the right of the stage. I managed to get his attention, and he waved, but I'm not sure if he recognized me," he chuckled. "Phillip's a fine fellow – a bit of a recluse in his later years. I've seen him a few times at the Grand when he's come to see a show or two. I think he's one of the original season ticket holders."

"He doesn't play anymore?" she managed to ask.

"Oh, no. He hasn't played publicly in decades. Back in the mid-forties, he was real popular in these parts. I was just a boy back then, but my father often brought me here while he worked on the piano, grooming me until I was old enough to be his apprentice. I met Phillip several times during those early days and witnessed his amazing talent. Just like you, he was always complimentary toward my father and his job." He chuckled. "And a real sharpshooter when it came to marbles."

Kat's mouth tweaked in a half-smile witnessing the joy on James' face as he recollected the childhood memory. Clearing her throat, she leaned forward with intention. "Isn't his picture in the, um, Hall of Fame?"

"Yes!" James exclaimed. "After Phillip returned from the war, he accompanied many famous artists who came to town on the same piano I tuned today. The man could have toured the whole world with his amazing talent if he'd wanted to."

Kat swallowed hard. "Well, why didn't he?"

Shaking his head, James stood, and Kat followed suit. "No one knows. Pete might have more answers than me. Phillip dropped out of the performing world and became more of a private teacher. He's lived a pretty quiet life ever since." The frown on his wrinkled face suddenly changed into a happy smile. "But it sure was good to see him tonight in his regular seat. He's gotta be getting close to his hundredth birthday by now. Can you imagine?" James' bushy eyebrows arose comically from behind his glasses.

Her knees threatened to buckle as she gripped the top of her chair. "Well, what a feat…to live such a long life."

"I'll say." James' face softened. "I don't want to take up any more of your time. I just wanted to say thanks again for thinking of me and inviting me to your party. The shrimp cocktail was delicious." He winked. "I'll be back mid-week for another quick tune of the piano. I hope to see you again, young lady."

Kat nodded, not knowing how to reply, her mind reeling with thoughts of Phillip Gordon. Was he really the same man who gave her the locket? Even if it was Phillip, surely there was an explanation for his actions?

They said their goodbyes, and Kat watched James stop to congratulate Spencer with a pat on the shoulder, the two of them chuckling and nodding in the exchange. Spencer waved him off before turning his attention to her. Settling back onto her chair, she sat up straight and nervously smoothed her gown across her lap, trying to play it cool in front of him.

"Okay, I got you a little bit of everything. I know you don't like cauliflower, so I picked out broccoli and celery instead. And try the shrimp cocktail. It's good." He handed her a linen napkin with silverware rolled up inside.

Kat paused and took in the image of her ex. He really was a decent man, always looking out for her best interests while on the road, making sure she had everything she needed. Between him and Sasha, she was a spoiled princess.

Patting his arm, her lips trembled into a smirk. "Thank you, Spencer."

His blue eyes turned vivid with intention as he took advantage of her sentimentality and grabbed her hand, kissing her on the knuckles. Their gaze lingered, and she took in his boyish good looks.

His dark hair was always neatly combed back from his face, and his full lips had once rendered her speechless from his flaming kisses back when they were a couple. Now that the tour was almost over, would they continue to see each other as friends? Or would he politely disappear for a while until the next show was booked?

"Eat," he insisted with a devilish grin.

Kat rolled her eyes and turned her focus to the plate of food. "Simmer down, Spencer." She popped a green grape into her mouth. "I'm eating."

---

The boutique hotel where Kat and her crew stayed was within walking distance of the theater. Sasha had checked the group in earlier in the day so they could get situated in their rooms before they arrived for the soundcheck. With her arm looped through her friend's, Kat bristled against the unusually cold evening, burrowing her chin into her heavy coat. The sky was dark, the overcast night snuffing out the usual moon and stars lighting their path. The boys followed closely behind, everyone amped up from their performance, and excited about the end of the tour.

"Can you come to my room after you change?"

"Sure. What's up?" Sasha whispered closely.

"I want to show you something, but I don't want Spencer or the others to see."

"O-kayyy," she replied slowly with unease.

"No worries," Kat assured.

The group dispersed in the quaint lobby and headed to their individual rooms on the first floor. As Kat started up the stairs to go to her room on the second floor, Spencer was suddenly by her side.

"What are you doing?"

"Making sure you get to your room safe and sound."

His nose was red from one too many glasses of champagne, his current buzz making her cautious.

"I can manage myself," she responded with a pleasant tone laced with a dismissive hint. Spencer knew full well she wasn't one to enjoy late-night shenanigans after a performance, especially with more shows on the calendar. She was militant when it came to her rest schedule; the toll the tour took on her voice a genuine concern.

"I know. But who knows when we'll have another weekend like this? It could be months. Let me, please?"

Kat exhaled through her nose and looped her arm through his as they continued in silence. When they approached her room, she fished her key card out of her purse and turned to look at Spencer. "Okay, I made it safe and sound. Goodnight."

"Hold on," he requested, running his hand down her arm. "You need to hear this."

"What?"

"You need to know I'm extremely proud of you. You did it, Kat. You did exactly what you set out to do." Before she could respond, he moved forward and pressed his lips against hers in a kiss, causing her to squeal.

At first, she tensed, not sure if this was such a good idea. But when his fingers gently combed through the sides of her hair, and his tongue teased her own, she could feel her shoulders relax into the familiar trickle of warmth she coveted. It would be so easy to fall into his arms again and get lost in the passion. So easy, and yet, so complicated.

When he pulled back, he was out of breath and lightly ran the pad of his thumb across her lips. "I'm proud of you. And during our break, I want us to continue to see each other."

"Spencer…" she exhaled in response.

Placing his index finger over her mouth, he shook his head. "No. Don't say anything else right now. Just think about it - you and me giving it another go, away from all the travel and tour bullshit. Take all the time you need." His brow rose as he nodded a final time.

She was breathless from the kiss, tired from the exertion of the show, and confused about the newly gifted locket from a stranger burning a hole in her clutch.

Spencer cupped her cheek for a second more before he placed a final kiss on her forehead, turned, and walked away. When he suddenly jumped up and clicked his heels together in the carpeted hallway in a boisterous whoop, she laughed out loud.

The man was a charmer, especially when he was in a good mood or a tad tipsy. Shaking her head, she unlocked her room and swiftly went inside.

Leaning against the closed door, she pulled the locket out of her purse and stared at it in the palm of her hand. The piece of vintage jewelry didn't make any sense to her. She needed answers.

Her assistant and dear friend, Sasha, was the only one who might be able to shed some light on her confusion.

Grab your copy…
**vinci-books.com/lovesrefrain**

# About the Author

"The Singing Author," KG Fletcher, lives in her very own frat house in Atlanta, GA, with her husband Ladd and three sons. As a singer/songwriter, she became a recipient of the "Airplay International Award" for "Best New Artist," showcasing original songs at The Bluebird Café in Nashville, TN. She earned her BFA in theater at Valdosta State University and has traveled the world professionally as a singer/actress. She is a two-time Georgia Maggie Award Nominee and currently gets to play rock star as a backup singer in the "Remember When Rock Was Young – the Elton John Experience."

KG is a hopeless romantic. When she's not on the road singing, she's probably at home daydreaming about her swoony book boyfriends or arranging a yummy charcuterie board while sipping red wine and listening to Frank Sinatra. She's also a conference speaker and loves to interact with readers on social media and share about her writing and singing journey.

# Acknowledgments

I can't believe this is the end of the Bennett Family series. My emotions are all over the place. Thank you for coming along this journey with me!

This series of books would've never happened if it hadn't been for my Atlanta bestie, Anne. Girl! Our brain-storming sessions floating on Lake Appalachia are the only reason James's story exists. And thank you for introducing me to the magic of Linville Falls (the inspiration for Langston Falls.) Our book research trips to the Linville Falls Winery and Blowing Rock will forever be an indelible memory for me. Now that the series is complete, we MUST go back and take all the pretty pictures with all five paper-back books in tow. Maybe we'll run into patriarch Jack Wiseman again and share a glass of Big Red?

As always, I need to thank my rock star husband, Ladd, and my three sons who are my biggest supporters. I love y'all with all of my heart! To my Insta-author friends for sharing the love, and to my Slow Burn Sisterhood gals who helped me during our epic writer's retreat dig myself out of writer's block at the beach. I love you!

To the best beta readers on the planet, Heather, Ladd, Blair, and Craig, I know for the last year and a half all I ever talked about was the Bennett family. Thanks for putting up with me. I love you most!

To Vicky Burkholder, my long-time editor and friend,

thank you for making my stories shine. And to Gigi Blume, you are and always will be my author bestie.

Thank you to all the ARC readers who have read every single word in this series, and to the tenacious bloggers for your support. I will never recover from all the gorgeous posts, teasers, and positive reviews. Thanks for giving this indie-author a chance.

I have no idea what's next for me. I'm sure whatever it is will surprise us both, LOL! Until then, follow my indie-artist journey on social media – and come to a show if I'm near your town so we can meet in person.

What a magical moment it would be to hug you in person.

xoxo, Kelly